THE ACCIDENTAL UNICORN

DAKOTA CASSIDY

The Accidental Unicorn

Published 2019 by Dakota Cassidy

ISBN: 9781695697454

Copyright © 2019, Dakota Cassidy

All rights reserved.

No part of this publication may be reproduced, stored in a retrieval system, or transmitted in any form or by any means, electronic, mechanical, recording, or otherwise, without the prior written permission of Book Boutiques.

This book is a work of fiction. Any similarity to actual persons, living or dead, locales, or events is wholly coincidental. The names, characters, dialogue, and events in this book are from the author's imagination and should not to be construed as real.

Manufactured in the USA.

❃ Created with Vellum

ACKNOWLEDGEMENTS

Cover Art: Katie Woods

Editor Kelli Collins

AUTHOR'S NOTE

My darlings,

Here we are at book eighteen! I'm not sure how the heck we got here, but from the bottom of my heart, I thank you. Nina, Marty, and Wanda thank you for your ongoing love and support. I adore this world. I love its flaws, its outrageous cussing, its enduring friendships, its extended-extended family, and I love that you still keep coming back for more after eleven years. It means the world to me.

I know this has to end someday. I mean, eventually, there'll be nothing left to accidentally turn but the vacuum (hmmm…), but until then, onward to another adventure!

Also, please note, I've played fast and loose with the mythology of unicorns (which there isn't a lot of, by the by) and twisted it to suit my own selfish needs. Any and all mistakes or outlandish fabrications are mine and mine alone.

Last, but never least, to my BFF Renee George: This chipmunk's for you.

Love,
   Dakota XXOO

THE ACCIDENTAL UNICORN

CHAPTER 1

"Thank you for calling OOPS in the middle of the goddamned night when I was just about to go home, have a pint of blood, and finish my binge-watch of *Stranger Things*. I mean, Jesus on a surfboard. It's three o'clock in the a-m. Can't whatever the fuck is wrong with you wait until tomorrow?"

"I...I'm..."

"Never mind. My name is Nina Statleon. I'll be your guide to all things paranormal. For your safety, please keep your hands and feet inside the whacked-ass ride you're about to go on until we come to a full and complete goddamn stop."

"Um..."

"So how the fuck may I direct your call? Do you have a sudden urge to drink blood and rip someone's throat out? Because that's my department. Or are you spittin' hairballs and feeling like a rare steak might hit the spot? That's for Marty, or maybe even Wanda, but she's preggers and the size of a GD tractor-trailer. Probably not a lot of help at this point. Anywho, if it's brains you're craving, that's for Carl, but I warn you, he's not your typical zomb—"

"Brains? Why would I...?" Oliver Baldwin couldn't even finish the sentence, but he couldn't let her continue to talk, either, or he'd likely projectile vomit.

Who craved brains? Who? That was sick.

His stomach lurched a little before it settled to a nice slosh from the remains of the sticky-sweet Frapp from Starbucks he'd had earlier. Maybe this had been a big mistake. Maybe these people were fetishists who merely thought they were vampires and werewolves. People like that existed.

He'd seen them on some show he used to watch with his fiancée called *My Strange Addiction* or some such weirdness. And if they thought they were these supernatural creatures, they lived the lifestyle according to the folklore.

Slept all day, stayed up all night—maybe they even drank blood. But it would take some fancy footwork to prove to him they were immortal and preternaturally strong.

He was no fool. He knew about these things because of Denise.

"Tick-tock, buddy. State your case and hurry the hell up. And I swear on all that's good and holy, if you're one of the flippy-dippy jokers who want to join us in our 'cause' or you're a crank call, I've said it before and I'll say it again. I can find you just by your scent. Yes. You heard that right. I'll sniff you out. Don't test that theory. Because trust and believe, you won't like how your esophagus looks on the motherfluffin' outside."

Oliver swallowed hard and rubbed the raised knot on his head just under the brim of his knit cap. He had some serious concerns here—one of which was the violence of not only the tone this woman used, but her actual words.

While true, he needed his esophagus…did he need it more that he needed an explanation for what was happening to him?

He was feeling pretty iffy about it right now.

The woman on the other end of the line rapped the phone on something hard. Probably her desk. Whatever it was, it brought him back to the present with a sharp jolt.

"Hello? I'm hanging the fuck up in three, two—"

"I'm sorry!" he rambled as quickly as he could before she disconnected and he was really left with no hope. "I got distracted. Uh… It's none of those things, ma'am. I am in need of none of those things."

There was a shuffle and a creak of something, probably the chair this surly woman was sitting on, before she said, "*Ma'am?* Did you hear that shit, Marty? We've become ma'ams. Ain't that some fuckin' shit."

"No," a melodic voice responded. The woman named Marty, he assumed. "That ain't *my* fuckin' shit, vampire. That's your fuckin' shit. He called *you* ma'am.

Not me." Then she giggled, and he found it was sweet and soft and pleasant to his ears.

Rolling his fingers over the mouse pad, he looked absently at the OOPS website and reread the part where it claimed to help anyone in paranormal distress. Oliver wasn't sure if this was paranormal distress, but it certainly wasn't *normal* distress.

It was just a lot of distressing stress, of that he was clear.

Clenching his fists, he refocused. "I'm sorry, Miss Statleon, was it? Maybe I've made a mistake. When I googled 'strange phenomena,' your website came up. Um, OOPS, right? I do have the right number, don't I? Can you define what strange phenomena means to you?"

"Can you define what the sound of hanging up means to you?"

He winced. He'd offended her. "I'm sorry, Miss Statleon. I know I must sound horribly rude. I'm a little mixed up right now."

"Forget it, and it's *Mrs.* Statleon—but preferably just fucking Nina, and yep. You got the right number. We deal in strange phenomena. That's just the fancy bullshit keyword Marty puts in the search engines to drum up business, but what it really means is we deal in the cuckoo. So forget that shitty phrase and focus on my next question: *What* are you? Or what do you *think* you are? If you're not a vampire, werewolf, zombie, cougar, bear, mermaid, skinwalker or a phoenix—oh, or a genie; sorry, I forgot that shizzle. That was some crazy, let me tell you—then what the fuck? We're runnin' out of shit to be, brother. Soon we'll have to shut this shit down because there won't be anything paranormal left to accidentally turn into."

"Nina? Put that call on speakerphone, please," another softly cultured voice demanded sternly.

"Why, Wanda? Don't you trust me to handle this?"

"No!" the two women said in gleeful unison.

Nina's raspy sigh grated in Oliver's ear. "Fucking fine. Listen, I said, state your case and state it fast. I got a full plate and you're holding up the buffet line."

He looked out the window of his house in Buffalo at the cold dead of night, watching as the leaves fell from his oak tree in soggy piles of gold and orange he'd have to rake come daylight. Under normal circumstances, that would make him happy. Fall was Oliver's favorite season. Whatever was happening to him was interrupting his favorite season and involved glitter—a buttload of glitter.

Suck it up, Baldwin, and tell the cranky lady what your problem is. Hurry, before she sniffs you out and does something to your organs.

"My name is Oliver Baldwin, and I have a problem. I don't know if you can help because I'm not any of the things you listed, but your website says you have a great deal of experience in paranormal occurrences. I also don't know if this is a paranormal experience in the truest form, but it's certainly not *un*-paranormal."

"Is un-paranormal a word?" a softly commanding

voice asked. "I'm Wanda Jefferson, by the way. Nice to meet you, Oliver Baldwin."

"Marty Flaherty here, too. And of course, you've already met our resident cranky pants, Nina. We're the three women who make up OOPS. So tell us what's occurring and we'll decide if it's un-paranormal or not."

Running a finger along the neck of his sweater, he pulled it away from his skin. Suddenly, he was very hot.

And glittery. Let's not forget glittery.

Worse, he was feeling like an idiot, but he was going to dive in anyway because there was nowhere else for him to turn.

But he needed to be sure he was talking to someone who wouldn't turn this into some huge joke. Because he didn't feel like laughing, and this was no joke.

"Can I ask you ladies a few questions first?"

"This isn't like a fucking job application, Oliver. We're not interviewing with you here, pal. You're interviewing with *us*. Got that shit? We're nonprofit. That means we do this fuckery out of the goodness of our hearts and we owe you shitballs."

"Nina," Marty chided. At least, he thought he had the right voice with the right name. "Don't be so obtuse. He's allowed to be concerned."

"Do you even know what the fuck *obtuse* means, Miss Clairol Number Three Fifty-Two?" the growly lady asked.

"You're the very definition, Elvira," Marty shot back.

There was another rasping sigh—one Oliver had the feeling happened pretty often with the woman named Nina.

"Ladies, are we still doing this? It's the same old song every flippin' time. Stop arguing. Listen to the client. Shut your faces, please and thank you." He assumed it was Wanda who cleared her throat. "Now, Oliver, please feel free to ask as many questions as you'd like. If, in fact, you are in paranormal distress, certainly we're happy to accommodate."

Pressing the heel of his hand to his forehead, he snatched it back when he ran across the bump under the edge of his knit cap. How the hell was he going to explain this?

Then he shook his head and took a swig of his beer. First, the questions.

"May I ask what qualifies you as paranormal experts?"

There was a scuffle of feet and a muffled protest he didn't understand before the woman named Wanda said, "Well, if being half-werewolf, half-vampire doesn't qualify me, I don't know what does."

He hissed through his teeth before he took a sharp inhale of breath. The room began to spin a little, but he righted himself by clinging to his dining room table.

"So you believe you're a were-vamp?" he asked, puffing out his chest as if doing so would convince him that, despite the weak squeal to his voice, he was still, indeed, a man.

There was a pause, and then a light chuckle. "You know the term?"

He sighed and looked at one of the two lone pictures he had left of him and Denise. "I do. My ex-fiancée used to watch a lot of paranormal-based shows. So I'm sort of familiar with the terminology."

"Fuck, Wanda! Is this dude gonna come at us with some *Vampire Diaries/Supernatural/Teen Wolf* bullstank? I'm bone tired of swimming around in the TV legend that is fucking Dean and Sam. Those two pussies wouldn't know a demon if they—"

More muffling of sound ensued before Wanda was back again. "I'm sorry for the interruption, please continue, Oliver."

He actually found Wanda's voice very soothing. "Your coworker Nina is actually correct on some level, I suppose. I do know a lot about Sam and Dean, too. If that makes a difference."

"Everyone does, Oliver. Everyone does. But it helps that you understand the terminology. So please, do continue to ask whatever will make you more comfortable about what we do here at OOPS."

Oliver licked his lips and sat back in his dining room chair. "Okay, so when you say you're a were-vamp, you mean you practice some sort of religion that supports blood-drinking and howling at the moon, right? Which, I'm assuming, at least means you know something about mythology and the habits of the paranormal."

Someone laughed, he wasn't sure which woman, but it was very definitely a cackle.

"Um, no. This isn't a religion, Oliver. Nor is it a cult or a group with a fetish for blood. I am *actually* a were-vamp. I can shift into a werewolf, though that's been quite a challenge at what feels like two hundred years pregnant. And I do drink the occasional cup of blood—synthetic, of course—to nourish my vampiric side. When I say I'm a were-vamp, it's a lot like you see on the shows you watched with your fiancée."

"Ex. She's my *ex*-fiancée."

"What the fuck does it matter, dude? Do you think we give a shit about the logistics of your sad-sack love life? Because you would be sorely mistaken, mother-fucker. Sorely."

She was right. Crass, maybe even a little too overzealous, but right. They didn't care about the woman who'd ripped his heart from his chest, and they shouldn't.

"I'm sorry. You're right. Anyway, where were we?"

"We were at the point where you were questioning the validity of my paranormal nature," Wanda reminded him almost like a gentle nudge.

He nodded as if there were anyone in the room who cared other than his rescue chipmunk, Baloney, who was currently in the pocket of his flannel jacket. He'd found her on his front porch one chilly, rainy day three years ago. Soaking wet, bedraggled, with a lame left hind leg and, worse, almost half dead.

He'd called up a friend whose wife specialized in

wildlife rehab and discovered Baloney was a she and a Siberian chipmunk—not typically indigenous to Buffalo—which led them to believe someone had either lost her or ditched her.

That also meant he'd be taking a chance if he tried to merge her back into the wild, and he'd fallen so deeply in love with the little critter, Oliver refused to take said chance.

Either way, the first sign she'd shown of any serious will to live had been when he'd left a bologna sandwich on the table while he grabbed a soda from the fridge, and even though Baloney didn't eat it, she was interested, and that meant she was hungry.

"Oliver?" someone prompted.

"Sorry. You're right. I mean, not exactly right. I wasn't really questioning the validity of your claim as much as I was *clarifying*."

"Bullshit, dude," Nina groused. "But whatever makes you feel like you can justify calling a bunch of women to help you out in your time of need. I don't care, Snowflake. Just move this fucking train along!"

By now, he didn't feel as much offended by Nina as he did worried she really could sniff him out. He wasn't sure if he wanted to come face to face with a woman so volatile.

"I don't think I'm like any of the people you claim to have helped overcome paranormal adversities. In fact, I know I'm not. I'm not any of the things listed on your website. Though, I'll admit, the mermaid really made me stop in my tracks, but maybe that's only because I recently saw *Aquaman*. Anyway, that's why I'm not sure if calling you was the right thing to do."

"What do you have going on, Oliver? Maybe we should start there? Some of the cases we've worked on were presented to us without our having any prior knowledge of the subject's paranormal existence. As an example, I ask you, who knew mermaids really existed? But they do. I assure you, they do. A gorgeous fin, underwater breathing, a faux Atlantis, and everything. Somehow we managed to slog through that just fine."

"Well, it wasn't *fine*-fine. Don't let Marty bullshit your ass, Ollie. There was a sea witch who nearly drown our fucking asses and a weirdo wannabe King Triton with a grudge. If that's your definition of fine, we have a serious motherfucking disconnect," Nina chirped.

Oliver blanched. That was certainly an outlandish tale, no pun intended, which sounded more like it had been ripped from a move theater screen than true reality.

But okay. In the scheme of where he stood right now, it didn't really matter. He definitely couldn't go to his GP. He'd be a science project in no time—not to mention, a laughingstock.

Likely, what was going on was some sort of weird anomalous occurrence. It didn't explain all of what had happened today, but it sure explained some.

"Oliver?" Wanda's soft voice whispered in his ear. "I don't know about you, but being pregnant makes me pretty tired and I'm well past my bedtime. I, of course, want you to feel comfortable, but I'd also like some sleep. So it would be so kind of you to simply tell us what you think you have, and then we'll carry on from there or we'll say good night as we wish you well."

Damn. He was a jerk. He hadn't once thought about how he was stalling because he had more pride than sense—and this woman was two hundred years pregnant.

Wait. Did were-vamps stay pregnant for two hundred years? Maybe that hadn't been an exaggeration...

Jesus. That was ridiculous. *Straighten up and fly right, Oliver.* That's what his memaw would say, were she here.

"Okay, here's what I think is wrong with me."

The silence on the other end of the line felt pulsing—almost alive—as the women waited and he squirmed.

He was about to revoke his man-card, for sure. Though, in this day and age of evolution and forward thinking, men could wear nail polish and mostly no one blinked an eye, right?

What was the big deal? He was just as much a man as he'd been earlier today.

Jesus, Oliver. You're no less a man for this, and no more, either. That's such a sexist thought. Evolved Twitter would eat your face off if you tweeted something so sexist.

Still, this made for an incredibly uncomfortable admission.

And who knew? He could be dead wrong. Maybe his guess about what happened—what *was* happening at this very moment—was one hundred percent incorrect.

But you won't know until you ask, will you?

And who better to ask than a group of women who claimed to be paranormal? Even if they weren't really paranormal—and c'mon, he wasn't falling for that; a were-vamp, seriously?—maybe they knew people who could help him. That's what he needed. Help. A whole lotta help.

"Oliver?"

A drumming of fingers on a hard surface swelled in his ears, if bated breath could be heard, he heard theirs.

"Spill, Ollie. Now, or we hang the fuck up!"

His heart crashed in his chest, his pulse slammed in his ears from the pressure of being forced to say the words out loud.

"Oooolllie-ooolllie-oxen free!" Nina sang out. "You've got three seconds. Three—two—"

"I think I'm a unicorn!" he blurted out, jumping up from his chair and scaring Baloney awake.

There wasn't even a pause out of respect. Not even a breath of recognition.

You know what there was plenty of, though?

Raucous laughter. Including, but not limited to, snorting, wheezing, and even some hyena-ish squeals.

Well, hell. So much for evolution, huh?

CHAPTER 2

When he clicked the phone off and threw it down on the table in a fit of anger he fully recognized as childish, Baloney skittered from the protection of his flannel jacket, hanging on the dining room chair before launching herself at him.

She clung to his shirt and scurried up his torso to burrow in the hair by his ear. Her little body shook with tremors of fear, making him regret his hasty behavior.

Oliver scooped her into his hand and held her to his cheek. "It's okay, Baloney. Daddy's just a little freaked out and annoyed. You want a peanut? That'll make it all better, right?"

She loved peanuts. She jammed them into her tiny cheeks and hid them all over his house. In his shoes, under the refrigerator, in the cardboard box his six-pack of beer came in—anywhere she felt they'd be safe from her perceived, albeit, nonexistent predators.

She twitched against his skin, which he took to mean she felt like a peanut was an acceptable trade-off for frightening her.

Setting her on his shoulder, Oliver headed into the kitchen he'd just remodeled as a "get Denise out of his system" project and went on the hunt for peanuts in his new pantry. He grabbed the bag he kept on the second shelf and pulled a couple out, handing one to her.

She snatched it from him with quick hands and drove it into the pouch of her cheeks, her small body quivering with delight.

He stroked her head and smiled. "That's nice, right, buddy? See? All better. I apologize for waking you that way. Now c'mon. We have to figure out what the hell to do about this thing growing out of my head. You in?"

Baloney rubbed up against his cheek, which was as much of a sign as any she was up for this adventure.

Yanking off his knit cap, he threw it on the countertop and made his way back through the dining room, through the living room, and into the half bath. Flipping on the soft globe lighting encased in burnt-copper shells shaped like bells, he smiled in satisfaction at another room he'd successfully remodeled via You Tube and a million trips to a big box store.

He liked the warm tones of the matte rustic gray and honey-colored wood flooring against the soft white of the antique dresser he'd turned into a vanity. It made him feel accomplished.

Until he looked in the oval white mirror, that is.

Then he forgot all about the pleasure he'd taken in

his grudge projects and winced, running his finger over the almost two-inch-long sparkly protrusion jutting from his forehead, just beneath his hairline.

Oliver pulled a dark strand of hair out of the way and examined his eyes, dilated and wide. The big black dot in the center of his blue eyes made it appear as though he'd been doing drugs.

Baloney skittered out from under the scruff of his hair and looked in the mirror with him, her eyes blinking as she cleaned her tiny paws.

"Yeah," he agreed with a smile when he looked at her. "It's a helluva thing, huh, B?"

She looked at him with her soft brown eyes as if to say, "Who do ya think you're telling, buster?"

Baloney was part of the reason he'd impulsively and —now, he felt—quite foolishly called OOPS to begin with.

Because when he'd arrived home after work, his head pounding, having spent the latter part of the afternoon trying to keep this sparkly rod under wraps with a hat, she'd greeted him with her usual enthusiasm.

Just like she was doing now as she scrambled up the side of his skull and went straight for the spot on his forehead, the same way she'd done earlier this evening...

Only then, her lame hind leg had dragged behind her.

He grabbed her by the loose skin of her back and

held her up, shaking his head, which didn't hurt as much as it had earlier today.

"Oh, no you don't, miss. We don't know what this will do to you. You mind your p's and q's until I can figure this out. Understood?"

Oliver dropped her back on his shoulder and ran a light finger over the hard, swirly nub, and blinked.

Baloney had immediately taken an interest in the thing—whatever this thing was. A horn, maybe? She'd jumped on it and began to gnaw, grinding her little teeth against it until he thought his head would explode and his body would follow right behind.

The vibrations screaming throughout his nerve-endings and limbs when she'd latched on were almost more than he could bear, they were so debilitating. He literally had to fight every instinct in him not to fling her tiny body off his head.

Somehow, he'd managed to get ahold of her and put her in her habitat while he got a grip.

When he'd gone to apologize and make it up to her with some late-in-the-season strawberries, she'd skipped out of her cage ten times as fast as she ever had.

And her left hind leg no longer dragged limply along.

In fact, she was running like the world's tiniest version of *The Flash*.

Oliver squinted into the mirror again, almost laughing at how ridiculous it was, trying to cover this up with a hat. There was no hiding from it. When it had popped out just after lunch, he'd been sitting in his office, going over some drafts for a new senior housing community he'd designed before stamping them with his final approval.

The horn, if you will, burst through his forehead with such force it had almost knocked him backward in his chair, leaving in its wake glitter in all the colors of the rainbow all over his shirt and forehead, and covering his desk.

He'd once heard his sister say glitter was the crafting world's version of herpes, and he'd proved her right. It had taken a metric ton of paper towels and spray cleaner to clean it all up.

Since then, the damn thing had grown at least another inch, and he had not an inkling how or why or even where it had come from.

Relieved he had a ton of vacation time saved, Oliver had called his boss once he got home and pleaded a family emergency.

The doorbell sounded, interrupting his desperate musings, a soft tinkling set of notes he'd decided he liked much better than your typical grating ding-dong, making him cock his head.

His eyes narrowed as he scooped up Baloney and dropped her in the pocket of his sweater. "You stay put. Christ knows who'd be ringing the doorbell at this time of night, but it's time I got my ass in gear and put in that new doorbell camera, eh?"

Leaving the bathroom, he padded softly back to the

kitchen, grabbed his knit hat, threw it on and glanced in suspicion at the front door—also new, thank you very much.

What a bitch *that* had been to get level, but he loved the oyster white of it and the rectangle of colored glass at the top.

He heard arguing female voices tussling with one another—and that made him pause before asking who was at the door.

Yet, he almost knew who was at the door.

"Shut the fuck up, Marty. JFC, you gotta lot to say for someone who was in a coma not too long ago. Makin' up for lost time, Ass-Sniffer? Just be glad we didn't have to drive here and quit moaning about shredding your nylons. Flying comes with collateral damage—especially when I have *both* your asses on my damn back. You're not exactly living off a grape and one fucking square of cheese a day."

"Did you just call me fat, you monster?" one of them squealed in outrage.

"The fuck I did, Marty! Don't start with that body-shaming bullshit. Stop turning everything into a Twitter feed of outrage. I said the two of you put together aren't exactly featherweights. I think it's safe to assume you both weigh more than a feather, yes?"

"Don't you turn this around on me, Mistress of The Night…"

No. It couldn't be. This couldn't be the women he'd just spoken to but fifteen minutes earlier. How had they found him?

Oliver froze.

Nina had said she could sniff him out...

No.

Now a hard fist pounded on the door, making the shelf with framed pictures of places he'd been bounce. "Open up, My Little Pony! I can fucking smell you in there. So quit hidin' your sparklies and open the GD door. I'm not gonna wait around all fucking night. You want help or not?"

"Marty? Would you put your hand over her mouth? I know it's going to be a stretch because your hand's so tiny and her mouth's so stinkin' big, but if you don't shut her piehole, I'll have to do it, and as she so kindly pointed out, I'm just so darn bulky these days it'd be like an elephant chasing a cheetah."

Boy, they sure could argue. Far worse than his sisters ever had. He'd grown used to the scuffling sound with these three, he just wasn't sure he wanted to witness it.

"*Please, Oliver,*" the voice he'd come to know as Wanda begged. "I won't sleep tonight for the guilt I feel at having laughed at your predicament. It was cruel, and we're so terribly sorry. Also, I'm pregnant and exhausted. After the mode of transportation we used to get here, precarious at best, I could really use the bathroom. Who am I kidding. I can always use the bathroom. So please, Oliver, open the door and let us explain, won't you?"

"Oh, fuck all, Wanda. I'm not even a little bit sorry.

Dude's a unicorn, for shit's sake. That shit is funny. F-u-n-n-y. *Funny.*"

"Nina, shut up!" Marty whisper-yelled. "You're going to wake all the neighbors and make this worse. God, what was I thinking when I decided handing the reins of the final stages of the merger between Bobbie-Sue and Pack over to Mara so I could spend more time devoted to OOPS was a good idea?"

Oliver couldn't take it anymore. They *would* wake his neighbors, and the last thing he needed was that soccer mom, Melissa, dropping by for no reason at all other than to slyly suggest they should sleep together as payback since both their partners had jumped ship.

But to be fair, she did always bring cookies when she made her advances, and they were good, but not good enough to coax him into bed with her errant husband, Cornelius "Corny" Fortinski, always lurking in the background.

He decided he couldn't take a chance they'd rouse his neighbors. His neighborhood was a quiet one, chosen especially for his future children with Denise in mind.

Without thinking, he popped the door open—so quickly, in fact, they all fell into his entryway like dominoes, stumbling and tripping as they went.

Baloney shivered in his shirt pocket, her fear of strangers, especially of the female variety, leading him to place a protective hand over the front of his sweater.

Planting one hand on his hip as they righted themselves and filed into a line, he kicked the door shut with his foot and got his first glimpse of the women who'd thought both he and his late-hour confession were pretty damn funny.

He gave them a real critical once-over, assessing them from the ground right up to their glittering eyes.

You know, for a bunch of supposed paranormals, they sure didn't look much different than your average homo sapiens.

They were all definitely very attractive and well groomed for almost four in the morning. From the blonde with the long hair curled into beachy waves—another term he knew because of Denise—to the outrageous, almost unearthly beauty of the brunette who, for some reason, he knew instinctively was Nina, to her very pregnant and elegantly coiffed friend, Wanda, Oliver decided they weren't what he'd envisioned in his mind's eye.

Wanda looked at him with wide eyes fringed with naturally long, thick lashes. "Bathroom?" she squeaked, hopping from foot to foot.

Oliver pointed over his shoulder, but he didn't say a word. Not a single word. He still felt quite grudgey about their gleeful mirth.

As Wanda went off to the bathroom, Marty held out her hand, the silver bangle bracelets she wore shimmering under the soft glow of the interior lighting of his house.

"Oliver, I'm Marty Flaherty, and from the bottom of my heart, I apologize. I paranormal-shamed you, and I regret it deeply. It was unprofessional and absolutely uncalled for. Let's start again, okay?"

He took her hand and nodded, but he didn't return her pretty, accommodating smile.

The brunette—tall, willowy-lean and supermodel gorgeous—gave him a glittery-eyed once-over, but she didn't offer her hand.

Nope. She jutted her chin out, pushed her hoodie from her head, let her brilliantly shiny hair spill over her shoulders, and thinned her lips in displeasure.

"I'm Nina Statleon, and I'm not all that sorry. I don't think I'm *ever* gonna to be sorry because, something you should know straight up? I'm an insensitive bitch, and it's all I can fucking do not to laugh right now because you're a *unicorn*." Then she snickered, not even bothering to cover her mouth with her hand to muffle it. "I'm gonna bet, you have a horn and it sparkles. That shit's funny."

Okay, so maybe everyone hadn't evolved as much as he'd hoped.

Wanda came up behind her and flipped a long length of Nina's hair upward. "Shake hands with the man like a good little vampire then quiet those dark forces within and behave."

Nina rolled her coal-black eyes at him and stuck out her hand. "Wanna be friends, Horned One?" Then she snickered again.

He was going to ignore the fun she was making of him and be a gentleman, but the moment he held out his hand, Baloney bolted upright out of his pocket and flung herself at Nina with a tiny screech.

Marty, whose pretty blue eyes went wide, opened her equally pretty mouth and screamed as Baloney became a blur of sound and motion.

"Oh my God!" she howled as she jumped on Nina, wrapping her legs around her friend's waist and clinging to her. "Ahhhhhh! It's a raaat! Get it out, Nina! Get—it—out! Eat it or something!"

As Baloney leapt off Nina and onto the floor, all he could think about was what she'd said about his esophagus, and he panicked. Visions of this violent woman with her terrified friend on her back, eating his chipmunk, as irrational as that sounded, whizzed through his head like a picture book of small woodland creature death.

Swiftly stepping in front of Nina, who'd swung around to see what direction Baloney had gone, Oliver shouted in her face, "No!"

To which Nina gave him the oddest look, a look that said how dare you have the audacity to tell me no, right before she grabbed his wrist, twisted his arm around his back and gave him a shove so hard into the wall, he dented the sheetrock of his entryway—the sheetrock he'd just damn well painted.

While he was busy being utterly astonished at her strength, she howled, "Get off me, Ass-Sniffer!" Swinging wildly, she grabbed Marty around the waist and virtually pulled the woman up over her head, dropping her on the floor with such force, it made the entire room shake.

And then she went after Baloney, her nostrils flaring, her eyes on fire. She dove for the floor in the living room to the left of the entryway and scrambled her way to a big rustic wood buffet, reaching behind it with a blurred swipe of her hand.

He'd recovered enough to bellow, "No! Please don't hurt her!"

But Nina had her between two fingers, rising as quickly as she'd dove to the ground. "Well, look at you," she cooed at Baloney, her once hard eyes now soft and warm.

It was all he could do not to stalk to her position in the room and snatch Baloney away from her, but he was afraid she'd eat her before he could get there.

"Please don't eat her," he begged. There wasn't much in this world he'd beg for, but Baloney was like his kid. It had been just him and Baloney since he and Denise had broken up.

Nina held up her free hand, her long fingers pointing in his direction. "Shut it, Unicorn Man. I'd *never* hurt her." She made kissy noises in Baloney's direction, her eyes soft and welcoming. "I would never hurt you, little lady. I love all the tiny babies. All of 'em! Now, who's a good-good chipmunk?" she cooed in a sticky-sweet voice. "You are, Nugget, that's who. Now, don't be afraid, okay? Come see Auntie Nina and we'll get to know each other. We'll be friends, even if your dad's a sparkly freaked-out mess."

Then she set Baloney in the palm of her hand and stroked her striped back with two gentle fingers.

And Baloney, president of the female woman-haters club, rolled over on her back and offered Nina her belly as though she'd never been terrified of every woman since Denise had lived with them.

Son of a bitch.

CHAPTER 3

While his mouth fell open, Wanda patted him reassuringly on the back. "She'd never hurt any animal, Oliver. Nina's a monster with people—almost all people until she gets to know you. But give her a child, the elderly, or any animal…and I do mean *any* animal. She has an opossum that lives in her backyard maze she built a heated hut for because she couldn't talk the poor thing into coming inside and she was worried he'd freeze. She'd nurture it to death before she'd hurt it. Your chipmunk's safe with Nina. Your anything that walks on all fours, wears a diaper or is defenseless is safe with her. *Promise.*"

Oliver inhaled deeply, his chest stinging from the crash against the wall. Still, he was afraid for Baloney. He didn't want to have to tussle with this freakishly violent woman, but he would if it meant saving Baloney. "Are you sure?"

Marty scoffed as she flanked his other side. "Are we

sure? Her hamster, Larry, before his untimely demise, lived like a king. What hamster do you know who has an entire room devoted to his habitat? Well, Larry had one. She's a beast, but she's mostly a good beast."

"Now," Wanda said gently. "While Nina makes lovey-dovey with your chipmunk—"

"Baloney. Her name's Baloney."

"Baloney? Who the fuck names a pretty-pretty princess like you Baloney?" Nina cooed as she stroked Baloney's back. *A man. A stupid man with a stupid sparkly horn. That's who.*

"Of course," Wanda agreed. "*Baloney*. While Nina plays with, ah…Baloney, why don't we sit in the other room and talk about what's happening? Would that be all right?"

Oliver scratched the side of his head, still bewildered. "I think… I think so. Let's go to the kitchen. I have plenty of seating there."

Yeah, he did. Denise had wanted a big kitchen to entertain family and friends, so the plan had been to knock out the wall between the dining room and living room and extend the kitchen. And he'd done that. *Alone*. All alone.

He led the two women to his sprawling kitchen and offered them each a chair at the wide island with the muted gray-and-black-veined sandstone countertop—just like Denise had wanted.

"Do you have tea, Oliver?" Marty asked, her hoop earrings glittering under the recessed lights as she tucked her hair behind her ears.

He felt so unsure about these women, yet they were now going about this with such warmth and sensitivity. Well, except for the demon in the living room, currently wooing his baby. They were pretty understanding for crazy people.

"Oliver?" Marty prompted.

Instead of speaking, he pointed to the cabinet by the six-burner gas stove.

But Marty just smiled and headed that way. "Good enough—and oh, my goodness, your kitchen is magnificent! Did you pick everything out, or is there a lady involved—or a man, for that matter—we should offer our compliments to?"

"Most of it I did on my own," he muttered, jamming his hands in the pockets of his jeans.

"It's breathtaking," she responded with another smile as she stood on tiptoe and reached for the teabags. "Tea, Mama Wanda?"

Wanda nodded to Marty with a smile of clear gratitude then patted a spot on the island across from her, setting her very pregnant body on one of the high-back chairs opposite him. "Sit, won't you?"

He did as he was told, but he still wasn't offering anything more. He was so freaked out by the range of emotions they'd evoked, he though it better to stay silent.

"So, Oliver, first, let me apologize again for how utterly shameful we were on the phone. How crass of us to behave the way we did. My only excuse, and it's a thin one, is that we were caught off guard. We've dealt with a lot of things, but never—"

"A *male* unicorn," he offered dryly.

Wanda gazed at him for a moment, the smile never leaving her pale-pink glossed lips. "Well, you have to admit, unicorns, as sexist as this sounds, are geared mostly toward young girls."

Oliver lifted his chin, adjusting his knit cap and trying to avoid blowing upward at his nose to remove any glitter that had fallen to its tip. "You know of any young girls who'd like to trade places?" he asked. "Because I'd be happy to take a step back."

"Either way, we're incredibly remorseful. Nina is, too—"

"The fuck she is!" Nina singsonged from the living room. "This shit is funny!"

Both Marty and Wanda heaved a resigned sigh. "Okay, she may not be right now, but she will be. Anyway, the moment you hung up on us, and deservedly so, we straightened up and flew right—right over *here*, that is."

"Yeah," Marty agreed as she set the kettle on the stove. "Did we ever."

Now he eyed Wanda, with her clear skin and even clearer eyes. For someone who claimed to be so tired, she looked great. They all did, but that was a perk of being supernatural, right? Eternal youth?

"You said you flew. I don't understand. I thought your offices were here in Buffalo?"

"They are. We just moved from the city to be closer

to our respective homes. Except Nina. She's still on the island—Staten Island, to be precise."

"So you flew here from *here*? That makes no sense."

Or he wasn't allowing it to make sense because the reality was too crazy. He wasn't sure. Either way, he couldn't possibly parse all the outrageous things they'd said on the phone as well as outside his door. It was too much right now.

Wanda reached across the counter and patted his hand with her delicate one, shooting him a sympathetic smile. "It will. All in good time, Oliver. I promise."

"How did you know how to find me?"

"Again, all in good time. We're here now, and that's all that matters. So let's get this show on the road, shall we? Can you tell me what brought you to this point?"

Dropping his head to his hands, noting a spray of glitter falling from the brim of his hat to the island counter, Oliver closed his eyes from exhaustion, trying to rub the graininess away. "I wish I knew."

When he lifted his head, Wanda was looking directly at him with thoughtful eyes.

"Let's start with this first." She pointed a finger at his head. "Would you mind showing me what's happening, Oliver? Then we can at least ascertain where we're at?"

There was a husky squeal of delight from the living room. "Is he gonna show you that shit, Wanda? I wanna see, too! And so does Baloney, don't you, Princess?"

Marty, in a blur of motion his eyes almost couldn't connect with his brain, set down the mugs she'd been preparing and zipped to the living room. "Stop being an insensitive goon, Nina!"

He looked at Wanda, his mouth open again. "How does she move…so fast?" Jesus, had he squeaked out that question like some chickenshit?

Yes, his inner coward muttered. *Yes you did, Oliver. But it's okay. You have every right to be scared. There's no other word to describe that woman but scary.*

But Wanda patted his hand again with her soft, smooth one. "As I said, explanations will happen all in due time. It's a lot, and for now, we don't want to overwhelm you. Moving forward, let's just see what we're dealing with. Are you comfortable doing that?"

What choice did he have? They'd come all this way—however it was they'd arrived. Wanda was pregnant and even if she didn't look so tired, she probably was. She was carrying around a life, for shit's sake.

He'd be a real dick if he didn't at least show them what he'd called about and explain what happened with Baloney. That alone was a miracle.

Pulling his bulky knit cap almost entirely from his head, Oliver took a deep breath, keeping his head low.

Marty was there at his side in an instant, patting his arm to console him. "It's okay, Oliver. Believe me, the mermaid story I told you was true. We've seen some things, some really crazy things you only see on TV and in movies. We're ready for just about anything. Promise."

Lifting his head with a raspy sigh, he looked straight past Wanda and at the side-by-side pictures of herbs hung on the far wall and pulled off his knit cap.

It was then that he heard the lovely, elegant, cultured Wanda fall off her chair.

~

Nina raced into the kitchen in another blur before he could even rise from his spot, catching Wanda before she hit the ground with Baloney tucked safely in her hoodie pocket.

"Jesus, Wanda! You have to be more fucking careful," she scolded, pushing her friend's hair from her face and peering into her eyes. "You're gonna have this damn kid before it's ready if you don't knock this ish off. You're like a frickin' balloon waiting to burst."

Nina was so tender with her friend and Baloney; he almost couldn't believe she was the same person he'd talked to on the phone. The same snarling, snapping, foul-mouthed person, he marveled.

She settled Wanda back in her chair with gentle hands as Oliver rushed to her side and asked, "Are you all right? Can I get you anything, Wanda?"

Nina gave him a nudge to the shoulder with the heel of her hand. "You can get me some Skittles, buddy. I wanna catch the rainbow." She cackled at her joke, laying her arm protectively across Wanda's shoulders.

"I'm so sorry, Oliver. I'm fine," Wanda finally said, tucking her sweater around her engorged waist before she ran her hand over her temple. "It's just so…"

"Shiny?" Nina crowed as she peered at his, for lack of a better word, horn. "That motherfucker's shiny and glittery as all hell. But I bet Marty'll tell ya the pink and purple are definitely in your color wheel. At least you got that going for ya."

Nina reached out and lifted a finger to touch it, but Oliver waved her away with a wince. "Please don't. It's very sensitive. When I touch it, my whole body vibrates so hard, it's like I'm a string on a bass guitar someone's plucked." Then he paused as her words impacted him fully. "Wait. What did you say? It's in my color *what*?"

Nina smirked, her face, if at all possible when smirking, even lovelier when she did so. "Your *color wheel*, My Little Pony."

Marty whisked across the room, her brown leather boots hushed as she dropped mugs of steaming tea in front of Wanda and Oliver.

"Ignore Nina. She wouldn't know a color wheel if it rolled her over, smacked her on the fanny, and called her dumplin'. It just means it goes well with your skin color, if that's any consolation. Now, let's discuss when this happened and what you were doing when it did. And Wanda? You drink up, and take deep breaths. Heath would set us on fire if anything happened to you." Marty held up the other mug and wafted it under his nose, encouraging him to take it. "Oliver? Answer the questions. When and where?"

He pushed up the sleeves of his sweater and shook his head. "I was in my office, going over some final blueprints for an affordable senior housing development when it nearly knocked me out of my chair with the force of it popping out of my head."

Marty leaned in close and examined the horn, holding her hands up in the air to show him she wouldn't touch it. "Wow," she murmured. "It's really quite incredible. I mean, I've never seen anything like it. I'm not surprised by it, I suppose, but…wow."

"So what the fuck were you doing *before* this shit happened, Ollie? Were you playing with your Barbies, maybe? You wanna borrow my kid's DreamHouse?"

Oliver was aghast yet again, not just about her sexist statement, but the fact that she was a parent, and though he should have tried to hide it, it came flying out of his mouth without warning.

"*You* have children?"

She leaned close and eyeballed him with a sneer. "I have *two* kids, Ollie. My Charlie, and a zombie named Carl. You got some shit to say about it?"

She had a zombie?

Instead of opening his mouth and sticking his foot in again, he threw his hands up in surrender. "Nope. I have no shit to say about it, Nina. You just caught me off guard. You know, like I caught *you* off guard with my girlie unicorn horn. Remember that? You know, when you laughed so hard you all sounded like hyenas?"

Nina's raven eyebrow arched. "Funny My Little Pony is funny. Respect, brother." She pounded her chest with her fist before she rocked back on her heels. "Now, answer the question. What were you doing before this happened? Like the day before yesterday or earlier in the day? Can you think of anything that prompted this shit?"

He'd racked his brain all day long and well into the night, trying to figure out what he'd done to get himself into this mess—where he'd been, whom he'd been with—but it had been a pretty dull week.

"I swear, I can't think of a single thing I did differently this week than any other. I got up, went to work, went to the gym with a couple of buddies. Came home, had dinner, fed Baloney, did some work around the house on renovations, went to bed. Got up and did it all over again. It's what I do almost every day."

"Got a sig other?" Nina asked. "Boyfriend? Girlfriend?"

He looked down at his folded hands. It had taken a long time before he'd remembered he was no longer part of a couple, but he had it down now. "No. No significant other."

"Then who's this?" Marty asked, plodding across the room and grabbing a 5x8 picture frame from the long countertop by the stove—one he'd forgotten to put away.

"Someone," he muttered vaguely, looking away.

"Someone who someone?" Nina pried.

"Someone I'd prefer not to talk about."

Nina moved closer. "Listen, Grudgy McGrudgerson, we need to know all the people you've been in contact with. *All* of the fucking people. *Who is she?*"

"A friend."

Nina poked a finger in his shoulder. "You kiss all your friends like that?"

He rasped a sigh, taking the picture from Marty and dropping it in a drawer in the island. She was the last person he wanted to talk about, but Nina was right.

"Fine. She's my ex-fiancée, Denise. Sore subject, I guess."

And the reason he had this house and the reason he'd renovated it as though he was coming upon his last dying breath.

Because he was gonna show her.

"So you parted badly?" Wanda finally spoke after finishing her tea.

"Well, it wasn't nice, I can tell you that."

Nina rolled her tongue along the inside of her cheek. "Define 'nice,' Sparkles."

Oliver was a private person. He wasn't one of those people who spilled their guts on social media and to anyone who'd listen.

But their parting had been ugly—very ugly.

"We had a huge argument. She left. I stayed. End of. Denise has nothing to do with this. She doesn't even live in Buffalo anymore. She lives in Manhattan. She couldn't possibly have anything to do with this, okay?"

Nina's glance was skeptical but when she was about to interrogate him further, and he knew that was her intent by the look in her gorgeous eyes, Wanda took over.

"So anyone suspicious hanging around? Anything

suspicious you've seen? Any enemies we should know about?"

He pointed to the horn on his head. "You're all making it sound like this was a malicious act. What would make you think this had anything to do with malice or revenge?"

Nina planted her hands on her hips as Baloney snuggled into the hair draping over her shoulder. "Oh, you'd be surprised the malicious shit we've seen. Wanda's sister was turned into a GD demon because she drank a drink meant for someone else. It was peppered with demon blood. Poof! Motherfuckin' insta-demon."

"That's true," Marty agreed with a jab of her finger to the air. "And that's not even the beginning of the wicked deeds we've borne witness to. So if someone wanted to do something to hurt you, cause you grief, wreak havoc with your life, whatever, it's not as outlandish as you'd like to think."

He was trying really hard not to buy into their outrageous stories. I mean, demon blood? Nina's flying? A zombie? These were the tallest tales he'd ever heard.

But how could he deny he had a horn with sparkles that had popped out of his head after lunch today? That was pretty outlandish. Why couldn't Wanda be a werevamp if he had a horn that had come out of nowhere?

Still, he protested. Whether he had it or not was no longer the issue. That someone might have tried to impose it upon him? That was a hard pill to swallow.

He made a face. "But a unicorn horn? Who gives someone a unicorn horn because they're angry with them? And who the hell has the ability to *give* someone a unicorn horn in the first place?"

"Well, Oliver, you have to admit, it would be the ultimate payback, right? A man with a unicorn horn? Whether we like to admit it or not, we still live in a pretty sexist world. Not everyone's evolved so much they wouldn't think it was a laugh-riot to give a big guy like you a sparkly horn, sticking out of the front of his head. But it could also have been an accident and not meant for you at all. As to *who* has the ability to give you a unicorn horn? Weeell," Wanda said with a wince as she rubbed her belly. "Do you believe in witches? Or genies? Or even wizards?"

He blinked, still dazed. "I don't know what I believe in anymore. I do know, I don't know any of those kinds of people—or if I do, I'm not aware of them. I mean, you all look like everyone else, but you claim to be a vampire and a were-vamp."

Nina gave him a slap on the back. "We don't just fucking *claim* it—we are it. Wanna see?"

Speaking of malicious, Nina took great pleasure in dotting all the paranormal I's and crossing all the T's, didn't she? She looked ghoulishly excited to "show" him whatever it was she thought she was capable of.

Marty frowned and shook her head of blonde curls, giving her friend a look of caution. "Nina. *Not now*. The man has enough on his plate. He's spitting glitter from his forehead, for heaven's sake. He's not ready for more."

Oliver squared his shoulders. Said who? He might be a little freaked out—uneasy even—but he could take whatever they had to dish out.

How much worse could it get than a unicorn horn?

So he eyed them all, standing in his kitchen in all their perfume, bangle bracelets and jeering gazes.

"Go ahead," he dared them. "Show me."

Now Wanda frowned and bit her lower lip. "I don't thin—"

"Put your money where your mouth is," Oliver goaded. "Show me or it didn't happen."

Nina lifted her chin defiantly before her beautiful face split into a wide grin. "Whoopee!"

CHAPTER 4

Nina stood beside him next to his beige sectional with the million and two pillows he hated, but bought anyway just to spite Denise, who'd said that was one of the many reasons she was leaving him—he was inflexible.

He'd shown her, hadn't he? His couch was a veritable treasure trove of soft-colored pillows in muted sage and fluffy cream.

Hah.

Nina pressed a cool cloth around the horn on his head—which, unfortunately, was still there, if the vibrations rattling his teeth and bones were any indication.

Marty stood over him, her clothes returned to their former places on her body, her hand on Nina's shoulder, her gaze one of blue-eyed sympathy. *"I told you."*

They had. She had. Wanda had, too. He'd chosen to

all but dare them to show him what he thought surely was utter nonsense.

But it wasn't nonsense.

It was real. Yes, Virginia, vampires and werewolves and half-breeds, maybe even gypsies, tramps, and thieves, were real. *Real*.

Holy frack.

"So are you ready to talk about this shit now, or do you need more time to change your man-panties and take a Xanax, Snowflake?"

Wanda came to stand next to Nina, taking Baloney from her shoulder and giving her an Eskimo kiss before she jabbed Nina in the ribs. "Don't be awful, Nina. He's no less a man because he screamed."

Oliver became a little more defensive than he would've liked when he protested, "I did *not*—"

"Oh," Marty said with a twinkle in her eye. "But you did. And it's fine. We're used to it. Everybody reacts differently. Some cry. Some rock in a corner. Some scream. No big deal. Now we need you to get past the shock, put on your thinking cap, and help us figure this out because you can't wander around like this—we need to know what it means and how you'll live with it. If you'll have to live with it forever."

Forever? He'd never considered this was permanent.

Pushing his way to a sitting position, Oliver tried to shake the cobwebs from his brain. "Why are you helping me? Why do you care what happens to me?"

Were they going to try to coax him into joining

their cult-ish movement? What motivated them if they didn't take money?

Wanda dropped down beside him on the couch, tucking a pillow behind her back before she patted his knee. "Because we know what it's like to be alone and have something so crazy happen to you, something so mind-boggling, you're terrified. You don't know who to tell or where to turn. You're horrified by the physical changes in your body. You don't know how to deal with them. We understand that because it happened to us, too, Oliver. But we had each other. We decided there must be other people out there like us. I mean, we—all three of us—had accidents within the space of a couple of years. Three accidents in as few years? That's a statistic that needed exploring. So we explored. And here we are, eleven years later and who knows how many accidents since."

"So it's true," he murmured, incredulous. "You really have seen a mermaid and a demon?"

Wanda chuckled. "That's one of my favorite cases of all time. Her name's Esther and she's amazing. I think you'd like her. There isn't anyone who doesn't like Esther, right girls?"

"I love that damn fish," Nina said on a snort. "Hated being wet all the frickin' time, but love my Little Mermaid."

He pinched the bridge of his nose, mostly because he wanted to avoid the area where his horn sprouted. "Did she really sniff me out? That was really true?"

"*She* is standing right the fuck in front of you," Nina

groused. "And I don't make idle threats, pal. After what you just saw, you still doubt I could sniff you out? Dumbass."

"Fair," he muttered. Dumbass was a fair assessment of his person at the moment.

He was having an extremely difficult time trying to clear his brain to make way for all that he'd seen and all he could potentially face, but he had to if he had any hope of figuring out what came next.

Nina nudged him with her knee before taking a seat next to Wanda, summoning Baloney by patting her shoulder. "So, let's figure this shit out, Ollie. That means going over everything you've been up to and everyone you've been in contact with for at least the last week."

Marty nodded as she sat in the chair opposite his sectional and pulled out her phone. "That's exactly what it means. So buckle up. Also, as a side note, I've invited a friend of a friend of ours to join us. She's a professor of mythology at the local college, understands the paranormal, and will keep this to herself. I'm just waiting on a return text."

"Which friend of a friend?" Wanda asked with one eyebrow raised.

Marty looked at her phone again. "Khristos's longtime friend. Her name's Vincenza Morretti, or Vinnie, as Khristos calls her, and apparently, she's well-versed in Greek mythology. I mean, she teaches it. So she should have a better understanding than we do, right? Also, she knows people like us exist. That's a huge relief when we don't have to explain. Now, I don't know if it'll help us, but it's worth a try because I don't know anyone else we know of who knows thing one about unicorns. The closest thing to mythological beings we have is Esther or Quinn. Esther's out of the country and mostly in the water and unreachable. But we can always find Khristos if we can't find Quinn."

Oliver gave them all a blank look as they chattered, but Wanda leaned into him and whispered, "Khristos is the husband of our friend Quinn Morris, and she's the latest incarnation of the Goddess Aphrodite."

He clenched his fists and tried not to react in stupefied shock. He'd seen what he'd seen and there was no two ways about it. So a reincarnation of Aphrodite shouldn't be a surprise, but he damn well had to fight not to visibly scoff at the very idea Aphrodite still existed.

He couldn't help but ask, "The Goddess of love still exists? What are her superpowers? Does she own magic Spanx or something?"

"So you *do* know a bit about mythology, then?" Wanda asked with a curious gaze.

"I happened to see some stuff while I was researching unicorns, and I read a bit about a magic girdle," he admitted.

He hadn't liked what he'd seen, but he'd seen it. It didn't help in his case anyway. Unicorns were rare. That was the gist of what he'd gotten from his research. So what?

Marty winked at him and chuckled. "Apparently,

the girdle thing is a total myth. Quinn told us so. No one ever owned a magical girdle that could make men fall in love with them, and she said if they had, she'd have outlawed them once she took over anyway. But she *is* a matchmaker extraordinaire. No one understands love, and the pursuit of, better than our Quinn. Think Meghan Markle and Prince Harry, as just one example. You might laugh at the idea that everyone has a mate, but ending up with the wrong person can be deadly. Her matches are forever."

Nina cackled and slapped him on the back, making a cloud of glitter spatter the air. "Oh, buddy. If you only knew the shit Quinn can do. She knows Cupid, BTW. Like, the real Cupid, golden arrows and all."

Oliver blanched.

"Why so green around the fucking gills, Unicorn Man?" Nina taunted, but then her face softened. "Listen, dude, you're gonna hear a lot of shit in the next few days. Things you won't fucking be able to wrap your pea brain around, but I promise you, if we can find out how to help you, we will. Just prepare for us to take over your life until we figure this out. Okay?"

He swallowed hard, his mouth dry. "Okay," he agreed.

What choice did he have, short of sawing this thing off his forehead, but to go along with whatever they said? He knew zero about unicorns other than they were among some of his niece's favorite toys.

The doorbell rang then, the sound more jarring this time around than it had been earlier, likely from his lack of sleep. As he rose, Nina rose, too, putting him behind her as she crept to the door.

"We don't know who the fuck's out there. It's near five in the morning. Who rings someone's doorbell at five in the morning? Let me answer the fucking thing. You stay behind me."

He couldn't deny that was the right thing to do. She was an ox times ten. I mean, she'd lifted his car to her shoulders right there in the middle of his driveway just to prove her strength in that spectacle of teeth and fur, but the chivalrous side of him, the one that was taught to protect a woman, fought the notion.

However, Nina was all business when she pressed her ear to the door before she sighed. "We have company," she sang out, swinging open the door to allow a redhead with glasses, holding a black cat, to enter.

"For Christ's sake," the cat said as it looked at him from the arms of the curly redhead. "Would ya look at that shit?"

Oliver almost fell on the floor. In fact, he had to press a palm against the wall to hold himself up. "You…"

"Talk," it said, hopping out of the redhead's arms and onto the floor to swirl its tail around Nina's legs. "Go on and let that shit sink in and then we'll do introductions and all that razzmatazz."

The. Cat. *Talked.*

Holy. Shit.

Nina scooped up the cat from the floor, its dark fur

blending in with her dark hair, and gave it a quick peck on the head. "Calamity, what are you doing here?"

"I heard unicorn and I came runnin'. So what in all of shiny is this shit? Is it real?" Calamity growled.

"It's about as real as it gets," Nina replied, then swung her eyes to the redhead in a bulky jacket, jeans and a pair of glasses that hid her pretty eyes. "So who the fuck is this?"

The cat rubbed its face against Nina's lean cheek. "I dunno. She was at the door when I got here. She picked me up and scratched my ears and didn't seem too flipped out that I can talk. So who am I to turn down an ear scratch?"

In fact, Oliver thought, she didn't seem too flipped out at all. Not by the talking cat or the violent vampire.

The redhead with the chocolate-brown eyes stuck out her hand to Nina, her cheeks pink from the cold October air. Night shrouded her pale face like a dark blanket as she peered at the vampire. "Who are you?"

Nina didn't offer a hand back. What she *did* do was loom over her in that defensive stance she'd perfected. The one with her legs wide apart, her face a seething mask of aggravated. "Uh, excuse the shit out of me. I didn't ring your doorbell. *You* rang *mine*. So who the fuck are *you*?" she sneered.

The woman, her face an ivory landscape of strawberries and cream with gorgeous dark eyes and a pair of softly colored pink lips, shrouded by a mop of unruly hair that easily touched the middle of her back, stared at Nina blankly as though the vampire should know exactly who she was.

"I'm Vincenza Morretti. Or Vinnie, if you'd prefer. You know, the mythology professor? I'm Khristos's friend. He texted me that you and your friends needed help."

"So you just dropped by at five in the fucking morning?"

Vinnie shrugged, pulling her bulky red coat off and tucking it under her arm. "I was already up. I got caught up in reading and happened to be awake when I got the text. Khris said it was urgent and you were up, so I figured why not pop over? If it's inconvenient, and you don't want to know about unicorns this second, I can go home."

"No!" Oliver almost tripped over himself to stop her. "If nobody else wants to know about unicorns, *I* do. Please come in, Miss Morretti." He held out his hand to her and she took it, curling her fingers into his palm.

They stood that way for a few moments, and he wasn't sure what the long gaze between them was about, but she pulled away first, tucking her hand under her jacket. And she didn't seem at all surprised by his horn. Were there others like him?

Nina had said there were tons of other vampires in the world—maybe there were more unicorns and what he'd read was wrong? Maybe he wasn't so rare after all and in no time flat, he'd have tons of little unicorn friends.

Like on Unicorn Island, Oliver? Where all unicorns gather to skip through fields of gumdrops and ride rainbows? Kewlio!

You, nitwit.

"So this?" she murmured in a hushed, almost reverent tone, pointing to his forehead. "*This* is it?"

Oliver spread his arms wide, catching a glimpse of himself in the entryway mirror without his hat before quickly looking away in horror.

"*This* is it."

Vinnie shoved her coat in Nina's direction, not even noticing the look on Nina's face when she behaved as though the vampire were nothing more than a coat check girl. Instead, she took Oliver by the hand, leading him to the living room, where she sat him down on the couch and she took the opposite chair.

She paid no mind to the other women—she didn't even bother to introduce herself—but she stared down at him intently for a long time, her dark eyes wide with interest before she sat across from him and said, "Interesting."

Nina glared at her with a scowl. "That's all you fucking have to say? Interesting? Who the fuck called this nincompoop? We need help, not adjectives, Marty."

But Vinnie almost didn't even notice Nina's ire, because she dared stick a finger to her mouth—and then she hushed her.

Hushed *Nina*.

Oh. Fuck.

"Shhh," she said absently, apparently unfazed by the flare of Nina's nostrils. "I'm working here."

Oliver leaned in close to her, getting a whiff of her perfume—plumeria, he surmised—and winced. "Just a small warning. She's very volatile and very, very easily riled."

Vinnie sighed, her shoulders lifting and falling with the deep breath she took as she folded her hands in her lap. "Oh, I'm not afraid of her. Khristos warned me she was difficult. Just ignore her."

Wow. This was one brave woman. A true warrior.

"Okay, it's your life. I hope you weren't too comfortable here with us folk who like living," Oliver warned.

Nina growled, but Wanda put a hand up in caution. "Nina," she whisper-yelled. "Let them…commune, or whatever's happening here."

But Vinnie still paid no mind. "So have you noticed anything unusual about your protrusion? I mean, besides the glitter? Khristos said there was glitter. Which, I mean, I can see, because it's everywhere, but anything else unusual?"

Sure he had, but he wanted to feel this professor out, and that meant not giving away too much. Did she really know something about unicorns or was she just curious? He needed help, not a rubbernecker.

"What do you mean unusual?"

Her eyes never once left his face, but he had the feeling she wasn't really looking at him, *per se*. He felt like a science experiment, splayed out on an eighth grader's desk, awaiting dissection.

"I mean anything out of the ordinary. Don't you know what 'unusual' means?"

Was she purposely being dense? Oliver tried not to sound offended when he said, "Of course I do. I'd just like to know your definition."

"How can I define what I mean when I don't know what you'd consider unusual? For instance, you have a horn poking out of your forehead, better known as an *alicorn*. That's an obviously unusual anomaly. But less unusual can mean something else entirely. Maybe you have stomach cramps. So do you usually have stomach cramps? Or did they just begin when the alicorn appeared. Do you understand what I mean?"

She peered at him as though he were a complete dolt then she tucked her hair behind her ears and waited for his answer.

"Look," Wanda said, her soft voice a welcome interference for his stunted speech and whirling thoughts. "Miss Morretti, Oliver's been up for ages now. He's tired, he's had a traumatic experience, and he's seen more than his fair share of *unusual* tonight. Let's take it easy on him. That would be the kindest thing to do at this point. While we appreciate you coming by at a moment's notice to help us, we don't want to insult our client."

Vinnie's face melted almost instantly as she bit at her lower lip and winced. "I came on too strong, didn't I? Shoot. Sometimes I get way too involved in my own thoughts and I forget to buffer my words, or I'm too anxious to say them at all. My mother used to tell me sometimes honesty isn't always the best policy. I fear that's true. Do you want me to leave?"

"Leave?" Oliver asked on a frown. "Of course not. Why would I want you to leave?"

Her face fell, her eyes growing round as dimes. "It wouldn't be the first time I've been too forward and someone's asked me to leave."

Nina popped her lips and planted her hands on her lean hips. "Nobody wants you to leave, Curly Sue. We just want you to slow your roll, and that's coming from an insensitive bitch who always says whatever the fuck she's thinking. Dude's all kinds of fucked up. He's still slogging his way through this shit. Go slow."

Oliver held up his hands to still everyone. "Let's start again, okay? I'm Oliver Baldwin, and I have an...*alicorn*, is it? It sheds pink and purple glitter as you can see, which, as my sister says, really is the herpes of the craft world, in case you were undecided. I don't know how I got it. I don't know why, but I have it, and I don't know what to do to get rid of it. Anyway, under these trying circumstances, it's nice to meet you."

Vinnie finally smiled, her eyes lighting up with amusement as she absorbed his words. Her entire face changed with that one smile, making him smile in return.

She held out her hand with a shy gaze. "My name is Vincenza Raphaela Morretti. I'm twenty-eight, and I teach Greek mythology at the local college. I live here in Buffalo, and I have two dogs and a cat. Their names are Frank, Mario, and Brenda. I'm here to try to help, if you'll let me." Then she paused and looked at him again, shyer than ever. "Still too much?"

He grinned, her smile warming him from the inside. "Frank, Mario, and Brenda, huh? Are they okay if you leave them alone?"

She nodded, her eyes lighting up. "I have someone who'll walk and feed them for me. They'll be fine for now."

"It's funny you should mention your pets. I have a chipmunk. Her name's Baloney."

Vinnie gasped in clear delight, smiling wider, thereby deepening her dimples. "Do you really? Can I see—"

"Hey! Love Connection!" Nina threw a hand between them, her lips a thin line, her expression annoyed. "I have shit to handle at home. Let's get this sparkly show on the damn road. We need to get moving before you're forced to do kids' parties with Elsa and Belle as your damn sidekicks in order to put bread on the table. Do you wanna shit glitter from your head for the rest of your life or do you wanna figure this out?"

Nina was right. He let his head hang in shame before he straightened his shoulders and sat up, his spine rigid. "Sorry, Nina. I definitely want to figure this out. If for nothing else but the fact that I don't think I can keep up with the kind of effort it takes to deal with all this glitter. I mean, who could?"

"Okay then. She asked you if you noticed anything unusual about your fucking horn, Pony Boy. So have you noticed anything unusual about it other than it's fucked up? Like, when you wave your head around, does it turn into a magic wand? Light saber? Or does it just shit glitter on everyone and everything?"

He laughed at that because really, even if you had no sense of humor at all, this was some funny stuff. That's when he remembered a small detail. Of course, it was ridiculous, but it was worth mentioning because who couldn't use a laugh when they had a unicorn horn in the middle of their head?

"You know, Nina, this has nothing to do with light sabers, but I did just think of something. You know what I had after lunch today?"

"A rainbow?" she asked on a snarf before she grinned. "No, wait. Skittles?"

He chuckled again, because he had to or he'd fall apart, and there was no way he was going to do that in front of strangers.

"One of those unicorn Frapps from Starbucks. You know, the pink sugary drink? Ironic, right? Me, a unicorn, drinking a unicorn Frapp."

But no one laughed—not even a snicker. In fact, all the women looked at him as though he'd just made a joke at a funeral. Except for Vinnie; she flashed him a small smile, showing off her dimples.

"Man, you guys. Tough crowd, huh? C'mon. That's funny right?"

"Not so funny, motherfucker," Nina groused. "Don't

you remember what I told you about Wanda's sister Casey and how she drank demon blood and then, lo and flippin' behold, she became a demon?"

"But you said that was an accident," he protested. "That wasn't meant for her, right? You can't really think Starbucks is turning everyone into unicorns, can you? Is it some mass plan to take over the world by glittering everyone to death?"

Nina waved a finger under his nose. "Listen, Sparkle Man, you have no idea what's fucking out there. None. People will do a whole lot more for a whole lot less. Quit making jokes and start thinking of things to fucking help us." Looking at Baloney, she cooed, "Tell Daddy to get his shit together and tell us if anything weird's happened to him because a comedian he ain't."

Baloney.

Shit. He'd forgotten all about what had happened earlier with Baloney.

Leaning back into the couch, Oliver nodded slowly. "Something weird has happened, actually."

"We've been here two fucking hours, Rainbow Brite. What the fuck took so long?"

"Sorry. This thing sticking out of my head's a little distracting."

"Forget her," Vinnie ordered, all business. "Tell me what you noticed, Oliver."

He liked the way she said his name. "Nina? Would you give me Baloney, please?"

Nina plopped down next to him and peeled a

sleepy, protesting Baloney from her shoulder, dropping a kiss on her head. "It's all right, Nugget. Daddy needs you, but I'm right here to save you from his crazy ass. Just say the word."

Oliver made a face, but he took Baloney from Nina, to the oooing and ahhing sounds of Vinnie, and held her in the palm of his hand. "This is Baloney, and Baloney had a lame hind leg. I found her on the front porch three years ago, and as long as I've known her, she's always had it." He tickled his chipmunk's belly to rouse her from sleep.

"May I?" Vinnie asked softly, holding out her fingertips in a tentative gesture.

"Under normal circumstances, I'd caution you to be careful. She doesn't normally like females, but Nina's proven me wrong tonight. Still. I'm going to caution you anyway. Just be careful. She's skittish."

Vinnie leaned forward and lightly grazed Baloney's back, running her fingers over the white stripes adorning it with the lightest of touches.

When Baloney actually leaned into her hand, Oliver knew everything would be all right.

That's when she asked, "So this unusual thing has to do with Baloney? Who, as an aside, is perfect in every way."

Oliver nodded. "It does. She's always dragged her back leg behind her. She gets around just fine, mind you. But it's always been lame. Today, when I got home and pulled off my hat, the first thing she did was scurry up along my body, went directly for the horn, and chewed on it. It hurt so damn much, I almost fell over. But guess what?"

The women all looked at him with curious expressions.

He rubbed his fingers together, trailing them along his arm to call Baloney, who followed them, running up his limb with nary a hitch in her stride.

"Shut the fuck up," Nina murmured, her eyes wide in shock. "No fucking way! It must be a fluke. How do we know she was lame before we met her? Is your daddy lying to me, Nugget?"

Baloney looked at Nina, her sweet brown eyes adoring when she cocked her small head as though she were really listening to Nina.

Handing Baloney over to Vinnie, he rose and began to make his way to the kitchen. "Let's test that no-fucking-way theory, Nina."

There was the satisfying sound of rushed footsteps and Wanda calling to Marty to help her lift "enormous butt" off the couch as he went for the knife drawer, then turning to look at them all gathering around the island.

He pulled the sharpest knife he had from the drawer, the gleaming silver catching the recessed lighting of the kitchen when he held it up.

"Oliver, no!" Vinnie cried in protest, her pale face going paler still.

Nina was beside him in a flash. "Give me that fucking thing, you stupid lunatic."

"Why?" he asked, comically leering down at her. "Will the scent of my blood tempt you?"

Nina threw up both her middle fingers. "Fuck off with your nutty watch-too-much-shit-on-TV, weirdo. I'm not gonna let you mutilate—"

Before she could stop him, Oliver ran it over the palm of his hand, which stung like hell, thank you very much, and held it up as a crimson line of blood began to drip down his forearm.

Then, before he could chicken out, he slammed it against the horn on his forehead and tightened his fist around it.

And prayed.

Prayed it would work…or this was gonna hurt like hell come tomorrow.

CHAPTER 5

Vinnie gasped sharply, clinging to Baloney and tucking her close to her face. But the moment Oliver put his big fist around the horn was the moment the blood dried up and evaporated as if it had never been there.

Which meant the legend she'd thought was just a bunch of bunk was really true.

He could heal people with his horn.

Holy cannoli.

Everyone was so busy gawking at Oliver—who, as a side note, wasn't hard on the eyeballs. He was easily a good six-two, maybe three. His coal-black hair, a little longish for her taste, just grazed the bottom of his neck, thick and shiny, and she had to admit, the purple and pink glitter his horn spat everywhere did kind of go with his complexion. Which was deep and ruddy, clear and smooth.

His hands were huge as he gripped the horn, but it

was his thighs that made her weak in the knees. She was a sucker for thickly muscled thighs, and he had those in spades. When he moved, they bulged against his jeans, leaving her mouth watering.

However, the immediate problem wasn't how heart-stoppingly attractive Oliver was. The immediate problem was, he had an alicorn, and there wasn't a God or Goddess with ill intent on their minds left in the universe who wouldn't want him under lock and key *forever.*

The power he held in that branch of many colors sprouting from his head was enormous, and could be used for evil just as easily as good.

And that wasn't even the tip of the iceberg. If, for instance, the government found out about this, the havoc they could wreak was something she couldn't even ponder without shuddering. They'd turn him into the biggest science project yet.

Yet, the real question? What made Oliver Baldwin the chosen one? What made him so special? No one suddenly turns into a unicorn for no reason. No one. Not ever. There were no recorded records of any living unicorns in this day and age. Not since the twelfth century. That left her with only legend and myth to go on.

Yet, there was no denying Oliver Baldwin was a unicorn.

So now what, Vin? What do you do now? You know as well as anyone, there are plenty of people who want what Oliver has, they've just never been able to find it.

So when half of the Underworld could potentially come looking for him, with vengeance in their hearts and death on their minds, how do you protect him, Vinnie? How do you prepare him for that kind of battle?

Worse, how could she tell him there might be a battle at all?

Her stomach roiled, the glass of wine she'd had earlier sloshing in her stomach.

For right now, until she understood more, she'd keep that under her hat and pray her forthright, some would say boldly single-minded nature stayed quiet and she was able to keep her mouth shut.

So rather than speak at this point, she merely observed. Observed these fierce women both Khristos and Quinn had spoken so fondly about over a bottle of wine and a charcuterie plate, as they gaped at what his horn had done.

Because neither Khristos nor Quinn could be here, she wanted to help in their stead. She wanted to do them proud.

That they'd thought of her in a time of such immediate crisis left her flattered. Her admiration for Quinn having taken over none other than Aphrodite's position knew no bounds. It was one of the tougher jobs a Goddess could endure, in her opinion. Going to battle was all well and good. But it was usually one and done. Fists flew, fire raged, and it was over.

But dealing with matters of the heart?

That was so very complicated. Even though Quinn had inherited the job by accident, she'd really stepped up to the plate. The love she shared with Khristos was enviable. It made Vinnie sigh every time they saw each other at a gathering at the college or some charity function.

She really wished they were here right now because she didn't know what to do or where to turn.

Vincenza Raphaela Morretti was probably one of the very few people on earth who knew almost everything there was to know about the elusive unicorn... and truth be told, there wasn't a whole lot to know, or at least she didn't think there was.

Khristos had a call into his mother, who'd been around for centuries. Maybe she could help. Still, who'da thunk she'd ever need to use what little information she had?

When Oliver pulled his hand from his horn, all the women backed away except Nina, who grabbed his fingers and examined his palm, her jaw unhinged.

But she gathered herself quickly. "Dude, you fucking healed your hand! What the shit?"

Oliver shrugged his linebacker shoulders, his face a little pale. "Your guess is as good as mine."

Wanda ran a hand over her very large belly and blew out a breath. "You do know what this means, don't you, ladies?"

Marty narrowed her eyes in Wanda's direction. "Please don't say it."

Vinnie silently prayed with her, wincing. *Please don't say it.*

Wanda licked her lips. "You guys remember what

happened with Quinn, don't you? She had the power. Somebody wanted the power. It's the same old, same old. If anyone finds out, human or paranormal, that Oliver has this kind of power, he's stewed."

Marty sighed long and loud as she tucked her arms under her breasts. "The truth. There's always someone waiting in the wings to snatch up something that isn't theirs. Whether it's because of jealousy or money or vengeance, there's always someone.

Nina dropped her hand on the gorgeous countertop like a hammer, making some residual glitter spray everywhere. "Fuuuck. You're right. He's a walking advertisement for easy money. Jesus. Christ. It's not like we can hide this shit."

But Oliver wasn't grasping the entire concept. "Hold on. What happened with Quinn? She's a matchmaker. How is that a superpower?"

Marty twirled a fat blonde curl around her index finger. "I told you before. Matchmaking isn't just some fluffy, vapid thing Aphrodite does, Oliver. She makes matches with the end game in mind. Matches that will produce future powerful leaders, negotiators, fixers, if you will. She ensures these people land in the same place at the same time in order to *produce* those people—or sometimes, on a much more emotion-based level, in order to simply bring two people together who would have left this life alone, sad. What she does is insanely important to the world. *The world.* And had someone gotten ahold of that power…"

By now, the wan sun was just beginning to rise,

breaching the bank of floor-to-ceiling windows in the kitchen, and Vinnie was feeling it. She was suddenly quite exhausted, but Marty's words made her stand straight and pay attention.

She couldn't have said it better, but she held her breath for what was to come.

Nina rolled her head on her shoulders and cracked her knuckles. "So here's what my favorite ass-sniffer's tryin' to tell you. There's always someone, someone shitty, lurking out there in the fucking shadows like a GD grease spot, looking to take that power. You understand? You have the power to heal shit. I don't know *all* the shit you can heal. I don't know if it's only cuts and scrapes, or it's big shit like cancer or tumors or what all else. I only know this: somebody will want it. Someone will find out you fucking have it, and they'll try to take it. I don't know if it'll be a human, like maybe someone from the government, or a paranormal, but somebody's gonna want that sparkle baton on your big-ass head. You mark my flippin' words, Ollie. *Mark 'em.*"

Vinnie squirmed. She'd have preferred to tell him in a less abrasive way, but Nina spoke the truth.

Suddenly, Oliver's blue gaze swung to her, pinning her to the spot, making her cheeks hot. He stormed over to her, those thighs she'd admired flexing and bulging as he went.

"So what they're saying is true?" Then he shook his head, sending yet more glitter shooting everywhere. "I mean, of course it is, right? Who wouldn't want something like that in their arsenal? I realize that sounds like a stupid question. I could totally see someone in the government wanting it, but someone paranormal?" He looked to the three women. "Don't you all have immortality on your side? Why would they want this horn if they can't get sick to begin with?"

Vinnie licked her lips and tucked Baloney closer to her neck as the room closed in on her. "Almost all of them are immortal, yes. But Marty will tell you, not so long ago, she fell into a coma because she's half human. Her turning was an accident and, as a result, she has human properties."

"And that's not even taking into consideration the loons who track and hunt myth shit like they breathe," Nina reminded. "We've had a fair amount of crazy Bigfoot lovers at our doorstep since we started the website, just hoping to catch us in the act of being fucking werewolves and vampires. There's one who calls the hotline all the damn time. Don't know who the fuck he is, but I can always smell a bullshitter. So I never give too much away. I'd hunt his ass down if I knew it wouldn't make more trouble for our kind. But I'll tell you this, he's hellbent on proving we exist."

"Because you do exist," Oliver murmured.

"Yeah, and now, so do you, pal," Nina replied grimly. "That's not taking into account the other paranormals who think they want in on this gig with us because it sounds like a fucking adventure, but what they really want is to find a way to exploit your ass. Believe me, we've had plenty of the vampire community offer to 'help,' but it's all just bullshit. They just want to take fucking advantage of a pool full of fresh newbs who have no idea what they're doing or the first clue about how to live as a paranormal."

Oliver gulped. "So you're telling me, someone might hunt me for my unicorn horn?"

"There are bad paranormal people as well as good, Oliver," Vinnie reminded. "And like humans, they come from varying socioeconomic walks of life. So I'm sure if a bad paranormal got wind of this, they'd use it to their advantage for financial gain."

He pressed his hip against the island and inhaled a deep breath. "But how would they do that when I'm attached to the damn horn?"

Her breathing sped up and her hands grew clammy. "They would—"

"Detach it. Which—let me take a wild guess—would kill me, I suppose," he replied woodenly.

Yeah.

Yeah. There was that.

～

The morning had arrived, chilly and overcast, a perfect fall day as far as Vinnie was concerned. Like Oliver, whom she'd discovered shared her love of autumn, she adored the leaves, the crisp weather, a nice warm jacket, and a healthy fire.

Unlike Oliver, she didn't have a horn, but she was trying desperately to find a way to figure out how to deal with his new appendage and to keep him safe.

That left her staring aimlessly out of his gorgeous windows in his beautiful kitchen at his backyard full of leaves in a state of semi-panic.

The OOPS women had put a call in to their friends to help them, because Oliver was going to need round-the-clock supervision, and with Wanda on the verge of giving birth, they wanted to have backup available.

In a matter of moments, a huge man with gold chains and high-top sneakers named Darnell had arrived, along with Carl, a pale green, childlike zombie, and the cutest elderly gentleman—in a sharp black suit and ascot—Vinnie had ever seen, named Archibald. The manservant, as he called himself, whisked in with a recipe book and bags of groceries and a vacuum, handing out orders to everyone who stood in the kitchen.

They'd swept in like a tour de force and taken over Oliver's lovely home. Archibald had begun cooking breakfast, Carl played with Baloney, and Darnell kept watch by the windows.

She'd heard all the stories about them from Khristos and Quinn, so when Oliver began to balk about the time he was taking from these strangers' lives, Vinnie reassured him this was part of the OOPS package. It might get loud, it might get messy, but they'd do their best to help him find his way through this.

Now, as Vinnie sat at the island, straightening the salt and pepper shakers so they aligned with the napkin holder, Oliver leaned over and asked, "I sense a fellow organizer in my midst."

Yet again, she'd forgotten not to fiddle with other people's belongings. She was a horrible fiddler. She liked things in order. For instance, her canned goods were stocked in her pantry in alphabetical order, her clothes were arranged in her closet by color and season, and her shoes were lined up, toes facing forward.

For some—okay, most—she was unnerving. She left people feeling like they couldn't measure up to her standards. If she were honest, mostly men felt that way. Women seemed to take her quirks in stride, but tell just one man he'd put away a can of creamed corn in the wrong place, and you were suddenly akin to having the plague.

Along with her anxiety, she had a touch of OCD, both of which made for a difficult time in the dating pool. So she'd stopped dating altogether.

Vinnie moved her hands away from the salt and pepper shakers and back to her lap in guilt. "Sorry. It's a bad habit."

"Oh, I don't mind, and I don't think it's bad. I like things in order, too," he assured her, his voice husky and warm. "Since I've been doing renovations on this place, it's been a fight to keep things together so I know where everything is. It makes me nuts when I can't find a tool or a list of what comes next."

"Lists!" she almost shouted in joyful agreement. "I love lists. They make everything right."

"I have a list for my list," Oliver joked, sipping his coffee.

She nodded her head with a return smile. He got it. "Organization gives me life." And it was the truth. She began to feel overwhelmed when things were out of order.

Likely because her childhood, while happy enough, had always been in complete chaos. Her mother was a clutter bug, she was always late, and there were always endless piles of things everywhere.

Vinnie lost track of the times she'd heard her mother yell across their living room, "Honey? Have you seen…?" fill in the blank.

It made her anxious, but she could appreciate someone who didn't think she was rigid and inflexible because she liked her kitchen faucet to sit squarely in the center of her farmhouse sink or the pillows on her bed to meet equally in the middle.

Oliver grinned, and even though he really looked ridiculous, he was so attractive, the horn was easy to ignore and she couldn't help but respond.

"Same here. I can't breathe if things aren't where they belong. According to Susan Baldwin, my mother, I've always been this way."

"Some might call you rigid." She chuckled, twisting a strand of hair around her finger. Had that sounded stupid? She was so awkward around the opposite sex—she'd always been—but Oliver had this calming nature that drew her to him. She couldn't explain it, but she'd felt it when they'd met at the front door

He winked. "Oh, believe. Some have. Some have even called me inflexible." His blue eyes grew a little distant when he said it, but when they returned to focus on her, he was smiling again.

She mock gasped. "No! The heathens."

"You've heard that before, I'm guessing?"

Sucking in her cheeks, she bounced her head. "If you only knew how many times I've heard that. But then I don't spend my weekends having to do a ton of housework because I didn't keep up with things all week, either."

He cocked his head, his dark hair gleaming and shiny as it fell around his horn. "How *do* you spend your Saturdays?"

"Ahem," Nina said, jamming her face between them. "I hate to interrupt this touching moment from Adrenaline Rush Dating, but didn't you fucking say you had a client you have to meet today before you can hand this shit off?"

Oliver winced and ran his hands over his thighs. "I do, and I love her, and I'm not handing her off to the dick I work with. Excuse my language. I took my vacation time, so I'm good, but I have to do this one thing. I have to go because she's a cute little old lady, and I won't have her badgered by my colleague, who's more interested in saving a buck than finding ways to give her as much as we can squeak out."

He sounded very passionate about whatever it was he did for work. She liked that because she was passionate about her work, too.

"What do you do for a living?" Vinnie asked with interest as she found herself leaning into him in order to take another whiff of his cologne.

He smelled clean. She liked that. Maybe she liked that too much. He had a horn, for the love of Zeus, and plenty on his plate. He didn't need her sniffing his hair, for cripes sake.

"I'm a housing developer." His answer was simple, but she had an idea what he did was anything but.

"Do you mind if I go along? I can't be a lot of help in the muscle department. I'm just plain old me. Though, I think you have the brawn covered with Nina. But I'd like to grab some things from my office at the college that might help us to decipher what to do next. Why go alone when I can conserve gas and go with you guys?"

Marty returned to the kitchen with a huge wad of gauze and some tape, her blue eyes shining as she held it up. "You ready?"

Oliver gave her a skeptical look. "I feel like telling everyone I'm concussed is going to be a stretch. A concussion usually doesn't come with a protrusion from your forehead."

The plan, in order to give Oliver the chance to handle this client he refused to leave to his co-worker, was to wrap his head and pretend he'd been in a minor accident, resulting in some head trauma.

Now, granted, this might stretch the boundaries of believability, but it was worth a shot because he wasn't letting this issue go, and the worry he might run into someone dangerous, who'd find out he had the mark of the unicorn, was too worrisome to let him go alone.

"Well, we'll just see about that," Marty muttered as she began to unravel the gauze with determination in her eyes. "I mean, it's not like anyone's going to wander up to you and ask you if you're hiding a unicorn horn, right? Most people will likely just look away, and maybe some will even laugh a little behind your back as they wonder what's going on under your bandages. But so what, right? It's nothing compared to the spectacle you'd make of yourself if you wandered around with it uncovered. But unfortunately, this isn't just the best idea any of us have had, it's the *only* one any of us have had. If you're determined to make this meeting, we don't have many options."

As Marty lifted her arms to begin her work camouflaging his horn, Oliver grabbed her hand and squeezed it before letting go. "Thank you, Marty. I don't know if I've said that yet, but I appreciate this. I know you're all doing your best to help me and I don't want you to think I'm not grateful—because I am. I really am."

He was kind, too. He loved animals. He was organized. He had a sense of humor.

He was super attractive on all fronts.

Marty tweaked his cheek and grinned, making Vinnie admire the fact that they'd been up all night and her makeup was still impeccable. "It's just what we do, Oliver. We help. Well, Wanda and I help. Nina taunts and calls names, but eventually she'll help, too."

Oliver laughed, the lines around his eyes wrinkling. "And threatens. Man, she's good with a threat."

Marty snickered before she said, "Now, listen, I'm going to try and be gentle. I know this is very sensitive, but give a yell if I hurt you."

As Marty wrapped his head, making it almost resemble a crooked turban, Vinnie watched the activity of the household, listened to the sounds of the women and their newly arrived friends chatter, smelled the scent of the delicious breakfast the cute elderly man was making and wondered why she'd always turned down the invitations from Khristos and Quinn to join in the events they attended with these people.

You know why, Vinnie.

Fair enough. She did know why.

She absolutely did.

~

As they stood in the square in front of the tall glass and steel building where Oliver worked, Vinnie fought to ignore the strange looks he kept getting from people strolling through the industrial park.

Marty had taken her job as Head Camouflage Designer above and beyond the call of duty. No one would ever guess by the heavy wrap of endless reams of gauze and medical tape that underneath, Oliver hid a horn.

In fact, Vinnie wasn't sure how he was able to keep

his head from falling backward, he had so much gauze around his skull. To make matters worse, the construction of it was crooked, so it looked as though he had a big, unevenly melting marshmallow on his head. Though, to Marty's credit, the gauze had managed to stifle the fall of all that glitter.

But he'd taken it in stride when Marty hesitantly showed him with her compact mirror. Oliver had done the kind thing and smiled and thanked her for making his upcoming meeting less worrisome, while Nina and Wanda fought not to burst out laughing.

Darnell simply slapped him on the back and told him to avoid short doorways so he wouldn't lose his head (har-har!) and Archibald had handed him a cinnamon roll with a smirk.

Now, as they waited for the person Oliver was meeting, Vinnie tried to soak up the beauty of their surroundings. Buffalo in the fall was quite glorious, and looking at the trees helped her to avoid thinking about the impending doom Nina repeatedly warned them could happen.

So far, all was quiet. No weirdoes crawling out of the woodwork. No one running at them with a saw in hand, prepared to hack Oliver's horn off and sell it on the black market.

However, things took a real turn when, as they crossed the square, a group of people stopped and stared at Oliver, whispering and nudging each other.

"Hey!" Nina yelled out to a passerby who had the audacity to cruelly snicker as she stalked toward them.

She yanked her phone from the pocket of her hoodie and held it up. "What the fuck is wrong with you? Are you checking to see if your eyeballs work? Or are you staring, punk? Because I fucking know you're not staring at my friend like you just saw a goddamn alien. He has a head injury, you insensitive asshole. Don't be so fucking rude, shitbird, or I'm gonna put your lame ass in a video and post it all up and down Twitter. You'll have a nickname in no time, you dick!"

"Nina," Oliver leaned in to whisper in her ear, as the group of people moved away as quickly away as their feet would carry them. "It's okay. Please don't start a war on my account. I can take care of myself."

"The fuck you say!" she ranted up at Oliver, standing on tiptoe, her eyes hidden by dark glasses but surely flashing fire in the morning light. "Maybe you can take care of yourself, Jolly Green Giant, but what about the people who can't and are just gonna suffer in silence because they have no voice? Bullshit! Those motherfuckers have no damn manners, and I'm gonna show them the inside of their assholes if they don't get some!"

"Nina?" Vinnie intervened, hoping to thwart the stares from more people who'd begun to gather when she'd started to rant, and to save Oliver the embarrassment of a colleague accidentally seeing this.

"*What?*" she yelled into the square, her voice echoing, her eyes bulging.

Vinnie held out her hand. She might be socially awkward, mostly riddled by anxiety when it came to male relationships, and so organized it actually stressed people out, but there was one thing she did know how to do. Fake an illness to get out of an awkward situation.

She was the bomb.com at that. She was also—due to the fact she spent more time observing people than actually getting in the thick of things and interacting—pretty darn good at gauging a person. Nina, though a beast, was an easy mark in terms of reading.

This vampire was a protector. She was a lot of bluster, but mostly no action unless necessary. She was banking on her character assessment skills now as she held out her hand to the vampire and put the other on her tummy.

"I don't feel so great. Could we go sit while we wait for Oliver?"

Nina's face instantly transformed as her attention fell on Vinnie. She looked down at her with eyes full of concern. "You okay? Did you have anything to eat before we left? I hear it's important you fucking eat in times of crisis, but it's been a long time since I ate, I forget."

Just then, a flurry of noise erupted from behind them, making them both turn around and stare.

By the fountain with the modern art sculpture made of steel in the middle, there were a few curse words thrown into the wind, followed by the rustle of a bunch of papers as they escaped someone's grasp.

"There she is," Oliver said, his tone warm as he pointed his finger in the direction of the person by the fountain who was cussing up a blue streak and chasing the escaped papers.

Vinnie squinted her eyes, a sudden burst of sun pushing through the clouds making it difficult to see. "Who is that?"

"My mid-morning date," Oliver said with a fond smile. "She's the liaison between the investors and me for the senior housing development I'm working on. She's been a huge help in keeping it affordable but with enough bells and whistles to attract folks."

A senior housing development that was affordable? Gods, he really was dreamy.

As Oliver began to move with quick strides toward the person swearing, with them following hot on his heels, Vinnie caught her first good glimpse of Oliver's morning date.

Which stopped her cold in her tracks and made her grind her teeth together.

Oh, this was bad. So very bad.

Nina pulled up short behind her and gave her a nudge to the shoulder with the flat of her palm. "You okay, Proff? Still have a stomachache?"

"Oh, I'm fine. Just fine. I don't have a stomachache anymore. I have a whole different kind of ache," Vinnie hissed, narrowing her eyes as she stomped toward the fountain while papers flew up in the air, mimicking the thousand thoughts whirling through her head.

None of them good.

When she reached the fountain, Vinnie was so close

to blowing her top, she had to clench her fists and her jaw to keep from going directly into attack mode.

Oliver's date's head popped up when she heard the footsteps, her eyes zeroing in on Vinnie.

And then she smiled wide, her blue-gray eyes lighting up as she held out her arms, so very clearly pleased with herself.

If steam could emit from one's ears, it would come out in big shooting gusts from Vinnie's as she stopped short in front of Oliver and his date.

From tight lips, she eyeballed her foe, whose face fell when she saw the look in Vinnie's eyes and the crimson red spotting her cheeks.

But she wasn't going to fall for that innocent fawn-in-the-woods look.

No, that didn't stop her from growling the word, *"Mother."*

CHAPTER 6

*O*liver ran his hand over his face and stared down at them with confused eyes. "You're Vinnie's mother, Mrs. Costas?"

Oh. My. Goddess. She was going to kill her. She was going to wrap her fingers around her mother's delicate neck and choke her out. Yes. Alice Marie *Costas* was her mother—her married-for-the-third-time mother. Which, when asked, would explain why her last name was Morretti and her mother's wasn't.

She looked to Oliver, her eyes warm and attentive. "I thought I told you to call me Alice, dear boy?" Then she licked her thumb and reached up. "You have a little something purple riiight there," she said, swiping her finger on the side of his mouth before wiping the glitter on her thigh.

Oliver's eyebrows smooshed together, or at least they tried to, but he had so much gauze on his head it looked like it made the task difficult. "Okay, *Alice*. Are you Vinnie's mother?"

But her mother, always quick to divert, reached up and cupped Oliver's cheek, her hands, though quite old —far older than anyone would guess—still making her look like she was in, at best, her late fifties.

"What happened to you, Oliver? Are you hurt, son?" Alice asked, concern in her eyes.

Vinnie couldn't help herself. Her head tipped backward and laughed as the sharp wind blew her hair around her face. She laughed so hard, she started to cough and she couldn't stop.

Nina slapped her on the back with such force, she almost passed out. "What the fuck's happening here, All Things Expert On Olives and Ouzo? Why the hell are you laughing?"

Vinnie held up a hand to signal she needed a second as she gathered her wits, tucking her jacket tighter around her. When she finally caught her breath, she narrowed her gaze in her mother's direction and shook her finger.

"Why don't you tell everyone what's going on, Mother? Because you know *exactly* what's going on, don't you? You did this, didn't you?" she yelled, waving a finger upward at Oliver's crooked head. "*It was you!*"

Her mother, with her sweet eyes, graying hair she refused to dye and braided to fall down her back, and quivering bottom lip, looked at her as though she'd gone mad. She held out her hands imploringly. "Vincenza, I don't understand. What have I done?"

Leaning in close, Vinnie fought not to scream the answer to the question in her mother's face. "A spell, Mother. A love spell, to be precise. Sound familiar?"

Alice's hand went directly to her throat in a clutching-her-pearls gesture. "I don't know what you mean, Vincenza. What exactly are you accusing me of?"

Vinnie planted her hands on her hips and made a face. "Oh, no. Nonononono! You don't get to do that, Mother! Don't you dare turn the tables on me, you meddler. *You* did this to Oliver. I know you did. I know it, but you don't have to admit it. Let me retrace your steps from the last couple of days. But first, let's start with when you met Oliver, then hold tight and prepare for your dressing down."

Nina's hand went up instantly as she wrapped an arm around Alice's trembling shoulders. "Hey, this is your fucking mother, Teacher. I get she probably has some shit to do with this, but she doesn't smell like somebody who does shit with malice. So relax, or I'm gonna fuck you up."

But Vinnie waved her off. She wasn't afraid of Nina. But Nina should be very afraid of her mother. "Oliver? How long have you known Alice Marie Costas?"

He looked at her, his handsome face blank. "Um, a couple of months, I think. Is that right, Alice?"

Alice licked her lips, her eyes darting around the square. "Give or take," she conceded.

Vinnie's eyes narrowed. "And that's probably how long you've been hatching this plan, right? You spent some time with him, you played the cute little old lady, you had a few lunches where you half paid attention to his suggestions for this senior development, all while you were investigating him, right?"

Alice gave her an affronted look and harrumphed. "I beg your pardon? I don't half pay attention to anything where the seniors are concerned, young lady! I know everything that's going into this development right down to which light switch covers were chosen. I take my job very seriously."

Vinnie rolled her tongue along the inside of her cheek and nodded. "Uh-huh. I just bet you did. If there's anything you're good at, it's the details, isn't it? You're also good at worming your way into any situation by playing sweet little old lady, and then shablam!"

Oliver, who'd stood rooted to the spot as papers flew around his big, yummy body and clouds rolled overhead, cupped his chin and rubbed the stubble growing there. "I don't understand where you're going, Vinnie. Your mother's been nothing but great during this whole process. If not for her and her details, I never would have thought to include—"

"Yeah," Vinnie drawled, unable to stop herself. "She's a real peach, aren't you, Mother? Know what else she is? A meddling monster! Did my mother bring you cookies, or a cake, maybe some pie? Or worse, the unicorn Frapp you talked about?"

Oliver gave her a blank look but he didn't respond. Still, she could see the wheels turning in his head.

"Now, if she didn't bring you the Frapp," Vinnie continued, "she still knew you'd drink it even if it is the worst-tasting Frapp in the world, because no one wants to upset cute little old Alice Marie Costas and you wouldn't dream of insulting her, am I right?"

Oliver frowned and rocked back on his feet. "Okay, that's probably true. She is really cute and sweet and I would never insult her, but she didn't bring me the Frapp, Vinnie. I was stupid enough to try it all on my own. So I'm not sure where you're going here?"

Vinnie pursed her lips as she looked up at him. "Ah, but I'd bet my collection of Encyclopedia Britannica you left her alone with it, didn't you?"

"You have a collection of Encyclopedia Britannica when there's Google? It's two thousand nineteen, Vinnie," Oliver quipped, his handsome face breaking into a smile.

"Not the point, Oliver!" she yelped, and then she softened her voice. "And I like real books. I like the way they smell. The way they feel. The way they look on a shelf. But that's still not the point."

"What the fuck *is* the point?" Nina yelled down at her with a clap of her hands. "Because you're not making any sense. Stop playing Sherlock Holmes and just tell us what the hell you're blaming your mother for, because I, for one, ain't a fan of publicly flaying a bitch…er, I mean, your mother. Get to the end of this lame story."

Vinnie waved the angry vampire away again. She wasn't afraid of Nina when there was an Alice Marie Costas roaming free. "Answer the question, Oliver. Did you leave my mother alone with your drink? Was she in your office at any time, alone with that Frapp? Was she anywhere in the vicinity of the unicorn drink?"

He paused and gazed off into the distance as if he were thinking, the sharp angles of his face even more handsome in the daylight. "Come to think of it, I guess I did. We had a meeting yesterday to go over some things, and then I had to grab more paperwork from my assistant. So I left her alone for about five minutes."

"I knew it!" she shouted, spinning around to face her mother, who did a nice portrayal of a little old lady cowering into Nina. Oscars all 'round for that performance. But Vinnie wasn't falling for it. "So, *Mom*, tell me. Did you put something in Oliver's unicorn Frapp?"

Her mother gave her a sheepish glance. "What do you mean put *something* in it? I don't even know what a unicorn Frapp is, Vincenza."

Vinnie grinned in irony and shook her head. "Oh, knock it off. You do so, and had I known Oliver knew *you*, I would have solved this mess much sooner. Now stop dodging the question and playing at semantics. Did you put something in Oliver's cup on his desk when he left you alone in his office yesterday?"

Now she became rather feisty as she rolled her head on her neck, gazing defiantly at her daughter. "No, I did not."

Nina glared at her, too, pulling her mother closer to her side. "See? Now back the fuck off. This is your mother, for Christ's sake."

Vinnie lifted her chin and crossed her arms over her chest. Okay. She saw the game, but she knew how to play. "Mother? Did you put a *spell* of any kind on Oliver's drink? Or anything he ate in front of you? Or anything he touched? Or his clothes? His aura? His anything, and I do mean *anything*—and if you value our relationship, you'll answer me truthfully. *Now*."

"My aura?" Oliver mumbled.

Her mother began to squirm as she listed all the viable portals acceptable for Alice to place a love spell.

"Mother?" Vinnie coaxed. "What have you done?"

Her mother crumbled then. Her face went soft and pliable, her eyes welled with tears. "I was just trying to help, Vincenza! I swear! Oliver's such a lovely young man and he's perfect for you. *Perfect!* I mean, look at how handsome he is, and he's single. His traitorous girlfriend Denise left him three years ago after *she* was unfaithful. Who leaves such a nice boy? Who, Vincenza? I tried to tell you about him, but you just wouldn't listen. You *never* listen. You'll be like this forever if someone doesn't do something. I just want you to be happy, honey!"

As the wind picked up and the leaves of the surrounding trees began to fall in orange and red drifts of color, Oliver pressed a finger to his mouth as though he were trying not to say something he couldn't take back.

And if it was because he was adhering to the age-old adage of respect your elders, Vinnie had to give it to him. His face contorted, his jaw tightened and he ground his teeth, but he didn't raise his voice.

When he finally spoke, he was deadly quiet,

unnerving not just Vinnie, but her mother, judging by the way she rocked back and forth on her feet. "So what you're telling me is, you put a spell on my unicorn Frapp, Alice? Am I hearing this right?"

Alice bit her lip with a grimace before jamming a knuckle between her pearly white teeth, but she nodded, and croaked, "Yes."

Vinnie clenched her fists so hard, she surely left half-moon shapes in her palm from her fingernails to keep from screaming.

But there was no stopping the eruption from her throat.

"Mother! Do you have any idea what you've done? Do you?" she squealed in horror.

"But—" she began to protest, and Vinnie cut her off with a glare and a shake of her finger.

"No, Mother. Don't you dare. No buts! You've really done it this time! Tell me, Alice, does Oliver *look* like he's in love?"

"In love?" Oliver repeated in astonishment. "But we just met this morning. I mean, you seem really nice, but aren't we putting the cart before the horse?"

Vinnie popped her lips and nodded her head, trying to ignore the compliment even if it made her stomach jump up and down. "Exactly. Which means *what*, Mother?"

Her mother frowned with guilt, twisting her fingers around her colorful scarf. "It didn't work," she peeped quietly, and then she made an attempt to defend herself. "I know I said the incantation correctly,

Vincenza. I don't understand what I keep doing wrong."

Vinnie gave all of them a *See? I'm not crazy* look.

"And why don't you tell Oliver what you were trying to do and what the outcome should have been?"

Wrapping her fingers around her long braid, Alice wrinkled her nose. "I...I planned to introduce you to Vincenza, and then you were supposed to fall wildly in love with her and live happily ever after. But... I guess it didn't work."

That's sort of when Vinnie *really* lost it.

Nina could balk all she wanted about her speaking disrespectfully to her mother, but she'd gone through this all her life. Her mother meddled in everything where Vinnie was concerned, and this time? This time she'd gone too far.

She'd put a man's life in danger—serious danger; as in, *death* kind of danger—which was a far cry from making him fall in love with her daughter.

Vinnie stomped her foot and stuck her face in Alice's. "That's right. It didn't work. It didn't work—because why?" she taunted. "Because they never, and I do mean *never* work, Mom! When are you going to learn you can't meddle in my life without consequences? You need to know your limitations as a, what is it, twenty-fifth-generation Goddess? You stink at spells, Mom. You've *always* stunk at spells, but this time? This time takes the cake. Wait until you see what you've done!"

"Hold up!" Oliver finally yelled into the rustling

wind before he took a deep breath. "Let's just slow this down for the mere mortal in the equation, okay? I don't understand some of the details. Are you paranormal, too, Alice?"

Her mother peered up at him with guilt-riddled eyes, her shoulders sagging. "I'm a descendant of Hecate. So yes, mostly I'm considered paranormal, but our powers have been diluted over the years, I suppose. Not all of us, but some of us."

"Holy motherfluffin' in deep dung, Alice," Nina muttered, pushing her sunglasses up her zinc-covered nose. "Man, you did it. I was all about lookin' out for ya, but this is some kinda somethin'. I'm not sure I can save you from yourself."

Vinnie rolled her head on her neck and stuck her chin out at Alice. "So, FYI, for the novices of the group, here's what my mother's trying to say. Yes. Technically, she's paranormal in that she'll live forever—unless I kill her. No, she has no significant power to speak of, but she'd sure like to. She's always known she was a descendant of Hecate, who once cast powerful spells. *Once* being the operative word here. She loves the idea of being able to make magic. But ever since she did the paranormal version of *23andme* and found out she actually has a *multitude* of Goddess ancestors, she's upped her spell-casting game. Obviously, we're of the low-rent Greek ancestry if what she did to you, Oliver, is any indication. In other words, she didn't inherit the skills to land a spell properly and they aren't worth the paper they're written on."

"Aha," was all Oliver said…and that worried Vinnie.

He was angry. Of course he was, who wouldn't be? But he was struggling with the fact that he was angry with a woman he truly liked and respected. Vinnie could see it all over his face, and especially in his blue eyes as they searched her mother's gray ones.

"Oh, Oliver," Alice whispered, reaching for his hand, a gesture he successfully avoided. "Am I responsible for that bandage on your head?"

Oliver looked behind him and backed up to take a seat at the fountain, his gaze dumbstruck. "Um, yeah. I think so. But it's okay, Alice. I'll be fine. It'll all be fine."

But Vinnie vehemently shook her head. There was no way she was going to let Oliver poo-poo this act of treachery because he was a nice guy.

"No! No, it is *not* fine, Oliver! She's upended your life, and all because she couldn't keep her nose out of my love life."

Her mother scoffed as though she hadn't done something life-altering with her tomfoolery. "You don't *have* a love life, young lady. Why do you think I went to such extreme measures?"

Vinnie threw her hands up in the air. Alice was hopeless. "And that's *my* business, Mother! Do you know what's under all that gauze and tape on Oliver's head, Mom? Do you have any idea how you've altered this man's life—maybe forever?"

"No," she murmured as she gave Oliver a worried look.

"Well, Alice," Nina drawled with a cluck of her

tongue and amusement in her tone. "I can promise you it ain't a declaration of love by way of a tattoo of your kid's name on his forehead. You fucked up—big. 'Scuse my language."

Alice's breath was a hiss as she inhaled and sat down next to Oliver. "Oh, Oliver, what happened? What have I done? You have to know I'd never intentionally do anything to hurt you. I need you to know that."

Oliver, in all his kind, sweet-natured, albeit misguided decency, took Alice's hand and patted it.

"Well, Alice. It seems I'm now a…" It was almost as if he couldn't say it.

But Vinnie could.

So she did, and she didn't even try to hide the venom in her tone. "He's a unicorn, Mother, with a big sparkly horn that's probably growing as we speak. *A. Unicorn.*"

With those words from her daughter, Alice Marie Costas did something she'd never done in all of Vinnie's life.

She clamped her mouth shut before she promptly fainted.

CHAPTER 7

Nina hauled her unconscious mother up over her shoulder right in front of anyone who cared to gawk while Vinnie and Oliver gathered her papers and her purse and they headed to the car.

"You sure we shouldn't take her to the hospital?" Oliver asked Nina, his voice worried.

"Nah. She just passed out from shock. She'll be fine," Nina reassured him as she put Alice in the big black SUV Darnell had driven to Oliver's, and buckled her in.

"How do you know? Are you also a doctor? A vampire-witch doctor? Did you add a PHD in there between accidentally becoming a witch and a vampire?" he asked, and he didn't even try to hide his sarcasm.

Hoo boy. He was feeling edgy. His lack of sleep wasn't helping, but Vinnie'd lay bets it was also due to deep disappointment in her mother. He liked Alice, that much was evident, and she'd taken that like and obliterated it.

Nina made a face at him, flicking her fingers in his face. "First of all, I'm more vampire than witch. Just like Abracadabra Alice here, I suck at spells. Ask my familiar, Calamity the talking cat about that shit. Second of all, I know because I can fuckin' smell it with my vampire nose. I might suck at being a witch, but I'm a badass vampire and I know scents. She's in shock. She'll be fine in a little bit. Let's get her back to your place, get her a cool cloth, and she'll be good as damn new. Trust me. I've done this a million times."

Oliver instantly shut his mouth as they climbed into the SUV, tucked Alice against Vinnie, and drove back to his house in silence.

Vinnie fought her anger with her mother the entire ride back. Her mother was a busybody, no doubt, but this was so extreme. She'd literally groomed Oliver for this moment. In fact, after spending a couple of months with him, Alice probably knew more about Oliver than he knew about himself.

She'd purposefully, willfully cast a spell over his drink to make him fall in love with Vinnie. Not only was that horrible, but it left Vinnie looking pathetically desperate, and she hated *that* almost more than she hated how socially awkward she was.

And while the last thing she should be thinking about was herself, she had to at least address the fact that she liked Oliver, and under other circumstances, because she felt an innate comfort with him, she might have liked to get to know him in her own time.

But that was all blown to hell now.

When they pulled up to Oliver's neat little Craftsman house, her mother began to stir, still tucked into Vinnie's side. Nina was there in a jiff, gathering up a groggy Alice in her arms, hoisting her over her shoulders and carrying her inside, where everyone waited to greet them.

Carl approached both she and Oliver with steaming cups of tea, offering one to Vinnie with a hand that had four duct-taped fingers.

She'd only heard a little about Carl from Quinn and Khristos, in that he was a zombie, but no one had told her how sweetly shy he was.

"For…you," he said with a little smile, his pale green face hopeful.

Vinnie took the mug and smiled warmly. "Thank you, Carl. This is so kind of you."

He turned and she followed him into Oliver's kitchen, where Nina sat Alice in a dining room chair and Archibald hovered over her with a cool cloth and some aspirin.

Wanda waddled up to her and gave her a sympathetic smile. "Don't say a word, honey. I heard all about it from Nina. Mothers, huh?"

Nina had called Wanda on the way back to Oliver's and told her, in her colorful way, what was happening, making Vinnie shrink with embarrassment.

Vinnie pulled her coat off and sighed. "I can't

believe how far she'll go to find me a husband. I don't know why I can't get it through her thick skull that being married and having children isn't the only life a woman can lead."

Wanda, who didn't look as though she'd been up all night and well into the day, nodded her head in sympathy. "She's old school—really old school if she's immortal, I'd guess. It's a hard mindset to break. There was a time when the *only* goal was to have a family, especially for a Goddess. Though, I have to admit, I don't mind having a husband and a child. It's been the best thing that's happened to me."

"But it's not *all* that's happened to you, right?" Vinnie asked. "There's more to your life than being a wife and a mother. I wish I could get my mother to understand that."

"If that ain't the truth," Marty said on a snort. "We have OOPS and various interests. I own a cosmetic's company. Wanda writes books and recently self-published. And Nina, well, she complains all the time. But she's damn good at it."

Vinnie almost laughed…until she remembered her mother had turned an unsuspecting man into a unicorn in order to marry her off. "I have a fulfilling career. I own my own home. I like my life, but my mother seems to think the only thing I have are my pets and some dusty old books, and that's just not true."

Or was it? Maybe it was a little true. Sure, her life was isolated from a social standpoint—she didn't love parties and crowds because she was so damn awkward, but the other parts of her life—her students, her hobbies—those brought her immense fulfillment.

Marty's face softened, her pretty blue eyes warm as she ushered Vinnie to the kitchen island and pulled out a chair. "But was there ever a time you wanted to get married? Have children?"

That deep yearning in the pit of her stomach, the part of her that used to think about a husband and a family, pinged her gut, but only briefly before she remembered, she'd built a life she truly loved, anxieties and all.

Vinnie looked at her hands before she redirected her gaze to Marty. "I did, but they've evolved, I guess. For now, anyway. I really do like my life. But my mother thinks there's a better one in store for me, and if she could just tweak it to satisfy her grandmotherly needs, everything would be right in her world."

"My mother's like that, too," Oliver stated as he leaned into her with just enough pressure against her shoulder to leave her warm before he moved away, taking the chair beside her.

"Your mother casts spells, too?" she teased. "We should introduce them."

Oliver barked a laugh. He'd removed his gauze, and he looked crazier than ever with sprinkles of pink and purple glitter on his cheeks, but somehow, he managed to pull the look off and still be handsome.

Oliver leaned forward, bracing his elbow on the island with a grin. "Maybe our mothers could get together and make a living garden gnome?"

"Bite your tongue and thank your lucky stars you didn't turn into Frankenstein." Vinnie paused for a moment as the full weight of what her mother had done sank in, and then she placed a hand on Oliver's big one, liking the way the contrast of their skin looked, and said, "I'm really sorry, Oliver. I don't know if we can fix this, but I'll do my best to try to find something. Even if it means shaking the answer out of my mother."

"Okay, no murdering mothers today," Wanda ordered with a smile. "How about we have some lunch? Arch made a batch of French onion soup and grilled Brie and Gouda sandwiches. Put a little something in your stomach on this chilly fall day. Anything Arch cooks always makes it better. Then we'll try and find an answer to this mess."

Was there an answer? But Vinnie smiled anyway. Food in her face would certainly temporarily keep her from murdering her mother.

"*Ahhh!*" Archibald howled from the stove as the crash of pots resounded through the kitchen, cutting off their conversation.

He'd knocked over the steaming pot of French onion soup, fresh from the stove. The contents dripped down the front of the steel oven and to the floor, leaving a puddle at the manservant's feet.

"Arch!" Nina was beside him in a flash as he held up his hand, now beet red and dripping with onion soup. "Jesus! You burned the shit out of yourself!"

Marty threw the tap water on, probably to run his

hand under it, but Archibald's skin had begun to bubble and water wasn't going to help that.

"Nooo, Marty!" Wanda bellowed. "He needs more than cold water! Get the SUV, Darnell. He needs a hospital!"

"Nay, miss," Arch protested, but it came out as nothing more than a whimper, his gentle eyes watery and red. "It's nothing, really. Please don't make a fuss."

Oliver popped up from his chair and, without saying a word, grabbed Arch's wrist, wrapping his long fingers around it gingerly.

Nina clapped him on the back, digging her fingers into his shoulder. "What the fuck are you doing, dude? We have to take him to the friggin' ER!"

But Oliver didn't listen. Instead, he bent his big body over the dapperly dressed man, making him look smaller than he really was, raised Arch's wrist and slapped it against the horn. "Grip it, Archibald. Grab on tight," he ordered gruffly.

But Arch looked at him as though he were insane. "Sir?" he cried weakly.

"Trust me. Grab on!" Oliver insisted.

Arch's round face, wrinkled like fine leather, went pale and chalky, his jowls shaking, but he latched on with a whimper of obvious pain from bending his fingers even just a little.

The moment Arch grabbed on, his aging hand twisting around the horn as best he could, Oliver's big body shook. His knees began to buckle as he grabbed for the counter to brace himself while Archibald clung to him.

But Oliver's complexion, normally ruddy and healthy, worried Vinnie the longer Arch held on.

He began to take on a pasty pallor, gray around the edges, making the veins bulging in his neck bluer.

When Oliver began to sway, Vinnie ran up behind him, reaching around his waist to steady him. He wasn't a small man, and he was heavier than he looked, making it difficult to brace him without collapsing herself.

Oliver's well-muscled body vibrated against her almost violently, so much so, she virtually felt the hum of electricity he emitted before he began to buckle, his knees starting to cave while sweat dripped from his forehead.

Vinnie gritted her teeth and dug her feet into the floor, her ballet slippers sliding as she pushed back against the bulk of him with a roar and her last burst of energy.

"Jesus Christ, his eyes are rolling to the back of his goddamn head!" Nina yelled, pushing Vinnie aside and taking her place. "Marty! Grab Arch! Make him let go!"

"Let go, Arch!" Marty ordered with a scream, reaching for Arch's arm and forcefully pulling him from Oliver until they both fell backward to the floor, the manservant's body flailing on top of Marty's.

Darnell rushed in from outside, where he'd been standing watch, his eyes wide. "What are y'all..." He didn't even finish his sentence before his big, lumbering body was across the kitchen, scooping up both Marty and Archibald in his arms. "What's goin' on in here?"

But it was Nina who yelled for help as Oliver began to convulse harder, making them both crash to the floor.

She was out from under him in seconds, rolling him to his side and yelling to everyone, "Stay the fuck out of the way! He's having a seizure!"

Oliver's long torso twisted for a moment like a fish out of water, slapping against the floor, making Vinnie's pulse slam in her ears before he arched his back and raised up on the heels of his feet, his black boots literally digging holes into the floor.

It was all Vinnie could do not to help, but she knew it was best not to touch him.

Yet, the moment she was about to yell they should call 9-1-1, was the moment his convulsions were over. Oliver's wide chest expanded, letting escape a long sigh before his eyes popped open and his vision appeared to clear.

"What the hell?" he murmured, trying to lift himself up on his elbows.

Vinnie was instantly at his side, brushing his sweat-soaked dark hair from his forehead, her heart crashing in her chest. "Are you okay, Oliver?"

"*What happened?* Why am I on the floor? Last thing I remember was telling Archibald to grab my horn."

Vinnie put a hand on his shoulder, the thick cord of muscle warm beneath her palm. "He did, and then you fell on the floor. Have you had seizures before, Oliver? Do you have a history of them?"

He shook his head, bewildered as his eyes roamed her face. "No. Never. But forget me. Did it work? Is Archibald okay?" he asked, his voice weak.

Arch stood over Oliver, his gentle face contorted with worry, his eyes deep with concern as he held out his hand, his fingers splayed. "You healed me, sir. You healed me," he mumbled, dazed as he held his hand higher to show Oliver. "How can I ever thank you?"

Nina's eyes went wide when they all looked to Arch, whose hand looked as though it had never been burned. "Holy fuck. He healed Arch. Holy-holy fuck. Like, I know he healed his cut, but I guess the breadth of his abilities didn't sink in. I mean, holy shitballs."

Her mother, who'd stood on the fringe of the chaos —and appeared fine, just as Nina predicted—whispered in clear terror, "What just happened to you, Oliver?"

Vinnie tapped Nina's work boots to move her out of her mother's line of vision, so she could see what happened—what she'd done.

She pointed at Oliver's forehead to the horn that now glowed so bright, it was like one of those light sticks kids used when they played hide and seek in the dark. The pink and purple glitter swirled around and around like a pastel neon sign.

Vinnie's lips thinned. "This, Mother. This is what happened. This is what *you* did."

Her mother cried out, gripping the edge of the

countertop, but Nina grabbed her this time and gave her a light shake as she threw Alice's arm around her shoulder and helped her back to the round dining room table.

"Oh no, Unicorn Maker. You stay upright. Time to face the music and help us figure out what the fuck to do."

Vinnie would have laughed at Nina's joke, but she was more concerned with how wrung out Oliver looked as Darnell latched onto his hand and pulled him upward from the floor where a pool of glitter scattered across the floor.

He gave Oliver a light pat on the back and smiled, his white teeth flashing as he wrapped his arm around Oliver's waist to help him out of the kitchen.

"Man, you need a lie-down, brother. You don't look so good. C'mon, I'll get you settled and we'll get ya some food. Big guy yo' size needs food and a lot of it, I'm bettin'."

Vinnie was ready to blow a gasket, but she fought that urge when she finally approached her mother, now sitting at the dining room table. Pulling out a chair, she sat down beside Alice, who looked positively horrified.

As well she should.

"Mother—"

The moment she spoke, Alice burst into tears, but Vinnie, while she was certain her mother was remorseful, wasn't up for her histrionics. The time for remorse would be later. Now, she needed some answers about whom they could talk to—who might know how to reverse this spell.

So she handed her a cloth napkin from one of the place settings and patted her mother on the back, making soothing circles with her palm. "We don't have time for tears, Mother. Did you see what just happened to that man?"

"I don't understand what I did wrong," she moaned, her gray eyes watery as she pressed the napkin to her nose. "I read it exactly as it was written."

"Let's start at the beginning. Where did you get the love spell, Mother?"

The guilt that spread across Alice's face almost made Vinnie crumble. It was how her mother won every argument ever—guilt. The guilt she felt for making her mother cry. The guilt she felt because guilt was her middle name. But this time she wasn't going to cave. This wasn't about her. This was a man's life her mother had tinkered with.

Vinnie took a deep breath, collecting her patience. "Where is the spell, Mom? Who did you get it from?"

"In my purse," she huffed. "But what difference will it make anyway, Vincenza? Seeing the spell on paper won't change what I've done. I couldn't fix it if I wanted to!"

Vinnie grabbed her mother's large tote-like purse and began digging until she found a wrinkled piece of paper with some words scribbled on it, words she couldn't even decipher but for maybe one. Vinnie squinted and still couldn't be sure she was reading the word correctly, but it was the only one that looked even a little like unicorn.

Biting her tongue before she spoke, she pointed to the word and showed it to her mother. "Mom, I think this says unicorn."

Her mother wouldn't even look at the paper. "No," Alice insisted with a shake of her head. "No, Vincenza. It's says *lovelorn*."

"Um, I don't think so. Had you worn your glasses, you would have known. But that's neither here nor there. Still, I can't read the rest of this. Can you?"

Her mother twisted her fingers together and looked out the bank of windows overlooking the dining room. "No…"

Vinnie let out a little gasp and tapped a finger on the table. She knew *exactly* what her mother's inability to decipher the spell was about. "You couldn't read *any* of it, could you? I'd bet money on the fact that you hurriedly copied it from somewhere you absolutely should not have been, and couldn't read it because you forgot your glasses, so you said whatever you could remember and filled in the blanks with made-up words, didn't you?"

Her mother threw her hands up in the air in defeat. "All right, fine! I blew it! I was so nervous I'd get caught, I might have put some words in there that didn't belong, okay? Are you happy to know I made an utter fool of myself, Vincenza?"

"You didn't just make a fool of yourself, Alice. You fuckin' gave a dude a horn. That's the shit," Nina said with a snicker as she strolled back into the kitchen and sat across from them.

Wanda, who'd made a bowl of soup for her mother, set it in front of her and sat down, too, reaching for Alice's hand. "I'm going to stick my nose in just a little bit here. I'm pretty sure Vinnie's not happy about how poorly this makes you feel, Alice. It's unfair to put that sort of burden on her shoulders, wouldn't you agree?"

Her mother crumbled once more, her eyes falling to her lap. "Of course it isn't fair," she sniveled. "I'm sorry, Vincenza. I only want your happiness. I swear, I don't do these things out of anything other than love."

Vinnie sighed. This vicious cycle would never end, would it? "I know that, Mom, but I also know you don't want it at the expense of someone as nice as Oliver. He now has something a lot of greedy people will want. You've put his *life* at risk. That's why everyone is here. To make sure no one tries to hurt him and to protect him, because how can *he*, a mortal with nothing more than human strength, protect himself from a demon or a vampire? You saw what his alicorn can do, didn't you? He healed someone with it, and Archibald isn't the only one he's healed."

"I'd take it back if I could, honey. Surely you know that," she sobbed.

"Where did you get the spell, Mom?"

Alice flapped her hands dismissively. "I can't exactly remember. I think it was at Goddesses' Night Out."

"Mom, your powers are so weak, they're almost nonexistent. Do they still even let you attend

Goddesses' Night Out? We only get invited to some of the functions out of some misguided courtesy. You do understand that, don't you?"

Alice's face collapsed again. "Of course I do, Vincenza! Do you have any idea what it's like to be overlooked time and again because you're nothing more than a token Goddess with no real power? Knowing they only invite me because it's the *right thing* to do? It hurts my feelings."

"So why would you want to bother going to an event that's for Goddesses only, Mom? If they don't think you're Goddess enough? Do you need to be part of that gaggle of Goddesses that badly? So badly you'd go and then let them ignore you? I don't understand why they're so important, Mom?"

Her mother's frustration level ratcheted upward. "Because when you have no one, you're happy to fit in anywhere, Vincenza—even if it's as the token handicapped Goddess!"

Her mother's life in a nutshell. Always trying to fit a square peg in a round hole. Her first marriage, fresh out of high school, had been to a man who'd verbally abused her. But he was a warm body and that was all she'd needed until he up and left and was never heard from again.

Alice's second marriage, to Vinnie's father, Norman Morretti, had lasted about as long as it took to find out having a baby meant sleepless nights and a steady job—both of which Norman Morretti was incapable of.

They'd divorced when Vinnie was three, and she'd

only seen him sporadically over her twenty-eight years of life.

But then, Agnew Costas had come into their lives when Vinnie was fifteen, and he'd been the best thing to happen to them. He was warm, loving, honest, and he made her mother feel like the most important person in the world. But he'd died two years ago, and her mother had been having trouble finding her footing ever since.

Nina pushed her way out of her chair and came around the table to hug Alice. "Any friend of Khristos and Quinn's is a friend of ours, right Wanda? You can be a part of our family, Alice. It's fucked to shit. We're about as dysfunctional as it damn well gets, but we'll never make you feel like a fifth wheel and we always have good eats. Everybody's welcome."

Alice wiped a tear from her eye and patted Nina on the arm. "You're very sweet. Thank you."

All warm squishies aside, they still needed to talk to whomever her mother got that spell from. Maybe they could help.

"Listen, Mom, I know they treat you poorly, and if you want to be a part of that group anyway, fine, but we need to know who you stole that spell from. Maybe she can help us fix this so we can let Oliver get back to his life."

"Hold up," Marty said, entering the dining room by way of the kitchen. "I just got a text from Khristos and Quinn."

Vinnie sat up straight. "And?"

"Khristos said he got in touch with his mother, the ex-Aphrodite, and she said this: *The only thing I know about unicorns is the legend as follows. A unicorn's alicorn can purify drinking water, nullify poison when dipped into it, and heal disease of any kind. But there is a price.*"

Vinnie held her breath, but Wanda didn't. With her elegant face a mask of worry, she asked, "What's the price?"

Oh, God...

Marty swallowed hard, her voice trembling as she read, "*If Oliver uses his horn to heal too often, it won't just debilitate him, it will kill him.*"

Oh, sweet mysteries of life.

CHAPTER 8

Well, that explained his seizure. It was as though using the horn was draining his life force or something. He felt weak as a kitten as he lay on the couch like some helpless lump of laziness, unable to do anything but listen to the conversations around him about how he was going to die if he overused this superpower that had so haphazardly been thrust upon him.

Hearing he could die unsettled Oliver, but he was too exhausted to do much about it.

Just then, Vinnie came to stand over him, her fiery-red hair falling around her pale face as she hitched her jaw. "May I sit?"

"Sure," he whispered, his voice husky and raw.

Everything on him hurt like hell. He felt like he'd been run over by a semi then squeezed out of a sausage casing, but somehow, for this woman he found so intriguing, he managed to inch over and pat the space beside him.

Her pretty brown eyes oozed sympathy as she settled in beside his hip, smelling of pears and cinnamon. "Did you hear what Marty said?"

He inhaled a ragged breath. "I did."

"That's why you feel the way you do right now. You'll recover, of course, but you can't keep doing that, Oliver. It hurts you to heal people."

Oliver struggled with this diagnoses on a million levels. "I heard. So I have this power by way of a sparkly horn on my head that makes me look like a horse on a merry-go-round." He used his fingers to make air quotes. "But I'm supposed to look away when someone is hurt? How does that work?"

She licked her peachy lips and took his hand in hers…her warm, soft hand…and attempted a smile. "You can't save everyone, Oliver. *That's* going to have to be how that works. You have a good heart, I suspect and it won't be easy. Listen, I realize it's a crappy position to be in, but do you want to die? Every time you use your horn, it's a death wish. Every time you use it to heal, you'll feel worse and worse. It'll take longer to recover, and if you keep doing it, someday, you simply *won't* recover."

Oliver blew out the breath he was holding. "Okay, that aside, what do I do about my horn? If I stop helping people heal, I still can't go to work like this or even out in public. I look ridiculous. Who's going to take me seriously with a unicorn horn?"

"What do *we* do about this?" she gently reminded him with a soft smile that lit up her eyes. "We're in this *together*, Oliver. My mother did this to you, and that means I'm going to comb the ends of the earth to find out how to make it better. I don't know what we'll do about your horn, but there has to be a solution."

Oliver shook his head. He wasn't so caught up in this mess that he didn't see how Alice felt about her daughter. She'd done this from a place of love. "You don't have to do that, Vinnie. I'm sure you have a life and a job to get back to."

But she shook her head right back at him. "I'm on fall break right now, which is why I was up so late reading last night. I'm at your service for as long as you need me."

"As much as I appreciate that, I need you to look at this from my POV, a more objective one, if you will. Alice meant no harm. I'm not angry enough not to see that. She loves you a lot. She talks about you all the time, even though she never mentioned your name. Not once. She simply called you her daughter. In fact, I thought you didn't even live in New York, the way she talked about you. But talk about you she did. How smart you are, how pretty you are. What a good person you are. She loves you, Vinnie."

Vinnie looked down at the floor for a minute before she gazed at him, her brown eyes filled with guilt. "You probably thought I lived somewhere else because I put a lot of distance between us. My mother is infamous for her nutty bid to be a part of the paranormal world.

It's been this way all my life, and it makes me so crazy. As a result, I sort of had to give her some boundaries. But in the process, I forgot to keep a closer eye on her. The way she feels about the Gods and Goddesses, at least in my opinion, is obsessive and unhealthy."

He liked hearing Vinnie's voice. It was soft but strong, warm but authoritative. "You don't feel the same way? I mean, about the paranormal?"

She shrugged her small shoulders with an indifference he knew she meant. "I'm not dying to be one of them, no. I've accepted that my line of ancestry is watered down. I'll live forever and that's that. That I can't make history-defining matches or shoot golden arrows or do any of the things Gods and Goddesses do doesn't bother me the way it does my mother. I don't feel the need to fit in, and I don't go where I'm not wanted. That's what troubles her more than anything, I guess. I mean, look at the lengths she was willing to go to in order to prove she could find me a husband. She pounced on a spell she knew nothing about, repeated it incorrectly, and boom, look what happened."

"But look at what she managed," Oliver said, pointing to his horn. "She *did* turn me into a unicorn. It might not have been the right spell, but it was a spell, so maybe you're all not as watered down as you think."

Vinnie's lips thinned in clear disapproval. "Maybe. I've never tried to cast a spell unless she forced me to practice an incantation, and that never went well. Still, the fact remains, she didn't make you fall in love with me, which was the intention of the spell. Mom just can't accept that she didn't inherit the magic of Hecate, or *any* of her ancestors' powers, period. They'd laugh her right out of Goddesses' Night Out if they knew what she'd produced from that half-assed spell, and I hate that for her."

Oliver drove his free hand behind his head to prop himself up and looked at her thoughtfully. "Here's something to think about. Do you think what she did has more to do with the fact that she loves you and she really just wants you to be happy, than it does proving a point to anyone, herself *or* her fellow Goddesses?"

"You weren't at my tenth birthday party…"

"Nope. But I'd love to hear all about it. What happened?"

On a sigh, Vinnie shook her head. "This isn't about me. It's about you and finding a solution to your predicament."

Oliver smiled. "Well, if we're going to be stuck together for who knows how long while we un-unicorn me, Vincenza Raphaela Morretti, we might as well get to know each other. So spill the beans."

She looked as though she gave it some thought, and then decided to throw caution to the wind. "It was a disaster. A total mess. Instead of doing what I wanted, which was to go to a movie and out for tacos, she invited a bunch of junior Gods and Goddesses and gave me a surprise party."

"Junior Goddesses?" Damn, this world got stranger and stranger. The image in his head of all these omnipotent people floating around with average humans was almost comical.

"Children of undiluted Gods and Goddesses who have real powers."

"Ah. And?"

"And they were expecting magic and fairies, the way all junior Gods and Goddesses do, and all they got was a really drunk Barney in a smelly, worn costume and some homemade chocolate cake with sprinkles. There were no dancing carousel horses come to life. No fairies with gossamer wings, spinning sugary spools of cotton candy. I mean, how exciting is a drunk Barney when you can have real-live fairies? Needless to say, no one ever wanted to come to another party of mine, and I knew that would happen. It's why I asked her to take me to the movies." Vinnie paused for a brief moment and shook her head, her eyes shimmering as she remembered. "No. I didn't ask. I *begged*."

He heard the disappointment in her voice, and Oliver found it upset him, too. Which made him want to fix it for her, even though he knew he couldn't. "But doesn't that say more about the snobs these Gods and Goddesses raised than it does about your mother, who only wanted to give you something nice?"

Vinnie's smile was vague and sad. "It's not about what she could or couldn't give me, Oliver. It's about her *listening* to what I really wanted. I really wanted some one-on-one time with her, not a party where I knew all the other parents would mock her at school the next day during drop-off."

That stung Oliver's heart. "So you were trying to protect her."

Vinnie's eyes went hard like granite. "Not just her, Oliver. I was trying to protect me, too. And yes. I hated the way they talked in hushed whispers about how she tried so desperately to fit in, or how they joked that she was the black sheep of Goddesses and she'd never be like them, no matter how hard she tried. They giggled about it more often than not, and it made me angry. I didn't know what to do with that anger. The paranormal can be elitist at the worst of times. Ask the ladies of OOPS."

"But the OOPS women are paranormal," he insisted, not fully grasping the hierarchy of supernatural beings.

Vinnie clucked her tongue and put her hand back in her lap. "But it was an accident. They're not pure by a true paranormal's standards. It's sort of the age-old story. You know, new money, old money. Rich, poor. They've managed to pave a way for themselves because they've done a lot of good, and they don't seem to give a flying fig about acceptance. They pave their own way because they're strong, feisty, empowered women, but I think even *they'll* tell you they've been snubbed a time or two."

"And I suppose Nina couldn't care less about fitting in anyway. She'd just beat the acceptance into everyone, huh?" he joked.

Vinnie giggled, and he liked the sound in his ears. It made him happy, but then she grew serious. "Well, there is that, but I'm not like Nina. I'm not as pushy or as vocal. I got angry, but I kept it on the inside. I didn't come out swinging. The end game of this is, I never fit in—*we* never fit in. We were misfits, but I accepted that from a very early age. My mother just couldn't. She said it was like giving up and dying. She said we belonged whether they liked it or not."

"So she sort of dragged you along behind her and forced you to be a part of something you wanted nothing to do with."

"She was like the ultimate pageant mother. You know, like *Toddlers and Tiaras*? Except, there were no tiaras. She dressed me up to fit the part, but when you can't create a spell or make things disappear, there's no hiding it. I was always going to be a runner-up. So, I crafted a life with everyday people because that's basically who I am. Just an ordinary, everyday person."

He hated that she felt ordinary. Whatever this pull to her was about, Oliver sensed she was anything but ordinary. "Who'll live forever…" he reminded.

"And that's a very long time to live with the hope a group of people, who aren't that nice to begin with, will eventually accept you."

Oliver heard the hurt in her voice and was incapable of not sharing his experience with a similar personality. "You know, I had someone in my life who was a lot like Alice."

"Your mother? But no," she said, shaking her head while he watched her fiery-red curls float around her face. "That can't be right. You said *had*."

"Yep. Had is the correct word. We broke up. Or

rather, she cheated on me with someone who has enough ambition to suit her needs."

As he spoke those words, he realized the usual malice and anger of Denise cheating on him seemed a lot farther away than it ever had before.

She tipped her head, the light catching her eyes as they twinkled. "Ah, ex-girlfriend?"

"Ex-*fiancée*. Her name was Denise, and she was never happy with how little I wanted to climb the corporate ladder. She was always pushing me to be someone I wasn't. I like my job. No. I take that back. I *love* my job as an ordinary housing developer who works with various coalitions for seniors to build affordable housing. I make a decent amount of money. I don't make a million dollars a year, but I work hard and I'm paid well enough, have good benefits, can afford a nice vacation a couple of times a year. I didn't want what Denise wanted."

"Yeah, but at least Denise didn't turn you into a unicorn. She might have wanted to change you, but I don't think this is what she meant."

"Don't think for one second if it were possible, she wouldn't have. We'd be making a website with some kitschy name and culling our client list as we speak."

Vinnie chuckled. "That bad?"

He sighed. Maybe he'd let it fester so long it seemed worse than it really was. "I guess at the time I didn't really see it. Mostly because I, like your mother, didn't listen. I kept thinking my vision was the best vision. But when I caught her red-handed, cheating on me, that is, I saw all the signs I'd ignored before. Denise wanted everything, but I was content with what I had. Never the twain and all. I'm not afraid of hard work, but my goals were more humanitarian than financial. I don't need a big house and a fancy sports car."

"But Denise did?"

He shrugged his shoulders. He didn't blame Denise for wanting something he didn't anymore. He took partial blame for their breakup because he simply didn't listen to what she'd wanted.

"More than I did. In fact, I foolishly bought this house, thinking it would make her happy. I thought we could renovate it together. You know, a fun project for couples?"

Vinnie nodded. "I get that. I love DIY. I suck at it, but I love it."

"Denise? Not so much. When she said she wanted a house, she meant in a swanky suburb, move-in ready. Not a fixer-upper. But again, it's not as though she didn't tell me."

Vinnie looked around his living room with surprised eyes. "But it's so beautiful, Oliver. Are you telling me you did this with Denise?"

He snorted. "No. I'm telling you I did this *in spite of* Denise. A fixer-upper wasn't what she wanted at all. She had no interest in picking up a hammer. So imagine my shock when I surprised her with this house, which, when I bought it, was a dumpster fire."

"Well, to be fair, you didn't consult her. Buying a house should be a together thing."

"Where were you four years ago when I was making impulsive decisions based on the stars in my eyes and my big fat ego?"

Vinnie giggled. "Trying to keep my mother from blowing up the world." They both laughed then. When they caught their breath, she asked, "So did that end your relationship? Was that the straw?"

"No. The straw was coming home to find her in a compromising position with her boss in the middle of the rubble that was eventually going to be her sort-of dream kitchen. So I broke up with her and licked my wounds by turning this house into all the things she said she liked."

"Well, for a renovation done out of spite, you really nailed it. Denise had good taste."

He chuckled. "Fortunately, we had similar tastes. So when I was done wallowing, I dove in feet first and did all the things I thought we were going to do together—alone. But it helped me heal."

Vinnie frowned and squirmed a little. "So the boss. I'm guessing her boss had enough ambition for two men?"

He had plenty of all the things Oliver didn't. But he no longer felt like he had to measure up. In all this renovation, he'd learned to accept himself and discovered what he found important. He wasn't all the way there yet. Denise's betrayal still stung a little, but not the way it once had.

When he finally answered, he said, "It would seem so. She married him last year, I think."

"Oh, Oliver. I'm sorry. How awful."

He shrugged his sore shoulders. "Not really. I'm glad it happened now. We'd have fallen apart if she was expecting trips to Bali every year, and I was secretly planning a trip to Wisconsin for cheese-fest."

Vinnie made a comical face. "Cheese-fest? Seriously?"

"What can I say, she liked cheese," he defended. "I thought she'd love it. Turns out, I didn't pay close enough attention to what she loved. I heard what I wanted to hear."

She spread her arms wide, her eyes twinkling. "And in the process, turned into Chip and Joanna Gaines."

"Now there *is* that. I can sheetrock with the best of them," he said with a laugh. "But here's what I mean. I get that you just want to do you. Nobody gets that more than I do. You have the courage of conviction to stand your ground. I, on the other hand, just turned a deaf ear and a blind eye. But what I'm really saying is, I understand what it's like to be pushed in a direction you don't necessarily want to go, and I also understand what it's like not to truly listen when someone is clearly telling you how they feel."

"And now look," she said, pointing to his horn. "If there were ever a direction somebody didn't want to go, I suppose this is the one."

Feeling a lot better, he used his free arm to push himself up. "I guess it wouldn't be so bad if it weren't for the sparkly horn. Speaking of, have we had any luck finding anyone who might be able to help us get rid of it?"

Vinnie pulled her phone from the pocket of the soft blue sweater she wore and scrolled her texts. "Not yet. My friend Khristos, also a God, is asking around for us. He's really respected in the community, especially with the elder Gods. If anyone can find anything, it's him."

"How do you know Khristos?"

Her smile was fond. "We went to school together. In fact, he looked out for me a lot."

"Because you were Goddess-light and people picked on you?"

She let her head fall back on her shoulders with a tinkling laugh. "No. Because I was an overachiever and he was a good guy. He's several years older than me, but we were both in the same grade."

Oliver pointed a finger at her and teased, "You were one of those kids, huh?"

"Guilty. It's hard being eleven and a senior in high school. Khristos made it easier. He kept the jerks away. We've been friends ever since, see each other from time to time."

"And now he's married to Aphrodite 2.0?"

"Quinn, yeah. She's such a great lady, who stepped into some impossible shoes with style and grace."

"Isn't she, by the standards you explained, impure, too? Because she's half-human?"

Vinnie grinned and it lit up her entire face, making him inexplicably pleased. "Not if Khristos is your husband, she's not. He'd knock someone into the next century if they ever said that to him. But Quinn isn't the kind of woman who lets stuff like that get in her way. She knows she has a job to do that's of great import and nothing stops her. I have a lot of admiration for her. She stepped in, took her knocks like a true champ, and kept it moving. But she's the only one who should be doing any matchmaking. Ever."

A small lick of hope sprang in his gut. "Maybe she's the answer to this? Maybe Quinn can get rid of this horn?"

"That's not what her power's about. She can't reverse spells."

"Okay, so all that said, what's next? Do we even have a plan of action? Or do we just see how big this thing on my forehead can get before I explode in a blaze of glitter?"

"We pinpoint who my mother got the spell from and we talk to them. She's not very communicative right now, which leads me to believe she's afraid to tell us who she stole it from."

Oliver frowned. "Can she get into trouble for taking it? Is it the fear of repercussion she's worried about? Because if that's the case, we'll find another way. Despite what she's done, I like Alice, Vinnie."

"There's always the possibility she could get into trouble, yes, but life is about consequences, Oliver. She shouldn't have been where she didn't belong. What if it had been a spell that ended the world, would you be so forgiving?"

"I wouldn't have the chance. The world would be done," he joked.

Vinnie gave him a small poke to his forearm. "You know what I mean, Oliver. It could have been far worse and affected more than just one person."

"That's so black and white, don't you think? We can allow for a little gray in this case."

She wrinkled her nose. "Because you like my mother, you're willing to have a sparkly horn that drains the very life from you, possibly forever?"

"No. I'm just saying, I don't want her to go to Goddess jail for it. Is that so wrong?"

Vinnie sat quietly and didn't answer, obviously at war with what to do next. The air between them became a little uncomfortable.

No, it became a lot uncomfortable. But it was *his* horn, damn it. If he didn't want Alice to get into trouble for giving it to him, that should be his choice.

Just as he was about to suggest they take a step back, maybe have some lunch, Alice poked her head around the corner of the dining room, her eyes watery with worry.

She twisted her fingers around her long braid and looked at him with a sheepish gaze, her voice shaking and barely above a whisper. "I think we might have someone you can talk to, Oliver. It's just a small kernel of help, but it's something."

He sat up straight and tried to smile at her, even though he felt like the world was going to tip on its side. He couldn't bear the look of guilt on her face.

They'd worked well together these past couple of months. She had a strong work ethic, even if she was a little disorganized.

So Oliver smiled and asked in what he hoped was an interested, accommodating tone, "What'd you find, Alice?"

She came all the way into the living room, her face hopeful at his warm reception. "We're not sure it means anything, but it's a small snippet of a story a friend once head at a party. I hope it's helpful, anyway."

"That's awesome, Alice. Tell me," he encouraged.

She pulled her pink phone out of her sweater pocket and squinted at the screen as Oliver and Vinnie waited expectantly. "Okay, so it says here, *glad to hear you're well, blah, blah, blah.* You know, the typical pleasantries. *Donna's marrying the God of her dreams and they're having the wedding—*"

"Mom," Vinnie said with a warning tone. "Get to the point, please."

Alice sighed and looked back down at her phone, running her finger over the screen. "Sorry. Got off track. Okay, um... Wedding, Paris... Book club and your virginity." Then Alice looked up expectantly.

Oliver blinked. "Pardon me?"

Alice flapped a hand in Vinnie's direction as she looked once more to the screen of her phone. "This could have something to do with Vinnie's virginity."

Vinnie hissed a wheezing gasp, her face turning bright red, but Oliver didn't know what to do or say.

He did know this—he was going to call his mother

when this was all over and tell her he loved her, because man. All this time, he'd thought *his* mother was an oversharing drag.

But it looked like Alice was the clear winner of that race.

CHAPTER 9

"Mom!" Vinnie hopped up off the couch, her cheeks hot, her eyes blazing as she reached for her mother's arm and pulled her away to the hall by the entryway.

Alice's face fell. Obviously, Vinnie had crushed her again. "I blew it again, didn't I?"

Nina came up behind her mother and leaned around her body to nod her head. "Um, yup. You done fucked up again, Alice. I kinda get the impression Junior Goddess here didn't want anybody to know she ain't into the bedsport. It's personal."

Vinnie slapped her hands against her thighs in exasperation. "It's not that I'm not into it, Nina, it's that I just haven't found the right person."

Alice pressed her fist to her mouth before reaching for Vinnie's arm. "I'm so sorry, honey. I was just reading the text and…"

Okay, so yes. Vincenza Raphaela Morretti was,

indeed, a virgin. And also yes. She knew well the reaction when people found out she was a virgin at the ripe old age of twenty-eight. She had her rebuttal down pat, she knew the reaction so well. In fact, she didn't even blink an eye when she said it anymore.

She was used to what people thought and she was used to lying about why she was a virgin and it didn't really have anything to do with saving herself for the right person. Well, maybe it had a little to do with saving herself for the right person, but it had more to do with an embarrassing incident and her anxiety—or so had been her experience thus far.

But that didn't mean she wanted everyone privy to something so personal.

Nina gave her a light punch to her shoulder. "Hey, who gives a fuck if you're a virgin? I don't give a fuck. You do you, boo. Unless it has some shit to do with the Glitter Shitter. Then I want to know all the fuck about it. Otherwise, whatever."

Licking her dry lips, she swallowed hard as she leaned up against the hall entryway wall and tried to explain while keeping her complete and utter humiliation to herself.

"There are a lot of legends about virgins being the keepers of unicorns, which I'm sure is what my mother was reading when she read that text, but it doesn't really have anything to do with helping Oliver—or I don't think it does. Am I right, Mom?"

Alice nodded, swiping at a tear. "You're right. It was just part of the legend Dorinda sent me, along with the other information she found. It has nothing to do with what happened to Oliver. I'm so sorry, honey. I would never want to share your embarrassing secret without permission."

Ugh.

"Mom, it's not so much that I'm embarrassed to be a...um, virgin, as I am that you just told a roomful of people we hardly know. I've told you that a million times. Why don't you ever listen to me?"

This was their problem in a nutshell. Her mother never heard what the real problem was between them.

"Either way, fuck that noise." Nina said, her face genuinely sympathetic. "Listen, if there's one thing I've learned over the years, and because I'm not exactly a warm-fuzzy, is this—do what's right for you no matter what. Do what's healthy or whatever the hell everyone says when it comes to crap like that. That self-care bullshit I hear so much about? It's important. You ain't got shit to be embarrassed about, kiddo. Not that you need my approval, but stick to your guns, whatever the fuck your guns are. Now if we could just get Mom here to keep her big yap shut, we'd be good to go."

Vinnie's smile was tremulous, but she giggled. "Thanks, Nina." Then she turned to her mother. "Well, now that the cat's out of the bag, what else did your friend Dorinda say?"

Vinnie wasn't exactly aware of all her mother's friends or what their names were, but she did recall Dorinda—an uppity descendant of Venus. From here on out, she was going to make it her mission to learn who her mother's "friends" were.

Alice sighed, closing her eyes. "She said there is no one else like Oliver. Not one soul alive, which as you said, makes him very valuable."

"Did you tell this Dorinda what you did to Oliver?" Nina asked. "Because we don't need a bunch of crazies running around, looking to profit from our boy here if she spreads the word. You understand, Alice? We can't afford to take any chances."

"I tried to be as careful as possible," Alice responded. "But if we're to have any hope of helping Oliver, I might not have a choice but to share what I've done with the person I took the spell from."

"Why would Dorinda even have a love spell, Mom? That's not her area of expertise."

"Because she's an ancient Goddess, Vincenza. Those annals have been passed down to her from generation to generation. The books don't only include love spells. That just happens to be what I found."

"When you were snooping in someone else's house," Vinnie reminded her, because she couldn't help herself.

Alice frowned with guilt all over her face. "Yes. Yes, I snooped, okay. Does it really hurt that I want to see the inner workings of how the other half lives?"

"I dunno, Alice," Nina quipped with a chuckle and hitched her thumb in Oliver's direction. "Does it?"

They were getting off track again. Vinnie redirected. "When did you get the spell from her anyway?"

"She had a Tupperware party, and I don't really care much about Tupperware—"

"But you went to the party anyway because any access to that group of snotty elitists in okay by you, right?" Vinnie chided. Of course her mother didn't care about Tupperware. She didn't care about anything that organized your life.

But Nina whipped a hand in the air. "Okay, enough with the blame. What's done is done. Now you accept it's fucking done and we move on and try to do better. Right, Alice?"

Her mother looked down at her feet. "Yes," she whispered, the shame in her voice crystal clear.

"How did you get the spell, Mother?" She had visions of her mother creeping around Dorinda's bedroom, opening drawers and sifting through the Goddess's belongings.

"I was bored, so I wandered off to her library and took a peek around. Dorinda has a massive house, as you know."

She sure did. Dorinda's son Byron's birthday was right before hers, and her mother had made her attend his soiree, which compounded the fact that her sad Barney birthday was an epic fail. Byron had made fun of her at school about it for at least a month.

"And you poked around in her books and found a book of spells," Vinnie finished for her. She didn't really need to hear the details, but she wanted the rest of the gang to know what they were dealing with in Alice.

"Right. And I hastily copied it down on a piece of paper…"

Vinnie closed her eyes as her mother's voice grew sorrowful, steeling herself against the inevitable guilt she'd feel for calling Alice out. "What possessed you to do something so crazy, Mom? Do you have any idea the trouble you'll be in if Dorinda finds out what you've done and tells an elder God? You'll be sunk."

"All the best laid plans, right?" she replied weakly. "I truly believed I could pull this off and no one would ever know. I'd introduce you, Oliver would fall madly in love with you, and you'd ride off into the sunset."

"Did it ever occur to you I might not reciprocate those feelings? What if I didn't fall in love with him, but he was nuts about me? He would have ended up hurt, Mother."

Oliver was handsome and funny and obviously very handy, if the parts of the house he'd renovated that she'd seen were any indication. Vinnie had no doubt he'd be a great date, and they definitely had chemistry, if she judged the way her stomach had all those butterflies floating around in it when she'd sat next to him and held his hand.

But what if they hadn't? What if her mother's spell hadn't failed, and they'd met and hated one another—or worse, were indifferent?

"I guess I didn't think about that, Vincenza," she groaned. Quite clearly miserable. "I know I've made a mess of things. But I promise you, that was never my intent."

Vinnie rolled her eyes. "I know you don't mean any harm, Mom, but you didn't think any of this through. Life isn't all about instant gratification. You didn't think past *your* vision of what my life should be instead of hearing what mine is."

Alice huffed then, aggravated. "Do you always want to hide away in that cave with your pets and some old dusty books, Vincenza? Or do you want to live? Experience life with someone? Fall in love?"

Sure, she wanted to experience life, she just didn't want to do it on her mother's terms or on her timetable, and she'd stubbornly stuck to her guns.

But now, seeing the OOPS ladies, and overhearing snippets of some of the adventures they'd shared when they weren't helping someone in peril, hearing about their home lives, Vinnie wondered if she'd gone too far in the other direction in order to defy her mother's wishes.

She had a lot of good things in her life, but maybe she didn't have enough of them. Maybe there was room for more.

But that was neither here nor there at the moment.

"Let's not get into this now, Mom. We'll have plenty of time to talk about this later, after we figure out how to help Oliver. So what information did Dorinda have, if any, that could be helpful? Because we could really use a win here."

"She referenced an alleged incident that happened maybe a thousand years ago with an alleged unicorn who lost his powers after he found a troll at the end of a rainbow."

Vinnie let her head fall back against the wall, her shoulders sagging. "That's ridiculous, Mom. A troll and a rainbow? I mean, c'mon. And you used the words *alleged incident*. We don't even know if it really happened. Did Dorinda witness it?"

Alice dropped her chin to her chest. "No. She simply said she recalled there being a story about it."

Even Gods and Goddesses had their equivalent of Bigfoot, and trolls were it. But trolls didn't really exist unless you counted the ones on social media.

Vinnie crossed her arms over her chest. "So, I think it's fair to say we shouldn't go looking for trolls and rainbows. Did you ask Dorinda if I could drop by and talk to her about this theory? Maybe someone she knows from the era when unicorns supposedly roamed the earth is still alive."

"Well," Alice said with a snide smile. "She's certainly old enough to have friends from that era, so I wouldn't be surprised."

"Oooo, Alice is a comedienne," Nina drawled with a grin.

"I'm happy to go with you, if you'd like," Alice offered with a conspiratorial grin. "Because if I think you're going to do what I think you're going to do, I know exactly where to find the book."

"Um, no. As long as you stuck to the story we gave you about me teaching a class on urban legend and mythology, we should be fine. I'll talk to her about unicorns and trolls or whatever else I have to while Nina and Marty look for the book."

"Why can't we just ask her for the book, Vincenza? Do you really believe Dorinda would tell anyone about Oliver? She's been a good friend—"

"No, Mom. She *hasn't* been a good friend. I don't know what your definition of friend is, but Dorinda isn't it. I wish I could teach you the difference."

"Do you want to go to the clink, Mama Bear?" Nina asked, standing beside Vinnie. "If this Dorinda finds out why we need the book, and she's as much of a bitch as Vinnie says, she'll be all up in this mess. We don't need that. Listen, you let us handle this shit, Alice. You go sit with Wanda, have some lunch, and wait this one out. Me and Marty got this."

Alice gave her a skeptical glance and a wince. "You do know you won't be well received, dear, don't you? I'm sorry, but I'm only being truthful. Dorinda's a bit of a…snob."

Nina's raven eyebrow lifted. "You mean because I'm not a pure vampire, right?"

"Yes," Alice whispered sheepishly.

Nina grabbed Alice's hand and looked her in the eye. "You think that shit bothers me? Nah, Mama Bear. I am who I am. I didn't ask for this thing called vampire, but I have it, and I'm damn well going to use it. Sometimes I use it to help other people. I've found others who do the same thing and made them my family. So fuck the hater elitists. Just let this Dorinda give me shit, and I'll show her what the hell this impure bitch is capable of. You gotta march to the beat of your own drum, Alice. It's the only way to live."

Vinnie couldn't help but grin. She'd probably never be able to tell Nina in actual words, because her anxiety would take over, but she really was as much of a badass as legend claimed. Her mother needed to hear that kind of strength, the kind that cared only about doing the right thing and to hell with the whispers.

If even just a little of Nina would rub off on her mother, that would be half the battle.

Vinnie didn't care that Nina didn't love displays of affection; it was the only way she was capable of conveying her gratitude. Words were Nina's thing, and affection was Vinnie's. Thus, she put her arms around the vampire's neck and squeezed tight, dropping a kiss on her leanly chiseled cheek.

"Thank you. You said that perfectly."

She gave Vinnie a quick pat before she made a face of distaste. "Get the fuck off me, weirdo. We don't know each other like that." And then she laughed. "Now let's get Marty and go see a Goddess about a love spell gone fucking off the chain."

Vinnie wasn't looking forward to going to Dorinda and asking for anything. She was part of a group of people who'd mocked her very existence for as long as she could remember.

She most especially didn't like doing it after her mother had stolen something from Dorinda. It only supported the evidence that Alice was beneath them.

But they had no choice. If that book had a way to fix this, Vinnie was determined to find it.

But she still hated how small she felt when up against someone like Dorinda.

"You ready to go fuck up some elitist dumpster trash?" Nina asked Vinnie, pulling her hoodie up over her glorious mane of hair.

But maybe it wouldn't be so bad with Nina by her side.

Vinnie smiled.

Maybe it wouldn't be so bad at all.

They pulled into Dorinda's long, custom-paved driveway to the circle in front of her magnificent glass-etched double doors. Not much had changed about the place, Vinnie noted. They still had a line of manicured topiaries, their round tops covered in twinkling lights that winked at you as you passed by.

The fountain in the middle of the circular portion of the driveway was still as spectacular and lavish as it had been when Vinnie was ten and had attended Byron's magical birthday party. Colored lights sat deep in the water, each splash of the fountain bringing with it a rainbow of muted hues.

The lawn spread out on both sides and pushed well toward the back of the mansion where, upon arriving at Byron's bash all those years ago, jugglers dressed as court jesters had juggled sparkling balls and acrobats dressed in bright primary colors had tumbled and flew in the air to greet guests.

The lawn itself was as green as ever, despite the nature of the season. In fact, it was at this very spot where Vinnie had begged her mother to take her home, knowing she was out of place at such a lavish affair.

She inhaled a breath and let it out slowly while the women assessed the landscape of things.

Nina peered out the window, her eyes taking in the grandness of it all. "Fuck. I thought *my* house was big."

"You live in a castle, Mistress of The Night. It *is* big," Marty chirped from the driver's seat.

"*You live in a castle?*" Oliver asked, cocking his head so the streetlights caught the glow of his horn as he looked around at the enormous stone mansion with columns along the front porch as high and as far as the eye could see.

Nina turned around and looked at him, her eyes glittering. "Yeah. So?"

"You're one of the most fascinating people I've ever met, Nina," Oliver quipped as he looked out the window of the big SUV, his eyes wide.

Marty giggled as she put the car in park and turned to look at Oliver. "She's probably also the meanest. Now, you stay here, buddy. Do not move. I mean it. We'll be as quick as we can."

But Oliver frowned. "I don't understand why I can't go with you. You *are* helping me, after all. The least I can do is help you."

"We don't fucking need your help, Sparkle Tits. I think you know that."

Vinnie, who'd sat beside him quietly the entire ride to Dorinda's, thinking about what she'd say, dreading how much she hated that she had to say *anything*, patted his muscled arm.

"What Nina means to say is, clearly they're fully equipped to handle a situation, should one involving fisticuffs arise. But also, letting Dorinda see your horn, see that it actually exists, probably isn't a good idea. I don't know Dorinda well enough to know if she can be trusted. I'd venture probably not, because let's face it, she's all about appearances and showing us all how rich and Goddess-like she is. Imagine what she could do with this kind of information? You're rare, Oliver. There are no others like you. She'd have you in a gilded cage before you could say sparkle tits."

Oliver chuckled. "But we could just hide it like we did earlier today for my meeting with your mother. I don't feel good about you guys going in there when I'm the reason you're putting yourselves in danger."

"I don't think we can camouflage that horn anymore, Oliver. It's grown just over the course of the afternoon alone. What explanation will ever convince anyone you're not a unicorn when I'm asking about unicorns and you have a protrusion popping out of your forehead that, even with the gauze bandage, looks like *a protrusion coming out of your forehead*? You don't think that'll look at all suspicious to Dorinda?" Vinnie asked.

"Fine," Oliver said with resignation in his husky tone. "But I feel kind of stupid just sitting here."

"You look stupid, too," Nina said on a snort.

Marty drove a finger into her friend's shoulder. "Shut up, Nina. Listen, Oliver. I get that you feel helpless, but you're a handicap at this point just by the nature of how you look. If Dorinda's a gossiper, which from what Vinnie tells us is true, we can't afford to have her spreading your misfortune around. We have enough on our plate with just your existence."

"So even though I'm now considered paranormal just like all of you, I can't tell anyone because, one, I'm the only unicorn in the land, and two, rather than welcome me into the fold, my new people would put me on the auction block and sell me to the highest bidder?"

"Ain't that some shit?" Nina asked. "So stay the fuck here. Swear to shit, I'll kill you if you come inside, Oliver. If you hear anything fishy, text us. If you think we're eyeball deep in something, text Darnell and our husbands, understood? Do not make this harder than it has to be. We don't want you to get caught, but we also don't want Mama Bear to get fucked, either. So keep that damn hood over your head and lay low. We'll be as fast as we can."

Oliver's face said it all, but Vinnie gave him a sympathetic smile. "I'll go as quick as I can. See you in a bit."

But he grabbed her hand and tightened his grip, stopping her from exiting the car, the look on his gorgeous face one of concern. "Be careful, okay? All of you be careful."

She didn't know why he was so worried, but she sought to reassure him. "It's no big deal, Oliver. I'm just going to ask her some questions under the pretense of teaching a class about unicorns while Nina pretends to use the bathroom and hunts down that book. If Dorinda has a chance for an audience, she'll take it. It's going to be fine. I promise." She gave his warm, broad hand one last pat and slipped from the car.

As the three women approached Dorinda's massive front porch, their reflections in the tall sidelights beside the door, Vinnie caught a glimpse of the three of them as a trio.

Nina's hoodie had fallen from her head, leaving her glorious mane of black hair to billow around her shoulders and breasts, shiny and luxurious. Her legs were long and lean, taking extensive strides to the front porch as though she were on a catwalk, and even in jeans and a black T-shirt that read, "Keep It Up. You Could Be The Funny Smell In My Trunk," paired with clunky work boots, she looked like a supermodel.

Marty's hair billowed, too. Beautiful and blonde, the beach waves that blew away from her face kissed the cold wind, bouncing about her shoulders and back. Her hoop earrings dangled and glimmered, and though not as tall as Nina, she wore thigh-high gray boots with a stiletto heel, a chunky purple sweater and faded blue skinny jeans like they were made for her.

Vinnie, in comparison, felt a bit like the short, average-looking Charlie's Angel who was a fill-in until the beautiful, willowy costar could return from maternity leave.

She'd watched all the reruns as a child, and even in a day and age when misogyny was at its height, they'd still been pretty kick-ass.

And hello, as a kid, who didn't want the chance to be a Charlie's Angel—even if they were the dumpy angel?

As Nina pressed her finger to the doorbell, Vinnie felt her stomach lurch and her heart race. A sure sign her anxiety was going to rear its ugly head.

But then she asked herself, what would Jaclyn Smith, her favorite angel of all, do in the face of adversity?

Would she cower between Farah and Kate like a chickenshit? Or would she rise to the occasion?

Lifting her chin, Vinnie decided Kelly Garrett would set all her insecurities aside and show Dorinda she was a strong, capable woman now, and all her stupid snide remarks when she was a kid were the shit under her shoes.

Yeah.

CHAPTER 10

Okay, maybe Kelly Garrett would sashay her way into Dorinda's enormous mansion like she owned the joint, but Vinnie Morretti decided the second she saw Dorinda walking toward the big doors through the thick etched glass, she was no damn Kelly Garrett.

She wasn't even Shelley Hack.

But the moment Vinnie considered bolting, her feet doing a little shuffle, was the moment both Nina and Marty latched onto her and firmly kept her in place.

"Man, you guys are strong," she muttered, trying to remove her arms from their iron grips, but Nina leaned into her.

"Are you gonna let this bitch fuck with your head, Vinnie Morretti? Are you gonna let her intimidate you? The fuck I say. You stand right the fuck there and watch us work."

As Vinnie's knees began to tremble, Marty threw a

gorgeous smile on her face and extended her hand just as Dorinda, in all her aging Goddess beauty, flung the doors open wide.

"You must be Dorinda," Marty cooed at the woman, lifting her chin in the friendliest display of haughty to which Vinnie had ever borne witness.

Dorinda, her platinum-blonde hair piled high atop her head, her flowing red maxi-dress adorned with one jewel or another, took Marty's hand, the diamond and sapphire rings on her aging fingers sparkling under the porch lights. She was just shy a martini in one hand and a long cigarillo in the other.

Vinnie used to think she was chic and worldly, and she'd never failed to intimidate her whenever she crossed paths with the Goddess.

Dorinda smiled the smile Vinnie remembered from her childhood, fake warm, and condescending as all hell.

Cocking her head, she looked at both Marty and Nina, giving them a critical once-over. "I already know Vincenza, of course. You ladies are...?"

Marty smiled accommodatingly at her while Nina remained stone-faced and rigid. "I'm Marty Flaherty and this is Nina Statleon. We're friends of Vinnie. We happened to be partaking in a little girls' night out—I'm sure you know about those, right?" Marty winked an eye, batting her long lashes. "Vinnie was with us when she got the text from her mother, but she'd had a little wine, because you know, girls' night, and so we offered to drive her over here because we know how crucial preparation is for this class she's going to be teaching. Right, girlfriend?" Marty asked, wrapping an arm around her neck and pulling Vinnie close to her side.

"Right," Vinnie muttered.

"Yeah," Nina agreed with a grunt, giving Dorinda the business with her eyes. "Girls' night."

"How nice that you have friends *now*, Vincenza," the Goddess drawled.

Was that a crack about how friendless she'd been all throughout school? Because ouch.

Of course it was, Vinnie, because Dorinda's a stuck-up snob who likes to poke fun at who she considers the less fortunate, and she doesn't even bother to try to hide it.

"How nice that you still have the same hairdo you had when she was a kid," Nina said, her eyes glued to Dorinda's face.

Dorinda sucked in her cheeks and took a deep, haughty breath. "How can I help you ladies?"

Nina leaned forward just enough to look like she might eat Dorinda's face off. "Can we come in or do you wanna do this on the front porch?"

Dorinda's nostrils flared as she stepped back. "Vampire?"

"In the flesh," Nina responded, rolling her tongue along the inside of her cheek.

Dorinda took another small step backward. "Is the myth true about inviting you into my home?"

Nina's eyes narrowed, glittering under the porch's globe lights. "You wanna take a stab at it and see?"

Marty quickly put an arm in front of Nina to intervene. "No. It's not true. No more true than you'll turn a man to stone if he looks at you. Or will you?" Marty asked with a wink and a giggle. "Anyway, I'm a werewolf, if knowing our origins is your thing. I promise not to shed on your carpets. Now, shall we? We'd hate to take up too much of your time, Miss Dorinda. I'm sure you're as busy as we are. Running a cosmetics company while having just merged with another large corporation is exhausting. Surely you understand what it is to be a corporate woman in this day and age?"

Slam!

Vinnie fought not to laugh out loud at the look on Dorinda's face.

Dorinda hadn't worked a day in her life. Her husband was some big-time defense attorney—he owned law offices all over New York. She'd been an arm piece for her husband back in the day and not much more.

"Oh, I never worked. I stayed home to raise my son and daughter. It's so important to their development," she responded with a catty smile, her red lips only slightly tilting upward.

What she meant was, nannies and maids had raised Byron and Donna while she'd shopped in Paris and Italy and spent the days she was actually home at some fancy spa.

Even at ten, Vinnie knew Dorinda only played at being a parent when the situation called for one to show up. But she'd been no more involved in Byron's and Donna's lives than a deadbeat dad who's forced to pay child support. She was all show, no substance.

In that respect, she had to give it to her mother. She might have thrust a life on Vinnie she didn't want, but she'd always been there for her. Every award, every accolade, her mother had shown up.

Marty nodded as the roar of a sports car zoomed up the driveway. "Oh, absolutely. I couldn't agree more. It's crucial for their character, their work ethic, their integrity... Speaking of, is that your son?" she asked, pointing to the shiny red Corvette, where a lithe blonde holding a champagne flute hung out the window and waved a long arm.

Music blared from the radio as Byron stumbled out onto the driveway, tripping over his feet.

"Yep. That's Byron," Vinnie assured her. She hadn't seen him in what felt like a million years, but she'd know his slicked-back look anywhere.

Marty cocked her head, bringing her shoulder to her chin with a coy smile. "Staying at home to raise your son paid off wonderfully, didn't it? Now, shall we?" She swept her arm toward the entryway of Dorinda's mansion. "I have an insanely busy day tomorrow—at *work*."

Dorinda lifted her sharp chin, but she stepped back and let them all inside, pointing toward the room directly in front of them. "If you'll have a seat in the parlor, I'll have Mavis make us some tea. Excuse me."

As the Goddess took her leave to arrange refreshment, Vinnie exhaled a long breath. One, because she hoped Byron would go the hell away and she wouldn't have to see him. Two, because these women, or at least Marty, knew how to give you hell all while smiling in your face.

It had been such a relief not to have to deal with Dorinda alone while she stumbled over her words and felt like a big blob of stupid.

Marty hooked her arm through Vinnie's and pulled her to the opulent parlor. Who called their living room a parlor, anyway?

"You okay?" Marty asked, giving her shoulder a light nudge.

"I'm fine." That's what her answer was to everything. I'm fine. Everything's fine. Fine. Fine. Finer than fine.

"No you're not," Nina shot back with an impatient growl. "Stand up straight, Vincenza Raphaela Morretti. You're an adult now. You don't have to take Miss Highbrow's snide subtext and bullshit dirty looks like you did when you were a kid. You're an accomplished fucking adult who has an impressive job and a house and isn't stumbling the fuck around in your mommy and daddy's driveway with some blonde, higher than a damn kite."

Nina stepped in front of Vinnie, pinning her to the spot with her intense black gaze. "Listen, I can smell the anxiety on you. You reek of it, and I get it. I'm not bashing you because of it. I understand it's real. But I'm fucking here to tell you, you're worthy. Way the fuck more worthy than this piece of shit and her piece-of-shit kid and his Corvette. Okay? So you ask all the questions you need to and stall her while I do my thing, but do not—I repeat—do *not* let her make you feel like you're the shit on her shoe, because I won't have it. She can't make you feel that way unless you let her. Period."

Marty pinched Nina's cheek and blew her a kiss Nina made a face at. "I love you, vampire." Then she looked to Vinnie and nodded. "She's right, you know. I understand your anxiety plays a role in this, and how she made you feel as a child is rearing its ugly head, but she's not allowed to get in your head unless you invite her in. You're strong and smart and, most importantly, kind. Now, I know it's easier said than done, but I'm going to need you to at least try to hold your head up like you mean it. You're an accomplished woman. Not a washed-up Goddess with some twisted, misplaced sense of entitlement. Got it?"

Vinnie nodded, even though she didn't necessarily feel it. This was for Oliver. She had to make this right.

Squaring her shoulders, she looked past the baby grand piano by the floor-to-ceiling windows with elaborate silk curtains and readied herself for battle.

Why she felt like it was a battle made no sense. Dorinda was just a mouthy Goddess with a lot of time on her hands. But it felt like battle.

"Vincenza Morretti? Is that you?" a voice from behind them said.

Vinnie turned around, her stomach twisting into the knot she'd just begun to untwist. "Byron?"

"Daaamn, look at you," he crowed with a slur as he

entered the parlor, his steps crooked and wobbly as the lithe blonde in a tight dress meant for clubbing clung to his waist. His handsome features hadn't changed much in all these years. He was still good-looking in a very groomed way. His dark hair slicked back from his face and his tan healthy, despite the fact that he was blotto. "How the hell are ya? Haven't seen you in what, fifteen years?"

Actually, it had been more like eighteen, and it was on the playground at their school just before she'd shot up ahead of her class and been promoted to a much higher grade than her classmates, but who was counting?

"Something like that," she mumbled, wishing she could, just this once, find her voice. If only to show Nina and Marty she appreciated their belief in her more than they'd ever understand. But instead, she looked down at her worn brown clogs and swallowed hard.

Nina clucked her tongue as she stepped closer to Vinnie and loomed in Byron's general direction—because she was great at that menacing, deranged stance where she said absolutely nothing, but you felt sure at any moment she might go ballistic on you and wipe you off the face of the planet—which made Byron blanch, but only for a second before he tried to stand up straight.

"Who are *you*, beautiful?" he asked as he appraised Nina with a sly grin, his bleary green eyes roaming over every inch of her lean body with a lascivious gaze.

Oh, God. This would end poorly for him, they'd be booted out on their keisters, and they'd never get the book at this rate.

But the vampire simply yawned in his face as though she were bored, crossing her arms over her chest and giving him a totally devoid-of-any-emotion stare. "A friend of Vinnie's."

But he wasn't at all deterred by Nina's cool response. He continued to outwardly gawk at her, even with a woman at his side, his breath reeking of alcohol. Though honestly, Vinnie couldn't blame him. Nina was so beautiful, it was almost surreal.

He smoothed a hand over his tapered blue silk shirt. "Who knew Vinnie had friends that look like you?"

"Who knew Vinnie had friends your age who still live with their mommy's and smell like a Jersey dump?" Nina replied, narrowing her gaze until her eyes were but two charcoal slits in her head. She jammed her hands into the pockets of her hoodie and waited.

Now he leaned toward her, the confused blonde still clinging to his waist, clearly unfazed by his bold words and obvious attempts to come on to Nina.

He shook a finger at her and smiled a crooked smile. "Ah. You're salty, huh? I like 'em salty."

Nina clucked her tongue and cracked her knuckles as she stared at him until Vinnie squirmed uncomfortably. "And I like 'em when they pay their own rent. You know, like a big boy?"

"Byron?" Dorinda called out, whisking into the room in a swirl of perfume with a maid dressed in full uniform following her in hot pursuit. She latched onto Byron's arm and gave it an affectionate pat. "What are you doing?"

"I'm welcoming your guests, Mom," he said with a lascivious grin at Nina. "Where've you been hiding them all this time?"

Dorinda cleared her throat and smiled briefly. "We were just about to sit down and have some tea, dear. I thought you were on your way out with... Sienna, is it?"

"Ciara," the blonde corrected, blowing a strand of her feathery hair from her round blue eyes. "It's Ciara, and we *are* on our way out. We're going to a new club." She tugged at Byron's arm and gave him a coy smile. "C'mon, Byron. Let's go. We're going to miss the new DJ if we don't hurry."

He looked down at Ciara and tapped the end of her nose with a cheesy grin, flashing his perfectly white teeth. "Okey-doke." Then he turned to Nina, giving her another lustful gaze. He grabbed her hand and winked before he let it go. "It was *really* nice meeting you. Hope we see each other again real soon."

Byron turned and headed for the door with his mother trailing after him and hissing, "Call an Uber. You're in no shape to drive."

He waved a manicured hand at her and stumbled back out the door as Dorinda approached them again, her eyes a bit sheepish if Vinnie was reading them correctly.

"Nice kid you got there, *Dorinda*. Got a bathroom I

can use? I have a sudden urge to wash my hand," Nina said, her words dripping blatant sarcasm as she held up the hand Byron had latched onto.

Dorinda's cheeks flushed pink, but she waved to her right and down a long, semi-lit hallway with a bunch of carved-out nooks in the wall that held various sculptures. "Of course. Down the hall and to your left."

"So, that tea?" Marty reminded pleasantly.

"Of course," Dorinda murmured. "Please, follow me." She swept deeper into the parlor and pointed to a beautiful settee in teal green and gold chintz.

As they settled in across from her, Vinnie fought the clammy sweat of her palms, crossing her legs as Mavis, a sweet, elderly woman with kind eyes, poured them tea Vinnie would never be able to drink because her stomach was in an uproar.

Dorinda looked expectantly down her nose at Vinnie, folding her hands in her lap. "So what can I help you with, Vincenza? I think I told Alice everything I know about unicorns, and that nonsense story I heard at a party so long ago. What more is there?"

It was obvious Dorinda was agitated. Marty and Nina had called her out and Byron had only doubled down on the idea she wasn't who she pretended to be. But Vinnie was taking no pleasure in revealing the empress without her clothes, despite her past cruelties.

Vinnie went into great detail about what she knew of the origins of unicorns, and reminded Dorinda it was a very small amount indeed, asking questions and hoping to take up as much time as she could to stall.

When Nina appeared at the entryway and held up her phone, an indication she'd gotten what they needed, Vinnie nodded her head and pretended to listen to Dorinda's answers.

"Are you sure there's no truth to it? I'd...I'd like to have at least something a little more detailed to share with my students. Can you remember who was telling the story? It might be fun to have a name to attach to the folklore."

"I'm sure there's no truth to it," she replied curtly. "I only overheard bits and pieces of the story and it was some time ago. And I don't remember whom I heard it from. For all I know, they'd had too much to drink and were just carrying on, the way drunks often do."

"But you do remember them claiming a unicorn had lost his powers to a troll at the end of a rainbow?"

She barked a sardonic laugh. "I do, but come now, do you really think it happened? It sounds like something out of a children's book. I've been around for some time, Vincenza, at least as long as your mother. Does she ever remember hearing a story like that?"

"Well, probably not. I mean, how often was she invited to a party you all attended without horning her way in?" Vinnie blurted out, then fought not to clamp her hand over her mouth to keep from showing Dorinda how anxious speaking up had left her.

Instead, she straightened her spine, hearing Nina's voice in her head.

The Goddess squirmed on her throne in clear

discomfort. Marty, on the other hand, fought laughter with an obvious snicker.

Dorinda sucked in her cheeks and sighed. "I still don't understand why you thought coming here was going to change what I told Alice on the phone, Vincenza."

Vinnie shrugged, but for the first time, she smiled. "I guess I hoped something I said might jar your memory, but then, maybe not. I'm sorry to have wasted your time."

Nina entered the room on catlike feet, despite her heavy work boots. "Would ya look at the time? We gotta blow this mausoleum, girlies. Vinnie's got more friends we're meeting up with for the rest of girls' night."

Marty instantly rose and stuck her hand out to Dorinda. "It was lovely to meet you, Dorinda. I do hope we run across one another at a function somewhere along the way. In fact, I'm launching a new skin care line at the completion of my company's merger with my husband's. I'll pop an invitation in the mail. It's perfect for women of a *certain age*."

Dorinda took her hand, but remained silent with a smile that never reached her eyes.

Vinnie took one last sip of her tea, because Dorinda might be awful, but Mavis made a helluva cup of tea. She tilted the delicate cup in Mavis's direction, smiling at her sweet round face. "Thanks for the tea and your time, ladies, but Nina's right. We have to get going. G'night!"

As they headed toward the door, Vinnie could have sworn she heard Mavis chuckle under her breath.

Once they'd closed the doors, as the frosty wind whipped their hair about their faces and leaves scattered across the driveway, Vinnie was about to turn to them and thank them for making that experience as painless as possible—but what greeted them stopped her cold.

"*What the fuck?*" Nina yelled into the wind as Vinnie's eyes landed on the focus of the vampire's rage. "Hey! Who the fuck do you think you are?"

A man—a big man in nothing but a T-shirt, jeans and what looked like a miner's hat—was in the process of dragging a lifeless Oliver down the driveway toward a dark sedan.

CHAPTER 11

As they all began to run toward him, the man looked up, his eyes filled with fear, Vinnie managed to catch a glimpse of his T-shirt in the lights around the driveway. It read, "I Believe."

Her mouth fell open in shock as she tried to keep up with the women, but man, Dorinda's driveway was long and these women were insanely fast.

Just as the thump of Nina's boots almost hit the spot where the man had stopped with poor Oliver, he dropped him and fled on foot down the road.

"You go after him, Nina!" Marty yelled. "I got Oliver!"

Vinnie flew to his side, gathering him up as Nina went after the perpetrator who'd abandoned his car in favor of running away. Obviously a poor choice, because if he was human, he'd never get away from Nina and her super-speed.

But Vinnie was too worried about Oliver and his

apparent unconscious condition to fret long over Nina. She patted his cheek, pulling his head to her lap. "Oliver! Oliver, wake up!"

As the wind tore through her light sweater and stung her cheeks, she tried to haul him upward, to no avail, but then Marty was there in a swirl of perfume and blonde hair.

She grabbed one of his big arms and in one fell swoop, she hauled his enormous body over her shoulder like a weight lifter hefted a barbell.

And she did it all in heels.

Wow.

"Help me get him in the car, Vinnie!" she yelled on a grunt as Vinnie ran for the SUV's back door and yanked it open.

She ran around to the other side and opened the other door to climb in so Marty could lay him across her lap. Marty dropped him like a sack of potatoes and flew to the driver's side, hopping in and revving the engine.

Caressing his face with her palm, running her fingers over his smooth skin and trying to avoid his horn, Vinnie tried to jar him. "Oliver, wake up!" she cried—and that's when she saw the half-filled needle.

She gasped as she looked at the syringe. Her eyes went wide in horror. "He has a needle in his neck, Marty!" Vinnie grabbed it and held it up, catching Marty's eyes in the SUV's rearview mirror. "It's still got something in it. It doesn't look like he used the full dose."

"Shit! That maniac must have tranquilized him. Hang on, Vinnie, I'm going to try to catch up with Nina!"

But it turned out, it wasn't necessary. Nina banged her knuckles on the passenger-side window, motioning to Marty to open it.

"What's the hell's going on?" Marty roared to her friend, her face angry.

Vinnie's heart slammed against her ribs, fear for Oliver's health her first concern, but then he groaned and stirred. "Oliver," she whispered. "Are you all right?"

As the wind blew into the car, Nina held up the man she'd chased down by the scruff of his neck—and by no means was he diminutive in size—with one freakin' hand. She gave him a shake, his head falling back on his neck from the motion. "*This* is what's going on. This motherfucker is from one of those crazy-ass groups who chase down shit like Bigfoot and the Lochness Monster."

Vinnie inhaled sharply as Oliver tried to sit up, but she patted his jaw. "Stay put," she whispered, pulling her sweater over his forehead.

"How do you know?" Marty asked in disgust.

Nina used her other hand to dig a phone from her hoodie and hold it up. "Because his home screen says so."

Vinni squinted to read the phone with a colorful picture of an alien on it. The site was called Hit or Myth, and it claimed to be in pursuit of the truth of all mythical creatures.

Oh, Jesus. Her stomach dropped to the floor.

"So what do we do with him?" Marty asked.

"Pop the back. I'll throw him in there and sit with him until we can take him somewhere to find out how he fucking found us. He's passed out for now. I tackled him about a quarter of the way down the road, knocked his loser ass out cold. I don't think anyone saw me, but he won't stay this way for long, Marty. Either way...goddammit. *Goddammit.* God-fucking-dammit! I want to choke this freak out for making me do this, but I had no choice. He wouldn't slow his fucking roll—even with a damn warning."

Marty popped the back of the SUV. The thump of a body and Nina's pale face as she climbed in beside him made Vinnie's heart skip a beat.

What other reason could he have shown up here than he was hunting Oliver? Had he seen Oliver's horn? How had he found out about him? They'd all been so careful. Had Dorinda said something to someone about unicorns? And if she did, how could anyone have possibly known it had to do with a real unicorn? Shit, this was horrible.

Panic seized her gut, her mouth going dry, her hands clammy. A panic attack was sure to follow, but Oliver must have sensed something, because he grabbed her hand as he fought to sit up, his words groggy.

"It's okay, Vinnie. We'll figure this out," he soothed as he settled beside her. "Don't think about this; think about finding the calm in you. Take deep breaths and listen to me. This feeling won't last forever. It's just for now. I promise."

Just as her heart had begun to race—and it felt more like she was having a heart attack than a panic attack—it slowed at Oliver's words. Logically, she knew she wasn't having a heart attack, her therapist had taught her that, but hearing his soothing words made her cling to the notion.

"What are we going to do about this joker's car?" Marty asked as she looked at the end of the driveway in her rearview mirror, preparing to leave.

"Leave it. Let the fucking neighborhood association have it towed. Maybe that fuck Byron, whose soul smells like rotting dead bodies under the Texas sun in July, can take care of it. Or I'll send Darnell out to deal with it. We'll find out who the fuck he is and how he found out about us, and then I'll wipe his fucking memory. I'll drop him somewhere safe like a hospital or a police station."

Oliver blinked as Marty hauled ass out of the driveway. "You can wipe someone's memory?"

Nina thumped him on the shoulder and grinned her beautiful grin. "If I need to. We don't do it often because dumb-ass vampire rules and all that shit, but it can be done."

Oliver craned his head around and looked at Nina. "I think I said this earlier, but I maintain, you're one of the most fascinating people I've ever met."

The vampire's nostrils flared. "Yeah. I hear that a lot."

"It's usually just before she hears what a bitch she is, but she does hear it a lot," Marty said on a chuckle.

Oliver laughed with a nod. "I'm shocked anyone would say that about you, Nina," he teased, his voice husky. "Positively, utterly shocked."

Vinnie held up the syringe she'd pulled from Oliver's neck. "So what happened while we were in there? And what is this?"

His hand flew to his neck, his eyes wide. "Did he sedate me?"

Vinnie eyed the syringe, still half full. "That's what it looks like, because you were passed out cold and he was dragging you down the driveway. But it doesn't look like he used it all. It does mean he came prepared. So what happened?"

"You guys were in talking to that Dorinda, and I was hunkered down here in the car waiting. I heard someone pull up, thought it might be the guy who was here earlier with the blonde. I looked out the window and the next thing I know, this guy's pulling the door open and jabbing something sharp in my neck. No warning, no how do ya do, just bam. That's the last thing I remember. But that aside, do we know who he is and what he wanted with me?"

Nina rasped a sigh. "Never should have let you talk us into bringing you."

"You're sure you've never seen him before?" Marty asked.

Oliver shook his head. "Never in my life."

Nina held up the man's phone and tapped it with a

finger. "His name's Mikey Stillman, and he runs a website called Hit or Myth, for people who hunt mythical fucking creatures. He's one of those GD nuts who's always calling OOPS, talking about exposing us to the world."

"Except, he's not nuts. If he only knew how close he is to the truth," Marty commented as they flew through the streets of Buffalo toward Oliver's.

Oliver dragged a hand through his hair, his face worried. "How the hell did he find out about me?"

"I dunno," Nina replied. "But I'm gonna fucking find out."

"You won't hurt him, will you?" Oliver asked, his face full of concern.

"Do you mean like torture the shit out of him the way he was probably going to torture the shit out of you? Nah. But I *will* fucking knock him around to get info from his nosy ass if I have to. You're one of us now, Ollie. None of us can afford to have this motherfucker out there telling people he found a dude with a GD sparkly horn. So I'll do what I have to in order to protect us and our families."

Vinnie gazed at Oliver, her eyes full of worry. "Do you know if he even saw your horn? Your hoodie was still on when he was dragging you down the driveway."

Oliver shrugged his wide shoulders. "I have no idea. I had the hoodie on when he knocked on the window. I can't believe I forgot to lock the damn door, but that's all I remember."

"It doesn't fucking matter if he saw your horn, dude. I'll wipe his memory."

Yet, as they passed through a small suburb, the lamppost lights whizzing by, Vinnie couldn't help but wonder out loud.

"But what if he wrote something down somewhere, Nina? What if he has notes on his computer or wherever?" Vinnie asked, the worry she'd been feeling earlier creeping back into her words. "You can wipe his memory all you like, but if he's got other research somewhere, or he told someone about what he was going to do tonight, we're in trouble."

"Don't worry. I'll fucking handle it. You just worry about the shit I got from Dorinda's damn library. I got an assload of pictures from that book."

"In record time, too," Vinnie commented with a smile.

Nina shrugged it off. "Vampire speed. Works like a damn boss. I dunno if the pics will help, but we need a win here."

Vinnie reached over the seat and squeezed Nina's pale hand. "Did I mention how much I appreciate you guys coming with me tonight? It made seeing Dorinda after such a long time a whole lot less stressful."

Nina ran her knuckles over the top of Vinnie's head and winked. "I heard you give the snooty bitch a little subtle what-for while I was in the library doing the deed. Good on you. Somebody needs to take her uppity ass in hand."

Vinnie felt inordinately pleased with Nina's

approval. "Thanks. Seeing you guys in action helped me have the courage."

Marty smiled at her from the rearview mirror. "You held your own, Vinnie. Well done."

A sudden quiet came over the car then, as Vinnie—and she was sure everyone else—pondered this Mikey Stillman and the harm he could bring to their kind.

She sank deeper into Oliver, reveling in the warmth his body provided and how safe she felt with these people—even with a crazy unicorn hunter in the backseat.

~

Mikey Stillman, forty-one, who, according to a little research and some Googling, lived in a raggedy, rundown trailer on the edge of the woods, lie partially in the back of Marty's SUV as Oliver stood with everyone in his garage. He didn't want anyone to know how panicked he was that someone had tried to grab him. He was trying like hell to take this like a man.

But Jesus. Someone had literally hunted him down because he was a unicorn. This was crazy.

But then again, Mikey Stillman looked pretty crazy himself. His scraggly beard, dirty nails, holey T-shirt and paint-spattered jeans didn't do much but add to his wild appearance. He wore a skull-covered bandanna around his greasy hair and had the worn, round circle of a can of chewing tobacco in his back pocket even as he reeked of cigarettes.

As Nina tugged Mikey the rest of the way into the back of the car, throwing a blanket over his body, Oliver continued to stare at him in disbelief.

This man had tried to kidnap him. What had he planned to do once he had him in his clutches?

Oliver looked to Nina and Wanda, both of whom had questioned Mikey. Nina being the one who'd threatened his life while Wanda asked the questions. "So he was tracing you guys from the hotline?"

Nina climbed back out of the SUV and brushed her hands together before resting an elbow on the side of the car. "I have no clue. Tech isn't my shit. That's Darnell's shiz. The basic gist of it is, Mikey somehow managed to track my phone through the OOPS line... or something like that. He followed us to that bitch Dorinda's mansion, waited until we got out of the car, and planned to break in while we were inside and surprise us. Instead, he found you, Unicorn Man. Either way, not a very well thought out plan."

Oliver winced and blew out a pent-up breath. "Did he see my horn?" he asked, catching another glimpse of it in the driver's side window of the SUV.

It would have been impossible not to see the damn thing. It felt like it was everywhere.

Nina nodded her dark head, the silky curtain of her hair falling over her shoulders. "Uh-yup. But like I said, it doesn't fucking matter—"

"You wiped his memory," he finished for her, still unable to process that sentence.

Wanda tapped his arm in sympathy and smiled from where she sat on the folding chair he took with him to games. "She only uses that power for good. I promise. Mikey was mostly an easy mark."

"Yep. He gave his plan up real nice and easy. It didn't take much violence at all. Disappointing to say the fucking least," she groused.

Oliver understood why they had to be careful, but he worried about their tactics—even with the gentle, compassionate Wanda present. He didn't want anyone hurt because of him, even if the guy had wanted to hurt *him* first.

"May I ask why he gave up the info so easily?"

Nina pointed to her very white, very shiny teeth. "Because I showed him my fucking sharp teeth. After that, everything was cake. See, here's the thing about dicks like this, they *think* they wanna know about the paranormal. They're all assholes and elbows to hunt us like GD trophies in the jungles of Africa. They have big mouths, they talk all manner of inflated shit until they see us and they see we really do fucking exist. Then they're all assholes and elbows to hide under the fucking covers like little chickenshits. I just gave him what he wanted to prove we really do exist."

"Oh, Oliver, if you could have seen his face." Wanda laughed with a clap to her thigh. "There's no other word to describe it but hysterical. Either way, he got what he was looking for, but as Nina said, he wasn't quite ready for the terror an experience like that brings."

Nina jabbed a finger in Mikey's direction. "He's also the dickweed who's been calling the hotline these last few months. If nothing else, I'm glad he found us for that reason alone. He's one less freak we have to watch the fuck out for."

Oliver rocked back on his heels and let out a breath. "And the tranquilizer he injected me with? What was that? Do I have to worry about repercussions? Like, am I going to grow another head to match my new horn?" he only half-joked.

"Morphine," Nina provided. "He stole it from his grandmother when she died in hospice care. Which means he's a damn asshole on top of crazy. There's nothing I like less than crazy assholes."

"Was anyone else involved in this endeavor? Or was it just him alone? When I watch some of those YouTube channels, people like Mikey have an awful lot of support."

That scared him, too. He was no shrinking violet. If need be, he could handle himself. But what if this Mikey had been successful in tranquilizing him? What if he'd dragged him off somewhere and locked his ass up? What if someone who wasn't human did it? He might be able to hold his own with Mikey, but he was powerless against a vampire.

"Just him. Mikey here's a lone wolf, but I'm gonna go to his house with Darnell, wipe his damn computer, any electronic devices, and we're all getting new phones just to be safe. I'll look around while I'm there to be fucking sure this nutbag's telling the truth. I can usually smell a lie from a mile off, but this guy's just plain fuckwit-kooky. Sometimes that throws my ass off."

Oliver was long past being horrified at her vampiric skills and well into deep admiration—for all of them, in fact. So he didn't bother to concern himself with whether she was capable of scrubbing this event from Mikey's memory.

And he said as much when he peered down into her beautiful, eerily pale face. "Is there anything you can't do, Wonder Woman?"

"Sing. She's a dreadful singer," Wanda quipped, rubbing her belly with a protective hand as she pushed her way out of the chair with Nina's help. "It sounds like a seal mating."

Nina flipped Wanda her middle finger as she steadied her. "Fuck off. I can too sing, Wanda. I just don't wanna show you bitches up on karaoke night," she said, and then she chuckled.

Vinnie slipped out of the entry to the garage off the kitchen with Baloney sitting happily on her shoulder and held up a cup. "Coffee?" she asked him.

Oliver smiled at her in gratitude. He was going on almost no sleep for the past two days. At some point, even coffee wasn't going to keep him awake. But he didn't just smile in gratitude. He liked seeing her face in his doorway. He liked it *and* her...a lot.

She handed him the coffee and smiled, her pretty

face beaming up at him. "So is Mikey thoroughly interrogated? Why is there no evidence of waterboarding and a pair of rusty pliers to extract teeth?"

"That was why Wanda was involved. To buffer all communications. Anyway, he's finished and will be on his way back home like this never happened. Nina and Darnell are taking him."

"The power of the paranormal, huh?" she asked with a dimpled grin.

"Will I ever get used to it?"

"I don't know. I don't have any powers to speak of, so I can't say. I *can* tell you, I've seen a lot of it in my day, and if you're not careful, it can be intimidating."

"You're immortal. That's a power, if you ask me." Then he paused when he realized what he'd said. "Wait. Am I immortal, too?" Oliver blanched at the idea he'd outlive his parents, his sisters—*everyone*. It froze him on the spot.

Baloney took that moment to hop to his shoulder with such lithe grace, rather than stumbling because of her lame back leg, it punctuated this new journey he was on, and he had to lean back against the garage wall.

Vinnie reached up and ran a light finger over Baloney's back with a smile. "I don't know, to be honest. Maybe? That's our whole problem, Oliver. We just don't know about a unicorn's origins. What I do know is, what happened tonight is probably just a small taste of what could happen if we don't find a way to help you with this horn business. That doesn't even include figuring out how to hide it from people and how it brought you to your knees when you used it to help Arch."

Baloney leaned into Vinnie's fingers, and he couldn't help but comment on it because he didn't want to talk about his horn. "You know, she's not usually a fan of women, but she really seems taken with all of you."

Vinnie cocked her head, her eyes warm as she stroked Baloney. "Really? Why's that, do you think?"

"Denise," he said woodenly. He wanted to say her name with ease, and he'd like to think he was past his anger with her, but what she'd done still stung.

Vinnie peered up at him with critical eyes. "Baloney didn't like Denise?"

"Denise didn't like *her*. She called her a rodent, wanted me to get rid of her."

Vinnie plucked Baloney from his shoulder and rubbed her tiny face against her cheek. "Get rid of this little cutie? I guess some people can't see the value in them, but then, I had mice when I was little, so I'm not a very good judge. Though, in fairness, maybe Denise was afraid, is all. Marty told me she nearly jumped out of her skin when she saw her, and now she loves her. Sometimes it takes time."

"How can anyone be afraid of this little bugger?" Oliver shook his head to dismiss the notion that Denise was a bad person because she never liked Baloney. Some people didn't like animals. They were clearly not *his* people, and that was okay. "I guess it's just one of many things I'm only recently realizing were the problems between us. I love animals, she didn't."

Vinnie grinned, tucking her hair behind her ears. "I like animals, too. I don't like unicorn hunters. Which brings me to the book Nina took pictures of at Dorinda's. I found nothing that makes any sense at all in correlation to turning someone into a unicorn. I did find the spell my mother meant to cast, and holy candied nuts, did she hack that up."

Oliver winced. "So she copied it down wrong?"

"Probably because she was in a rush and didn't want to get caught, but ooo-wee, did she ever copy it wrong. I sure wish I knew what she said so we could make sure she never says it again. Who knows what could happen if she gets it right. I could end up with a serial killer. But all joking aside, I have a call into Khristos to see if he knows anyone who can discreetly find out if there's a spell to turn you back."

"So we're back to square one, and my situation forced you to face some demons you didn't want to face. I'm sorry for that, Vinnie."

As Nina and Darnell piled into Marty's SUV and fired it up to drop Mikey back at his house, Vinnie shrugged. "Maybe it was exactly what I needed to see to show me Dorinda wasn't as intimidating to twenty-eight-year-old me as she once was to ten-year-old me. I think it even actually helped a little."

Oliver gave her a lopsided grin. "Well, until otherwise notified, I'm part of the club now, too. So you're not alone in feeling like you don't fit in. We can be misfits together."

Her smile of acceptance made his chest feel tight, and with everything going on, he wasn't sure how to deal with the emotion. "Deal. Now, our next plan of action? Any thoughts?"

"Are fairies who spin cotton candy out of the question? Because that's pretty damn cool."

Vinnie let her head fall back on her shoulders, laughter gurgling from her throat. "I thought I told you, all I have is a drunken Barney."

Oliver mocked a sad face. "So no dancing carousel horses either, then?"

"Um, nope. Not a one. And listen, don't think I'm not just as disappointed as you because hello, dancing carousel horses come to life? It just doesn't get any cooler."

Now he laughed, and then rubbed his belly as it growled. "Then how about some food. I could really use some food. It's been a hella long day with no answers and despite my weird paranormal anomaly, I'm still a twelve-year-old boy on the inside. Which means I'm starving. Any leftovers from the dinner we missed?"

She hitched her jaw toward the inside of the house. "I hear Arch made spaghetti and meatballs with a sauce that's to die for, no pun intended. I think there's some in the fridge. Want me to whip you up some fresh noodles?"

"You'd do that for me?" he asked, feigning coyness.

"It's the least I can do, seeing as it was my mother who turned you into a unicorn. If she keeps this up, I'm going to have to take up cooking lessons for all her future victims."

As they laughed and headed back inside to the kitchen, where the warmth of the lights glowed and everyone had gathered around his kitchen table to have coffee and chat while they ate dessert, he smiled. This is what the kitchen was made for. People laughing and talking and having pie.

But there was someone missing. "Where is Alice, anyway?"

Vinnie clucked her tongue with a sigh. "She went back home. She said she had some work to do. The ladies felt like it would be okay to let her go. They don't think she's in any kind of danger, but Darnell promised to check in on her throughout the night. Honestly though, it's a relief. I haven't gotten past the blame portion of this adventure and I don't want to lash out at her anymore. She's taken enough of a beating."

"She didn't mean to cause all this trouble," he reminded. He understood the relationship between them was complicated, and while what she'd done was wrong, he hated seeing Alice so upset.

"I know that. I really do, Oliver. We just have some kinks to work out, but we left each other on good terms. Promise, your new buddy's safe. No worries. Now, that spaghetti?"

"Yes, please," he said as he followed her farther into the kitchen, and it was then he realized how much he missed sharing a meal with someone other than Baloney.

He'd isolated himself a bit since he and Denise broke up, unless it was family-related. He was seeing now that was a misstep on his part, and for the first time in a long time, even with a sparkly horn, he felt an invisible heavy weight lift from his shoulders.

~

Oliver woke with a start, his stomach still full from Arch's amazing spaghetti. Even reheated, those meatballs had been killer, but he was experiencing a bit of heartburn after eating well past his limit.

After dinner, when Nina and Darnell returned, they'd sat around and talked about what to do next, deciding they'd wait on Khristos because they didn't know how to approach this without sending out alarms in the paranormal world.

When Oliver had protested uprooting their lives this way and promised not to use his horn so everyone could go home to their families, no one budged. They were in it for the long haul, the way they'd been in every case before his, he'd been told. That meant they stayed the night in order to protect him—which felt weird as a grown man.

But then he reminded himself he was a grown man of average strength, possibly dealing with bad guys with super-human strength.

The choice of dead or alive became the question.

So they'd broken out some UNO cards and played a few rounds before he'd bowed out and gone off to bed, exhausted from the day's events.

But that burning in his chest because he'd overdone the delicious sauce woke him up, and that's when he remembered he hadn't taken out the trash. His world had been a bit upside down and his normal schedule, which he typically didn't enjoy having interrupted, was totally off.

Slipping from the guest bed and throwing on his jeans and sneakers, he tiptoed out to the long hallway, past the master bedroom where Wanda and Vinnie were sleeping, and away from the rest of the rooms, grateful he could at least provide a place for everyone to sleep.

He was glad they'd talked Vinnie into staying, too. Not just because he liked her, but because she was safe here with them. Wanda had warned that she had vital information about the existence of unicorns. If someone wanted that information, they might try and hurt her to get it.

Sneaking through the kitchen, Oliver popped open the door to the garage and headed to the other door leading out to his backyard, where he kept the trash cans.

He shivered the second he hit the backyard. Damn it was cold tonight. He should have put a shirt on. And maybe a hat because, shit, he'd forgotten about his horn.

Oliver looked around with haste, hoping none of his neighbors were up this late. There was no hiding this damn horn, especially under the shiny moon, so bright it gave him a headache.

Now, what he *should* have done was run back inside and grab a towel or something to hide the frickin' thing.

What he did instead? Decided to chance it by opening his back gate, grabbing the trash can and dragging it down to the end of the driveway at a light jog while surreptitiously keeping an eye out for the odd neighbor who'd be up at two in the morning.

Which, by the by, was an enormous mistake. Because the next thing he knew, someone had grabbed him—by his neck no less—and threw him up against the side of his house.

He had a feeling this wasn't a good sign.

CHAPTER 12

The instant he felt the hands around his neck —male hands, he discovered, by the grip of them—was the instant he came out swinging, but it was like hitting a rock when his fist met the guy's jaw. He reached up and tried to pry the man's fingers from around his neck, but it was like trying to break the grip of a steel band.

As Oliver's eyes bulged, he fought to remember what he knew about getting free from someone stronger. As the oxygen to his brain decreased, and his feet lifted off the ground, Oliver struggled, but he managed to lift his arms up enough to use his thumbs in an attempt to gouge the guy's eyes out.

The wind tore at his bare chest, his feet hung like icy stumps from his legs, but just as he pressed his fingers against the man's eyes, there was a blur of sound and noise.

"*Staaahp!*" he heard Vinnie cry out. Somehow, as

small as she was, she jumped on the man's back and got her hands around his neck, which deterred the maniac for no more than a few seconds before he was squeezing Oliver's neck again. "*Let go!*" she screamed, latching onto his hair and yanking so hard, his head jerked back.

Oliver saw her knuckles, white and straining as she latched onto his hair, but that didn't make him stop. However, it *did* make him roar his discontent and squeeze harder, but this time with one hand as he reached up behind him and grabbed Vinnie's hair.

She screamed so loud, it reverberated in Oliver's ears, infuriating him so much that, even though his hands and arms were becoming numb, he managed to grab at the madmen's shoulder and sink his fingers into his flesh.

Yet, that did nothing but make the man laugh, leaving Oliver helpless in his grip. He was no small man by any stretch of the imagination, and he could certainly hold his own, but whoever this was, he was insanely strong.

Though, note to self: not as strong as Nina and Marty, because here came the Calvary—and that's when everything went sideways.

He was still conscious enough to see Nina, her dark hair like a silky cape around her head, flying behind her, as she launched herself at the man who held him captive while Marty, in her silky nightgown, virtually plucked Vinnie from harm's way in one simultaneous act of harmonious rescue.

Oliver dropped to the ground, gasping and choking for air as Vinnie and Marty rushed to him. His throat ached and his heart pounded in his chest as he watched Nina drag whomever she had in her clutches into the garage as though she were dragging an empty plastic bag.

Marty threw her hand out and yanked him upward. "Come on, Oliver. Let's get you inside. It's freezing. Can you walk?"

He coughed and sputtered, but managed a nod. Then he looked to Vinnie, her hair flying around her face in the gusts of icy wind, her eyes wide with fear as she tucked her hands into her checked flannel pajama bottoms and shivered.

Oliver extended a hand to her, and she took it, her fingers like ice. "Are you okay, Vinnie?"

Her eyes, the terror slowly turning to concern, looked into his. "Don't worry about me; are *you* okay? He really had a hold of you. I couldn't get him to stop."

"C'mon, you two, let's get you inside," Marty directed, attempting to usher them into the house, but Oliver wanted a piece of whoever this was.

He shook his head and stalked toward the garage, but Marty tapped his arm. "Oliver, not a good idea. Let us handle whoever that is."

"With all due respect, Marty," he seethed, fighting to keep his temper in check, "whoever the hell that is, he had me in a death grip. Swear, I thought it was over. I want to know who the hell that is and have him prosecuted to the fullest extent!"

He didn't bother to listen to her rebuttal. Instead, he let go of Vinnie's hand and stomped toward the garage with the two women in tow. He didn't care how cold he was, he didn't care how ridiculous he probably looked. He wanted blood.

Not only had the man almost killed Oliver, he'd tried to hurt Vinnie.

That enraged him. It might be irrational, but she was nothing more than the size of a curvy minute, and with the kind of strength this shit had, he could have done some serious damage to someone who was half his size.

"Oliver!" Marty shouted, but he kept right on ignoring her, his feet clapping against the garage floor.

When he entered the garage, his eyes flew to the man Nina had in her grip. "Who the fuck are you?" he roared as he reached around Nina and tried to grab for the guy.

But Nina stopped him by grabbing his shoulders and literally setting him behind her before turning around, her eyes slits of coal in her face.

"Oliver! Calm your fucking shit, man. Let me handle this," she hissed, and then she grabbed the guy by his shirt.

The man, pale and shaking, his dark hair cropped short, looked no older than fifteen. He certainly wasn't a very big guy, but the way Oliver's throat felt after that iron grip, he could attest he had the strength of ten men.

"Shut the goddamn garage door, Marty, and come

meet Ezekiel. A risk-taking motherfucker who likes to get his ass kicked by a chick. Isn't that right, Ezekiel?" Nina cooed, leaning down to leer in his face as he cringed and shrank in her grip.

"What?" Oliver said, stunned at how small he truly was. "I don't understand."

Nina gave the guy a violent shake and dropped him on top of an old cooler Oliver used to take fishing. She pointed down at him. "Sit. Stay. Move, I rip off your balls, grind them up, make pâté and have them for lunch on some crackers. You got that?"

"*Who* is he?" Vinnie asked, her voice trembling as she shivered.

Marty looked down at him, his lanky legs splayed out before him, and shook her head. "He's just an overgrown kid, Nina."

"Nah. He's no kid. He might look like one, the crusty motherfucker, but he's older than me, aren't you, *Ezekiel*?"

"I'll kill you!" he hissed, flashing his fangs the same way Nina had yesterday to prove she was a vampire.

Nina leaned way into him, her voice husky and filled with dark menace. "The fuck you say, Dink?" She jabbed a lean finger in his face. "You'll do what now? Kill *me*? *Me*? How're you gonna do that when you're dead? Because trust and believe, I will light your ass on fire with a rope of garlic around your neck so fucking thick, it'll make your eyeballs pop right the fuck out of your wee head, and not a single soul in the clan will protest your fucking death. Now, *talk*, or I get the gasoline and a match. What the fuck are you doing here and how did you find out about this?"

Oliver's eyes flew wide open in surprise. He even made an effort to stop Nina from hurting the kid, but Marty intervened.

"No," she said sternly. "This is vampire business, Oliver. He's gone against the strict code all vampires have. No violence against humans. He has to be punished."

Suddenly, all the wind in Oliver's sails evaporated, and as Vinnie threw the blanket he used when he went camping around his shoulders, he gulped when he looked to Marty. "Vampire business?"

"Vampire business," she said firmly with a nod. "They have laws and rules the same as everyone else, Oliver, and he can be punished the same as any other lawbreaker."

"But..." He didn't know what to say. Ezekiel looked like a kid in high school.

But Vinnie sidled up to him and grabbed his hand. "Don't let his youthful appearance fool you, Oliver. Nina's well into her forties now, but she looks like she's twenty, right? Same with Marty. She doesn't look a day over thirty, but she's actually—"

"Thirty?" Marty squawked with feigned horror, planting her hands on her hips and glaring at Vinnie. "Why does Nina look twenty and I look thirty? I'm younger than she is by like a year, I think." Then she shook her head and wrinkled her nose. "I don't know. I

stopped counting years a long time ago, after I was turned."

Vinnie gave her a sheepish glance and an apology. "Sorry. You both look great is the point. They don't age the way humans do. Since they were turned, they stopped aging. They'll never look any older than they do right now. Which means, this guy could be a hundred, for all we know."

Oliver blinked down at her and frowned. He had so much to learn. "Will that happen to me, too?"

But Vinnie didn't have time to answer, because Nina tipped Ezekiel over backward and put her foot on his throat. "Where the fuck did you find out about Oliver, fucknuts? Say it, or I'm going to wipe your ass all up and down this garage floor."

"*Fuuuck you!*" he screamed at her, his pale face contorted with rage.

Ooooh. This guy really was crazy. He might be a vampire, too, but Oliver got the feeling that between them, Nina was the badder ass and she meant what she said—which made him wonder.

Should he hide the garlic, because he was pretty sure he had some in the fridge. That would make him an accessory to murder. He wanted to know what was going on as much as the next guy, but he didn't want to kill anyone over it.

Nina ground the heel of her work boot into the flesh of Ezekiel's neck without thinking twice. "Marty? Call Greg. Call your man, too, before I eat this fuckwad's face off and he has to live eternally with a goddamn chewed-off face!"

Almost as if Nina had asked Marty to call Satan, his face changed and he held up a hand. "Wait! Greg? Like, Greg Statleon? You're gonna fucking call Greg *Statleon?*"

Nina gave him a coy pout, but she didn't seem at all concerned he knew who Greg was. "Whassamatter, Ezekiel. You afraid? Tell me what you fucking know and where you found out about it and maybe I won't call him."

He glared at her with hatred so real, Oliver felt it. "How the fuck do you know Greg Statleon?"

"He's my life mate, you little asshole."

Ezekiel's face fell, but unfortunately, he decided to double down. "Call him—and fuck you!"

Nina flicked her fingers at his head and spat, "Then hold on to your skateboard, wank. He'll be here in five. If I were you, I'd start praying now."

Marty gabbed both Vinnie and Oliver by the arms and said, "We'd better get inside. You don't want to see this."

But Oliver wouldn't budge as he gave another glance over his shoulder at Ezekiel. "She's not going to… I mean, listen, yes, he almost killed me, and probably would have hurt Vinnie pretty bad, too. But I don't want to see him die, Marty," he hissed.

Marty gripped his arm with fingers that sank into his flesh, her eyes, once so warm, now hard chips of blue. "And I'm going to say this one more time, Oliver.

You will come inside the house and let the vampires deal with the vampire. They don't make a choice like that rashly, but I can't promise this will err on the side of Ezekiel, either. We don't know anything about him or his past behavior. We *do* know he was willing to kill you—probably for that horn. All of this is in an effort to keep you safe. Now, I won't say it again, but I'm not opposed to using force if I have to. *Go inside. Now.*"

Vinnie took his hand and gripped it, pulling him toward the door leading to the kitchen, and this time, upon hearing Marty's tone, he didn't protest.

As they stepped inside, Oliver heard Ezekiel's hoarse cry, "You can't do anything to me, you stupid bitch! He's not even fucking human!"

And that statement sent a swish of chills down his spine.

~

*A*rch and Darnell looked at him from across the table as they sipped their coffee with sleepy, sympathetic eyes. The garage had suddenly become very quiet, and it was all Oliver could do not to go see what was happening.

Greg, and Marty's husband, Keegan, had arrived two minutes after Nina had threatened they would, and then everything had gone hushed.

A little too hushed for his comfort. Surely if garlic and fire were involved it would be noisier…

Arch had stirred when he heard the commotion,

and Darnell had awakened to keep watch in case anyone else showed up tonight, wanting a piece of Oliver. Carl had been in tow, book in his duct-taped hand and Baloney in his pajama-top pocket.

When he could no longer stand the waiting, Oliver pushed his chair back from the table, but he found a gentle pale green hand on his shoulder. "No…stay. Please, Ol—Ol—"

"Ol-iv-er," Darnell interjected with a broad smile at Carl. "Say it with me, buddy. Ready?"

Carl nodded with a smile, opening his mouth to mimic Darnell and, in unison with the demon, he said, "Ol-iv-er."

Darnell held up a beefy hand and bounced his head in approval. "Niiiice! Up top, brother."

Carl leaned over and gave the demon a high-five before sitting down next to Oliver and patting his arm with his duct-taped hand. "It is…okay. Prom…promise."

Oliver couldn't help but smile at this sweet boy who was so fiercely devoted to these people. He genuinely liked Carl, and how kind he was to everyone. He was nothing like one would expect. Nothing at all.

Oliver patted his hand with a gentle thump. "It's okay, Carl. I promise not to cause trouble."

"The boy is correct, Master Oliver," Arch said, sipping his tea. "They are nothing if not fair, but this man came to harm you. They wouldn't be doing their jobs if they didn't handle this accordingly. Please don't fret, sir. All will be well."

Everyone was sitting around as though they weren't contemplating setting a guy on fire right out in his garage. "But…"

Darnell rested his round, cheerful face in his hands. "Look, Oliver. You're a good guy. Old Darnell can tell ya mean well, but this ain't like the world you live in no more. Bad stuff happens here, too. Stuff you can't even in your wildest dreams. Way worse than in the human world. If you don't want someone hackin' that thing off yer head, they have to protect you. That horn ain't gettin' any smaller. You gotta be looked after."

Oliver's hand went instantly to his forehead to find the circumference of his alicorn did, indeed, feel bigger.

Shit.

Darnell grinned at him. "Get used to this kinda crazy, because you in now. There's mostly no gettin' out. Not that I've seen anyways. But right here, right now? These are all good people. I promise you. So let it ride, okay?"

Oliver took a sip of his tea, but he was having trouble letting it ride. Still, he took Darnell's advice and stayed in his seat until he heard Wanda's voice come from the garage.

"Arch?" she asked, trailing into the kitchen, her face flushed, her hand on her hip as she hobbled to the chair. "Would you be a love and pour me some tea? I don't think I can stand up one more second. This child is truly sucking every last ounce of energy I have left like a straw in a cup of milk."

Oliver hopped up instantly and pulled the chair out for her, almost afraid to ask what was going on in his garage. But he was unable to help himself because every time he saw that kid's face, he felt riddled with guilt.

Clearing his throat, Oliver asked, "What's happening out there, Wanda?"

Wanda sighed, and then she yawned as Arch set a steaming cup of tea in front of her, clearly very unconcerned about Ezekiel's well-being.

"He's not giving up the name of whoever told him about you. So it's about to be very uncomfortable for him."

Oliver clenched his fists to keep from saying anything, but in reality, he reminded himself he was virtually helpless anyway. He couldn't stop them from doing whatever their culture required. They not only outnumbered him, but even Nina was stronger than he'd ever be.

Wanda leaned over and rubbed her shoulder against his. "I see those wheels turning, Oliver. They're not out there murdering him. At least I don't think so. Do you smell burning garlic?"

His mouth fell open until Wanda burst out laughing. "I'm kidding, Oliver! Listen, Nina's all threats and such, but she'd never really murder anyone unless her or one of us was in imminent danger. We'd all do that for each other, and I won't lie—we have. But it was never without reason. As in, our lives or a client's life was on the line. Stop behaving as though we're a bunch of mindless heathens. Nina was just threatening him. She was doing what she does best. Behave horridly. You'll get used to it."

His shoulders sagged and remorse hit him directly between the eyes. He was being rude with his assumptions. He had no right to judge a world he knew nothing about.

"I'm sorry, Wanda. I didn't mean to make it seem as though you all haven't gone to bat for me...it's just..."

Wanda looked him directly in the eye. "It's just that he looks twelve. Look, we were human once, too, Oliver. I get it. Some of the things in the vampire culture, or even things in a pack of werewolves, will upset you. No need to apologize. But we can't have paranormals running around doing unsavory things to humans. Not only do we risk being caught by humans, but there has to be a strict code of ethics just by virtue of the powers we have."

Oliver blew out a long held breath.

Wanda gave him a sympathetic look. "Ezekiel will be punished, no doubt, just like any other human would be punished for assaulting someone. But I highly doubt they'd kill him for what he did. However, none of that changes the fact that he's not telling us who told him about you. That's beyond dangerous for *all* of us. Vinnie included. You're going to have to trust that we know what we're doing, okay? Don't feel sorry for a guy who's two hundred years old and doesn't know enough not to threaten a human."

His eyes went wide. "Two hundred? Is that a joke?"

"Not a fucking joke, dude," Nina said, entering the kitchen. "He's old enough to fucking know better, that's for sure."

"Any progress, Mistress Nina?" Arch asked, fighting a yawn.

"Nope. Greg and Keegan are hauling that shitbird back to the elders of the clan. Let *them* deal with his ass."

A thought occurred to Oliver then. "Hey, why don't you do to him what you did to Mikey? Just erase his memory."

"Because he's a damn vampire, Columbo, and he knows how to block that shit. Otherwise, we'd be a bunch of fucking vampires wandering around not knowing we were GD vampires."

"Oh, right," he muttered, feeling dejected and stupider by the second.

Nina looked down at him, her eyes intense and hard. "Listen, Peace Lover. I get you have reservations and you want to fucking make nice because he looks like he's just a kid. But I got news for you. That little fucker is a piece of shit. The crap he's done to humans alone just because he can would be enough to make your big-ass horn curl. He's no saint, trust and believe. He uses his powers for gain—financial, political, societal. That ain't cool. He's a grifter who doesn't know the first damn thing about working for anything. So unless you want him hacking off your horn and selling it to the highest bidder, get your shit together, Sparkle Tits. I'm not gonna let you look at me like I just took a steaming dump in your mother's living room because I stopped him from choking you out. Feel that?"

"Let him be, Nina," Wanda chastised, and she wiggled her toes. "It takes a long time to remember all the ins and outs of the paranormal. Or are you forgetting the time you picked up Marty's clothes while she was on a full-moon run?"

Nina rolled her eyes and scoffed. "Fuck you. They were on the ground. I was just trying to keep them from fucking getting trampled with all those ass-sniffers running around, howling."

"Uh-huh. But the point is, it took a while to remember Marty's needs her clothes after the shift. It's the same for Oliver. It'll take a while to remember he's only half-human. Cut him some slack and ease off. And while you're at it, grab me that ice pack from the freezer, would you? My feet feel like ten-pound sausages."

"Yeah? That's not what they look like. They look like fucking Sequoia stumps," Nina teased with a snort.

He felt like a complete and total shit right now. "I didn't mean to question your methods. I'm sorry, Wanda."

Nina handed Wanda the ice pack for her feet and grunted, but Wanda reassured him. "Not a worry in the world, Oliver. I know this takes a certain amount of faith, but I swear, we really can be trusted to do what's right within the confines of our packs and clans."

Nina clucked her tongue and shook her head. "All well and fucking good, except that little fuckhead isn't talking. We don't know how the hell he found out about Oliver and who else he told, and he's not giving it up. We can't keep his ass here with us forever, so that means eventually that twat goes to council, which fucking means—"

"The council will find out about Oliver, too," Wanda finished with a frown. "Damn it!"

Oliver looked at both the women and swallowed hard at their tone. "Meaning?"

Nina gave him a pointed glance, her face hard. "Too many fucking people will know you exist, and we won't be able to contain this shit. When the council finds out you have these abilities—and believe me, they GD will—they'll want to investigate. Which means isolating your ass somewhere until they 'understand' your predicament. You get me? You'll be under what they call a 'soft lockup.' Sure, they'll give you nice meals and some magazines because this was an accident. Maybe you'll even get a TV. But make no fucking mistake, Unicorn Man, you're gonna have more tests done on your person than a hundred flippin' senior high students take in a year—because there's no one else like you. *No one.*"

Ahhh. Therein lie the hitch in this whole giddyup.

Shit.

CHAPTER 13

"Hey, Vinnie?" Marty whispered softly, sitting down beside her on the comfy sofa, her floaty ice-blue negligee and matching bathrobe swishing softly around her. "You okay? You've been very quiet since we caught Ezekiel. He was pretty scary, I'm sure."

Vinnie folded her hands in her lap and nodded. He'd definitely been scary. "I'm fine. Really. I guess…I mean, I guess the experience made me realize how little help I can be. For example, you and Nina? Zoinks. You two are a force, add in Wanda, and I'm sure there isn't much you can't handle. But all I was capable of doing was latching onto that bastard's hair and yanking, for all the good it did me."

Marty tsk-tsked her words. "Did you see yourself jump on that jerk's back? Who says you're no help? You distracted him for us. Not to mention, you held on to his hair for a pretty good amount of time. That was smart because it was just what we needed to get to Oliver. Also, you're no dummy, little lady. Even what little information we have came from you."

She shrugged her shoulders. She wasn't normally prone to pity parties, but she was feeling a little raw. "It mostly came from Khristos, but I'm doing my best to get more."

Marty patted her thigh and smiled. "Exactly. Listen, I know it sucks to be stuck here with nowhere to go, but it won't be forever. Soon you'll be able to go back home to your normal routine and your beloved pets. I know how hard it can be to be away from my daughter and my poodle, Muffin. Oh, and my DH, too." Then she laughed, a tinkling sound Vinnie liked.

Maybe that was part of the problem. Being with these people, people the paranormal world considered half-breeds, made her feel like she finally fit in. Maybe she didn't want it to end. It had only been a couple of days, but she felt a bond with them she'd never felt with a group of people before. Not in school. Not in college. Not until now.

Naturally, that didn't mean she didn't want to find out how to get Oliver's life back, but she was really, for the first time in a good portion of her life, enjoying the camaraderie of female friendship she'd lacked because she was too afraid to reach out to those who considered her less than.

It was her own fault, of course. Rather than give people a chance, even people outside the paranormal realm, she simply didn't risk it for fear of rejection.

But Marty intuitively sensed that, and when she looked into Vinnie's eyes, she smiled gently. "Is that part of the problem? You don't have to tell me if you'd rather not. But I don't think I'm wrong when I say your mother embarrassed you, and she embarrassed you quite often by inserting herself where she wasn't wanted, yes?"

Her heart clenched tight. "Yeah. You're right. It was always so awkward because we really didn't fit in. Not even a little. She foisted herself on people with the premise she deserved to be there because she's technically a Goddess and by birth, so am I. I knew it hurt her when she was rejected or left out. Yet, she never stopped trying. But the real problem was, she never stopped shoving *me* in their faces, too. She never listened to what I wanted, which wasn't to be forced into a situation where I didn't just *feel* inferior. I *was* in inferior, and that's not a plea for pity. That's the truth. I'm immortal and that's it. I have no real power."

Wow, she'd never said the bit about her mother to anyone out loud ever. Not anyone other than her mother.

"You know how I see this, Vinnie? Your mother has chutzpah out the wazoo. She's the epitome of try-try-again. My mom was a single mother, too, in a day and age when it was frowned upon, but she worked her butt off to give me everything. And yes. Sometimes it embarrassed the hell out of me. But now, as a mother myself, I think it wasn't just selfish motives that drove our mothers. They wanted us to belong in the same way I want my daughter Hollis to belong. I want her to belong to her father's pack, of course. I'd fight as hard as our mothers did for her inclusion in the pack even though she's technically a watered-down werewolf.

"But I also want her to understand she can make a place for herself the same way we did, and she's not less than because she's not pure werewolf, and neither are you. Because we fought to be a part of this, Hollis will always have a crabby Auntie Nina and an ultra-sophisticated, etiquette-minded Auntie Wanda. So the gist of all that is, I want her to belong to *something*—belong to a family so that if anything ever happens to me, she'll always have them. I think that's what our mothers wanted, too."

What an unusual perspective, but it rang crystal true with Vinnie. "That makes so much sense, it hurts my head."

Marty giggled softly, dragging a throw pillow to her lap. "Sometimes, it just takes a little perspective from the outside looking in. Listen, when this began for me, when I was accidentally turned, that is, my mother had passed and it was just my poodle, Muffin and I. I didn't really have anyone, and then I had *everyone* and their brother, and I mean that literally. And everyone and their brother didn't like me much because I was only half-were. It took some getting used to them and them to me, but as the years passed, in the midst of fighting for our own places in our respective packs and clans, we misfits formed an unbreakable bond—one I know I can count on until the bitter end—if there ever is one, that is. I mean, I was in a coma after suffering a heart attack, and Nina and Wanda refused to accept I wouldn't wake up. So what did my ride-or-dies do? They hired a doctor, set up a hospital room in my damn bedroom, and never left my side until I woke up."

Vinnie nodded. Marty's coma had filtered down to even her—someone who didn't attend many paranormal functions. "You were all the talk in paranormal circles when that happened."

She snorted. "I bet I was. The point is, there's no one I trust more than my husband, Nina, Wanda, Darnell, Arch and Carl. All of us, save for my husband, misfits."

"I guess it's hard to see you guys as misfits—with your capabilities and all."

"Well, if you ask some people in these parts, they'd tell you different. But ask me if I care. Part of this experience is bonding, Vinnie. We bond quickly because in times of crisis, or a traumatic incident—which an accidental turning certainly is—that's what happens. You cling to the people who get it. That's why we make ourselves available twenty-four-seven. We don't just understand what you're going through, we know how alone it feels to be labeled. Our goal—OOPS's goal—isn't just to help people find their way in the paranormal world. Our goal is inclusion. For all, because there's always room for more, and the door's always open. *Always.* All you have to do is walk right in."

Vinnie gulped as she fought tears. She wanted to believe that she could be a part of that. She only had to let herself. *"Thank you, Marty,"* she whispered, unsure how to process this new feeling.

"You bet." Marty gave her a squeeze with an arm around her shoulder. "Now, anything else you want to talk about?"

"Like?"

"Like the way you look at Oliver."

"Didn't you just say in times of crisis, people bond quickly?"

Marty grinned. "I did."

"Maybe I should wait and see if what I'm feel… experiencing…is all just part of the traumatic circumstances and nothing of substance?"

Marty batted long, flirty lashes at her when she winked. "You certainly should, but it won't change how he looks without a shirt, and I don't mind saying, he looks very nice. Very nice indeed."

Vinnie giggled. "Okay, crisis or not, that's a true statement." Man, was it ever true. Oliver wasn't hard on the eye, and her eyes liked him—all of him.

"Listen, I get feeling hesitant about what's going on with your insides in regard to our sexy unicorn. You don't want to upset his applecart further in an already explosive atmosphere by letting on that you find him attractive. Oliver's got a lot on his plate and you don't want to add to it. You're also worried about how quickly you found yourself attracted to him, and you're wondering if the circumstances are a part of that."

She hadn't been in such close proximity to a man, other than her students and fellow faculty, that she was interested in for a long time, and she was wondering if that was a part of it, too. "I don't know what I'm wondering, but I think when I parse this out in my head, that'll likely be on the list."

"Listen, chemistry is chemistry whether you're traumatized or not, and that's just the truth. You guys have it in spades. You can't fake that, crisis or not. And if you're doubting," she said with a grin, "I'm pretty sure he likes you, too, judging by the way his eyes smile when he sees you. All I'm saying is, don't rule it out because you're in the height of a crisis. Instead of overthinking it, breathe through it. Don't add to your plate either, and if you find yourself overwhelmed by how you're feeling, just tell us you need a time out or an ear or whatever. Will you do that?"

Vinnie nodded. "I can. I will, but..."

"But?"

She'd never talked openly to anyone about her virginity, and it had been a long time since she'd had to explain to a man. How did you broach that—even though it was already out in the open?

"My virginity..."

Marty shrugged her shoulders. "What about it?"

"Well, I guess I would have preferred I be the one to share that with someone I was interested in, but now that it's out in the open... I mean, I'm twenty-eight, for heaven's sake. I feel—"

Marty flapped her hands in the air dismissively. "So? There's no age limit to choosing the right time and place to become intimate, honey. You're *you*. You made decisions that were right for you and *only* you. So just keep being you, Vinnie. When you decide you want to change something about that part of your life, you go at your own pace and find the person who's willing to do the same. It's not something to be embarrassed about. And look at it this way—Mama Bear took any embarrassment you might have experienced out of that conversation if you ever chose to have it with Oliver, right? It's over and done with."

Vinnie giggled with a wince. "That did happen."

Marty patted her knee and slid to the edge of the couch and rose. "It sure did, kiddo. Now, I'm going to see what the next plan of action is since that Ezekiel's made a bloody mess of everything. You sure you're okay?"

She smiled up at Marty in all her gorgeous blonde hair and swishy nightwear. "I am. I really am."

She felt somehow lighter. Her anxiety less than it had been a day or so ago.

Oliver entered the room then, his broad chest covered with a ratty T-shirt, which in Vinnie's personal opinion was a shame because he had a pretty great chest. One she'd like to test drive by way of resting her head on it as she slept.

Her cheeks turned red at her suddenly lusty thoughts, getting redder still when he looked down at her and smiled. He might look ridiculous with a big, glittery horn sticking out of his head, but she didn't have any trouble seeing past it. None at all, and that made her stomach feel a little wobbly.

Now, when the man was in severe crisis, wasn't the time to lust after him. That was definitely something she was sure of.

"Mind if I sit?" he asked with his handsome smile.

She started to scoot over, but he plopped down next to her, leaving their arms touching. In response, a shiver whizzed along her flesh and instantly she felt self-conscious. But Oliver didn't seem to notice, or if he did, he didn't care.

"Hey," he said softy, his husky voice resonating in her ear. "Thanks for what you did out there."

She flapped a hand upward. "It was nothing. I mean, it was *really* nothing. I didn't help at all."

"You stalled him long enough for Nina and Marty to step in. That's all it took."

She craned her neck to look at the marks on his neck and grimaced with a hiss. "How's your neck feel? It looks like it hurts."

Oliver literally had handprints on his neck, red, purple and distorted, Ezekiel's grip had been so tight.

He ran a big palm over the affected area. "Nah. It's okay, but man do I have a headache. He squeezed my neck so hard, I thought my eyes were going to pop out of my head."

For someone like Vinnie, who worked hard to keep her life uncluttered and calm, Ezekiel had been an eye-opener. "I don't think I've ever been so scared in my life."

Oliver smiled at her with a nod that had glitter falling from his alicorn. "Me either. I really thought it was curtains." And then he looked down at her hand and saw the bruise around her wrist.

He reached for it with a frown. "Hey, did he do this? Are you okay? You want some ice. I'm sure Wanda'd give up her ice pack for a little while."

She let him hold her wrist in his big hand and it felt good. Comfortable. Exciting. "I'm fine. It's just the bruise from where he grabbed me to try and make me stop pulling his hair, which he didn't have a lot to pull, by the way. But I showed him, didn't I?" Vinnie said on an ironic chuckle.

"Don't knock it, Vinnie. You were pretty fierce up against a guy with superhuman strength." He paused for a moment, before he asked, "What were you doing out there anyway?"

"Strange place. I always have trouble sleeping in new, strange places. I got up to get a glass of water and I saw him grab you from the living room window. I didn't think. I just reacted."

She didn't mention that his gallant gesture to give them his comfortable bedroom had also resulted in her senses being overwhelmed by the smell of him on his sheets, on his pillow, everywhere.

"So I guess you heard the ladies?"

Vinnie nodded her head, tucking a stray curl behind her ear. "If you mean about what to do with Ezekiel, I did. They're going to have to bring him to the council and when they do, this is all going to explode."

"What the heck is the *council*? I didn't want to ask the ladies because I've already jammed my foot so far in my mouth, it became uncomfortable to speak. But I don't fully understand."

"Each paranormal group has their own set of leaders. Think of these groups as separate countries, like Switzerland and England and so on. Each country has their own rules and laws governed by a body of heads of state, right? Be they prime ministers or presidents, whatever. So each faction of paranormals, like vampires, werewolves, shapeshifters, have their own people in charge. The clan, which is what Nina belongs to, by virtue of being a vampire, has a council of elders and leaders Ezekiel will have to face for punishment because he attacked you. What he did was an egregious error on his part, and he has to pay. I guess they'll have a trial or whatever vampires do. I'm a little sketchy on the details."

Oliver rubbed his free hand over the stubble on his chin. "I can't get over how young he looks. He looks like he should have a backpack and a skateboard under his arm."

"I hear your protest and feel your pain. I know it's upsetting, but he *attacked* you, Oliver. He could have killed you as easily as you stomp out a bug. I mean, who knows what he planned to do with you. Please remember that. He's dangerous."

"You're right. He's kind of a super-criminal, I suppose."

"Exactly. Now, we have bigger fish to fry. Like who else he's told about you, and who told *him* about you in the first place. Marty said they're going to double up on security here to make sure you're safe until the council speaks with him. She said maybe they can get him to fess up with the fear of imprisonment."

Oliver cocked his head and gave her a strange look. "What does vampire prison look like? Is it garlic and sunlight all day long?"

Vinnie snorted. "I don't know a lot about vampire prison, but I feel pretty sure it's not quite so brutal, or there'd be no vampire prison because all the bad vampires would be dead from exposure to garlic and sunlight."

Oliver nodded his head in affirmation with a laugh, and Vinnie noticed something.

In the midst of their chat, somehow, their fingers had entwined, and as they sat and talked, they held hands as though they'd always held hands.

And she liked it. She didn't feel pressured to talk or pressured to fill in the gaps—or pressured period, and she wasn't sure if that was because of the situation or that Oliver just left her feeling at ease.

His husky voice interrupted her thoughts. "I feel like I've really blown your fall vacation now that you have to stay here with our babysitters. I'm sorry you were ever involved in this, Vinnie."

"I'm not," she said, letting out a breath because it felt good to say it out loud. She even straightened her shoulders and tried to appear confident. "I was just telling Marty it feels good to belong somewhere with people who were branded misfits like me. I'm glad I met them even though I'm sorry the circumstances surrounding our meeting suck for you, but I'm also glad I met you, too, Oliver."

Oliver sat quietly for a moment, smelling good, looking good, shedding glitter all over his couch, but then he turned to look at her, his eyes gleaming and playful. "Hey, question?"

Vinnie looked down at her lap and licked her dry lips, her heart crashing against her ribs. "Sure."

"When this is over, or settled, or whatever happens, I was wondering if you'd like to maybe grab some coffee—or a drink? Even dinner, if you think you can stand all the stares and whispers about my sparkly horn for more than an hour."

Her heart clenched in her chest and her pulse raced in her veins, but she somehow managed to remain cool. A man she both liked *and* felt comfortable with was asking her out on a date. That felt nice. It also felt nice that he'd likely been having the same thoughts she had.

Which made it very easy for her to reply with a smile. "Yeah. I'd like that, Oliver. I know a great place for coffee right by the college."

"As long as there are no unicorn Frapps on the menu, I'm all in."

She giggled until she wheezed and Oliver laughed with her.

And when they were done, she smiled at him again.

And he smiled back.

CHAPTER 14

"You could have waited back at your house, Sparkle Tits," Nina chided.

He nodded with a glance at her face, which glowed eerily pale in the dark. "I could have, vampire, but what fun would that be? Then you wouldn't have a reason to use sparkle tits in a sentence, and we can't have that, can we?"

Nina cackled but she flipped him a middle finger while she did as they walked along the brick path to Vinnie's house. "Fuck you, Unicorn Man. You just want to see your girlfriend's house."

That was not a lie. After sitting on the couch these last few nights with Vinnie, he was more curious than ever about who she really was—how she lived—and he especially wanted to meet her dogs and her cat. They'd been with a pet sitter for all this time, but Oliver could tell how anxious she was without them, and he wanted her to be comfortable.

But more than anything, he wanted to know what this beautiful woman did day to day other than teach mythology and, as he'd later learned, philosophy. Alice was overbearing and pushy, and a lifetime of that certainly had to wear a person down, so he understood why she shied away from people, but you could only read so much, right?

Also, he was beginning to go a little stir-crazy being cooped up in the house and hidden away like someone's dirty little secret. They were on day five of this mess, and they hadn't heard anything more from this council the girls spoke of since Ezekiel was taken, but they'd also heard nothing from their friend Khristos, either.

There was nothing to do but wait.

So he was in limbo, and so was everyone else. They'd played cards, board games, watched a few movies, eaten some of the best meals he'd had in his entire life, but it didn't replace fresh air and new surroundings.

So he'd asked to come along for the ride when Vinnie mentioned she really needed to check on her pets. Nina, Marty and Darnell hadn't loved the idea, but according to Wanda, she was no help currently, and neither were Arch or Carl.

If someone was going to come for him, they could just as easily do it at Vinnie's house as they could at his —he'd still have the same amount of protection wherever he went.

So under the cover of night, after an amazing

dinner of bacon-wrapped scallops, Parmesan risotto, creamed spinach, and balsamic Brussels sprouts, they piled into Marty's SUV and drove to Vinnie's, which, ironically, was only five minutes from his house.

They'd even laughed about how close they lived to one another, yet they'd never run into each other anywhere before this week.

Also, he noted, her neighborhood was a lot like his. A mix of old and new with tree-lined streets, mostly manicured lawns and gardens, and a park one block from her house.

As Vinnie stuck the key in the door of her small one-level ranch, Oliver heard the rustle of tiny, frantic dog feet before she threw the door open wide and motioned everyone to go ahead of her.

From the darkness, Frank, Mario, and even Brenda emerged, all aimed directly at Vinnie, tails wagging, mouths open, barking and meowing in simultaneous joy.

She dropped to the floor to hug them and lavish them with kisses while Marty turned on a light in the living room.

It was then Oliver understood how she spent her spare time. In fact, he had to fight a gasp of awe.

Painting.

She painted. Holy cow, did she ever paint. And she didn't just *paint*, she immersed the viewer in her creations by creating such vivid images, they literally leapt off the canvas and grabbed you by the throat.

Powerful, raw, surreally beautiful pictures of all

sorts of things were everywhere. And they weren't just your typical sunsets and shoreline paintings. They were pictures of powerful superheroes; none Oliver recognized, but ones he'd be inclined to pick up a comic book to read about because they were so viscerally primal.

Darnell was the first to speak when he pointed at the unfinished picture on an easel of a woman with skin the color of eggplant, a curvy body, yet rippling with muscle, and hair the color of fresh corn poking out of her head.

"Miss Vinnie, did you paint this?"

She rose from the floor, scooping up Brenda as she went, a calico cat with round green eyes who rubbed her face against Vinnie's when she nodded shyly. "Yep," she responded, her eyes flitting toward the floor

Darnell's mouth fell open, and he squeezed her shoulder with a big hand, pulling her to his side. "It's incredible. *You're* incredible! Y'all seein' what I'm seein'?" he asked in wonder.

"Jesus fuck, kiddo," Nina said as her eyes took in the pictures hanging on the walls. "Why are you a college professor again? These are fucking brilliant!"

In the few days he'd known Nina, he'd observed she didn't hand out compliments often, but to hear the wonder in her voice made the compliment even grander.

Marty stooped and grabbed one of the two dogs, a tan speckled runt of a dachshund mixed with something else, Oliver assumed, pulling him to her chest and dropping a kiss on top of his head as she began to rub his long ear. "Vinnie, these are *stunning*. Why aren't you selling these? Or sending them to places that publish comic books? Your artwork is amazing."

Vinnie tucked her other dog, a tiny little bugger of a mutt with wiry white and black hair and unknown origins, under her chin next to her cat and snuggled him close while she dismissed their praise.

She gave Darnell's hand a squeeze with her free fingers before she said, "It's just something I do in my spare time to blow off steam. I'm not much of a social creature, as you all already know. So it's sort of my release. I'd never presume to ask for money for them. That never even occurred to me."

Nina came and scooped the small dog right from Vinnie's arms, and the tiny mutt, like most other animals when it came to her, was instantly in love with the vampire. He tucked his head right against her chin and wiggled against her in excitement.

Nina held him up, using the childlike voice she reserved strictly for four-legged creatures and children. "Listen, Whatsername, you tell Mommy it's a waste of goddamn time not to sell her shit and Auntie Nina thinks she's bananapants. Will you do that for me? Of course you will, because hims a good boy," she cooed, kissing the dog's nose while he happily wagged his short, stubby tail.

"That's Mario, and even he'll tell you, I'm not in this to make money. It's just a way for me to relax and be creative."

Darnell retrieved Brenda the cat from Vinnie's arms and hugged her close, scratching the top of her multicolored head. "That's a big ol' waste a' talent, if you ask old Darnell. I read comics all the time, and your pictures are some of the best I've ever seen."

Vinnie's cheeks blushed prettily as she made her way across the light oak floor of her living room toward her kitchen and turned on the lights to expose a space full of blue and gray cabinets and sparkling white countertops, free of almost everything but a Keurig and lush green plants in various decorative clay pots.

"Thanks, Darnell. That's nice of you to say."

"I ain't just bein' nice. I'm bein' real," he said with a wide smile. "Flat-out honest when I tell ya, you got somethin' special."

Vinnie came back around the bank of cabinets facing her living room, a cozy space with fuzzy blankets on her ivory brocade couch and, of course, plenty of throw pillows to spare in mint green and pale blue.

Leaning into him, she gave Darnell a quick hug, wrapping an arm around his wide waist. "You do a girl's ego good. Now, does anyone want coffee or tea while you wait? I have both."

Marty and Nina swapped dogs like they were passing each other footballs and Nina took Frank, cradling him against her face. "That's avoidance, right, you cute little fucking fur ball? Mommy's avoiding the nice things Uncle Darnell's saying because it makes her uncomfortable. But the truth is the truth, right, handsome?"

Vinnie giggled. "I'm not avoiding, Auntie Nina. I just like eating more than I like suffering for my art. Now, coffee? The blood of my neighbor's annoying wife, maybe?"

Nina chuckled. "Ahh, Almost-Goddess, you're not as shy as you fucking pretend, eh? Therein lies a crabby beast. The cranky in me honors the cranky in you."

Vinnie giggled with a grin as she set her purse on the pristine counter. "What can I say, you bring out the snark in me, and it's not so much that she makes me cranky, but she's a little overbearing when it comes to the neighborhood association."

"Your home is so lovely, Vinnie. It's like a cozy, warm cottage," Marty remarked as she stroked Mario's fur and looked around. "You really have a great eye for decorating as well as art."

Nina pointed to one picture where the woman had on a ratty T-shirt and a pair of yoga pants. "I like that the women in them aren't half fucking naked, kiddo. Who the hell fights crime, or fights *anything*, in a damn bathing suit that has D-cups made of farkin' steel? I'm not much of a comic book reader, but that always bugged the shit out of me."

Oliver nodded his head, still blown away by her incredible talent. "You really are amazing, Vinnie. I especially like that picture." He pointed to a picture of a woman in military style black boots, tentacles for hair and a royal blue coat that looked like it came straight out of the *Matrix* movie. "The detail is magnificent. Would you consider selling it to me? It'd look great in my den."

"Sell it?" She cocked her head and gave him a strange look. "You can just take it, Oliver. I can always paint another. They're no big deal. Now, you guys make yourselves comfortable while I pack a bag for these monsters, and then I'll grab some fresh clothes and we can get back to Wanda and the others, okay?"

Oliver found himself a little disappointed that she so easily dismissed the idea someone would pay for her art. As he bent to scoop up Brenda, who'd curled her tail around his calf, meowing for attention, he decided not to press.

Clearly, praise embarrassed her, and that wasn't what he wanted. Still, he liked her more and more with each passing moment they spent together.

As she rummaged around in the kitchen, and the others talked to each other while they played with the dogs, he watched Vinnie in her element, and he liked what he saw.

She'd made this house her haven, that much was clear. Every inch of it screamed calm and organized, something he knew she craved after the chaos of Alice.

The shake of a box of treats from the kitchen had Brenda scrambling from his arms and dropping to the floor in a cloud of fur to go see what Vinnie had to offer, leaving him to make his way to her fireplace and look at the construction of the stonework.

Like everything else, it was really well done and he

found himself envious. "Hey, Vinnie? Did you DIY this or did you hire out?"

She poked her fiery red head over the bank of floor cabinets and rested her elbows on the counter and grinned. They'd spent a ton of time talking into the wee hours of the morning these last few days, and DIY was a topic of some of their most spirited discussions.

"Do you have fireplace envy, Oliver Baldwin?"

He ran his hands over the muted white stone and nodded with a smile. "I damn well do, and if you tell me you did this yourself, I'm gonna hang up my tool belt."

She rolled up the sleeves of her bulky periwinkle sweater and chuckled. "Then fear not. Your tool belt is safe from retirement. I hired someone to reface it. I'm ambitious, but I'm not that ambitious."

"Then I suppose I can let you live. For now, anyway," he teased with a wink.

They'd developed this easy banter between them, one he relished after Denise. He found he didn't have to watch what he said to Vinnie. Despite her admission of social anxiety, Oliver didn't at all feel like he had to temper his words when he was with her, or that she went out of her way to temper hers.

And while their banter was easy, his desire to lay one on her was not.

In fact, last night, after they'd watched a few episodes of one DIY show or another, they'd realized the house had gone quiet and everyone had gone off to bed or, in Nina's case, gone to read with Carl, leaving them totally alone with nothing but Baloney between them.

What he'd found was an irresistible urge to kiss her beautiful raspberry-colored lips, but he'd fought it. He really liked her. He thought about her all the time, but Oliver didn't want her to think this was a case of him bonding because of dire crisis. He also didn't want to rush her into anything she wasn't ready for.

So he'd refrained, but it hadn't been easy, and as he watched her in her element, he could easily picture them sharing a bottle of wine by her fireplace while they discussed anything and everything.

"Okay, I'm going to let these little beasts out and then we'll go. Are you sure you don't mind me bringing them to your house, Oliver? I don't want Baloney to feel usurped."

"And I don't want you to spend a fortune on your pet sitter if you won't let me pay for it. Besides, Baloney could do with some socialization, and she seems okay with Calamity."

"That's because Calamity knows I'd kick her little furry ass if she hurt another living thing," Nina crowed from the couch as she put Frank, who knew what the bag Vinnie was packing meant, on the floor.

Oliver watched him prance toward the kitchen, his tail in the air, clearly excited by the prospect of Vinnie in the pantry that held treats

Vinnie pulled a tote bag from her pantry and yelled, "I'm not letting you pay for my dog sitter, Oliver!"

"But it's my fault they have to be uprooted in the

first place," he yelled back with a chuckle. "If it weren't for me and my horn, you'd be here with them, safe and sound, painting and reading, toasty warm by the awesome fireplace you outsourced."

"Ah, but would my life be as exciting as that of a guy with a horn that can heal people? I think not, Baldwin. Also, I don't mind watching all that DIY with someone who can carry on an actual conversation and form opinions about shiplap."

"Shiplap's dumb, Morretti! I don't care what Joanna says."

"Aw, look, Mistress of the Dark, the kids are flirting," Marty teased with a snort as she elbowed Darnell.

"All right, Paranormal Rom-com.com," Nina said as she jumped up from the couch. "Quit with the cutesy banter bullshit and pack 'em up. No way we're leaving these little buggers here, now that I've seen 'em anyway, but I don't wanna be here all fucking night while you two play footsie. I have a Skype with Charlie and Greg tonight and a book to read to Carl. Get a move on, lovers."

Vinnie laughed the laugh he liked the best. The one where she let it all bubble up from her throat, carefree and with total abandon.

"Hold on to your fangs, vampire. I'm—"

Oliver's head reared upward at the sudden silence as he looked to the entryway of her pantry—but Vinnie wasn't there. "What the hell?"

Nina was in the kitchen in a flash with Marty right

behind her, pulling the pantry door open all the way. "Vinnie? Kiddo? What the fuck?" she yelped.

Darnell stomped through the living room and into the kitchen, sniffing the air as the dogs began to run in circles and the cat howled mournfully.

He moved his big body with quick grace as he surveyed Vinnie's kitchen. "Demon, Miss Nina," he murmured. "You smell him, too?"

"He? You can tell it's a male demon by his smell?" Oliver fought not to screech the question as panic began to rise in his gut.

Whoever this was. They'd virtually snatched Vinnie up out of thin air.

Out of thin air.

Nina drove her clenched fists inside the pocket of her hoodie. "Which fuck is it, Darnell? What am I dealing with here?"

Darnell's face went dark, but he looked her directly in the eye. "The one who likes scarin' folks when he shifts…"

Nina's face went hard, her teeth clenching. "Jesus and fuck. Do you mean that bastard who shifts into that pus-dripping, red-faced fucking loon?"

Darnell bounced his head, totally avoiding eye contact with Oliver.

Nina's mouth fell open but her nostrils flared and her eyes went hard. "Motherfucker, motherfucker, motherfucker!" she bellowed, clenching her fists. "Darnell? Can you smell where the fuck he went?"

Darnell ran his palm over his shortly cropped hair

and grimaced. "I can. But it ain't pretty, Nina. You know what it's like there."

There? What did that mean? His stomach rolled in fear and his heart raced. "Where the hell is *there*?" Oliver yelled in frustration.

All this paranormal lingo, this quiet understanding amongst them, was beginning to feel isolating. They instinctively knew what they meant, while he was still stuck back on being able to smell the difference between a male and female demon.

But no one was listening to him. Most especially Nina, who didn't even acknowledge his questions with so much as a blink of her eye. "I don't give a shit, Darnell. He's got a defenseless kid who has no paranormal power to speak of and he knows it. Take my ass to wherever this fucking demon is. I'll kill the sonofabitch!"

Oliver was across the room in two seconds flat, latching onto Nina's hand. "Take you to wherever the demon is? Am I hearing that right?"

"Yes, Oliver, and we have to move fast! God only knows what's happening," Marty said with measured words, but he heard the tone of her voice. There was fear in it.

"Then let's go!" he said, knowing his tone was panicked. But he didn't care. Jesus Christ, a demon had Vinnie.

A demon.

Jesus Christ!

Nina gripped his shoulders, her fingers digging into

the flesh right through his Bills sweatshirt, and looked up into his eyes. "You can't go, Sparkle Tits."

"Why?" he rasped, his tone urgent to his ears.

"Why do you think a demon, out of fucking nowhere, took *Vinnie*, of all people? Because they can smell that you like her, Ollie—that she's connected to you, but she's weaker than they are. They took her ass because what they really want is *you*. She's just bait."

His mind raced and his pulse fired up. "But how do they even know about her? How do they know I like her, Nina? This is insane!"

"Remember when I told you that fuck Ezekiel was a bad dude? He found out about you somehow, didn't he? I told you we couldn't let him go because we couldn't trust he wouldn't tell other people you frickin' exist. How do we know he didn't tell *them* long before he ever got to you, and that's why the demon took Vinnie?" She shook her head, her silky hair splaying over her shoulders. "For fuck's sake, dude. It doesn't matter. A fucking cocksucking demon has her. We'd be playing right into its hands if you came. Now listen, I know you like her, but this is no time to play GD hero. You hear me? Stay put. Darnell and I will go. You stay with Marty. Understand me?"

"You need to hurry! Go!" Marty yelled at them. "I'll stay with Oliver."

Darnell grabbed Nina's hand and raised his fingers in the air as though he were going to snap them together. Somehow, it dawned on him that Darnell was going to zap them somewhere by clicking his fingers.

By holding on to Nina's hand, she'd be transported, too.

So the moment Darnell rubbed his fingers together was the moment Oliver foolishly, stupidly, grabbed on to Nina's hoodie and held on for dear life.

Which turned out to be a good thing.

Because when you land in hell, you want something to cushion your fall.

CHAPTER 15

Vinnie swallowed hard as the man—a man who was quite handsome, if she did say so herself—breathed into her face in a place she neither understood, nor would her brain allow her to process.

Flames sputtered and spat all along the walls and ceiling of the room they occupied. Even though the floor felt hard beneath her backside, it looked as if it rolled and receded in its fluid, gooey red motion, with puffs of intermittent smoke.

"So now we wait, right, Vinnie?" the man who'd snatched her right from her kitchen hissed, the air coming from his lips hot and dry on her cheeks. "But you're a lovely way to pass the time, kitten. You're so pretty. Are your insides as pretty? I bet your liver would be delicious with some fava beans and a nice Chianti." Then he slithered his tongue in and out of his mouth like a snake

Had he just done an eerily accurate imitation of Hannibal Lecter?

A shiver of dread scurried up her spine and terror settled in her belly.

As her head tried to wrap around her surroundings—her hot, hellish, flamey surroundings—Vinnie attempted to make herself small and force words from her mouth.

"Wait? I don't understand. What are we waiting... Wait for...*for what?*"

He trailed a finger down the side of her face, his beautiful green eyes scanning hers in a slow perusal of her features—until he suddenly wrapped a curl of her hair around his finger and yanked, and he didn't let go, not even when tears came to her eyes.

"You know what I'm waiting for, *Vinnie*," he crooned, letting her hair go and pushing her away. Then he laughed, showing his brilliant white teeth.

She shook her head, fighting tears. Who was this and why was she here? "No! I don't know what you're waiting for."

He booped her nose with his finger and shook it at her in a wagging motion. "Dude, don't play. I'm waiting for your unicorn. I mean, duuuh," he said, à la Sean Penn in *Fast Times at Ridgemont high.*

And then she understood. She was here as bait for Oliver, and if Nina and the rest didn't know how to find her, she had no doubt she was going to die. If he'd been motivated enough to snatch her right from her kitchen in front of everyone, he meant business.

As flames cracked and popped, as the embers from the fiery walls danced and flew into the air, Vinnie still feigned surprise as if someone were paying her to act, even as her body trembled and her heart raced.

"My *what*? What are you talking about?" she squeaked, her flesh hot and clammy. "Why would I...I mean, *me* of all people, have a unicorn? I'm a nobody. And besides, isn't their existence just a made-up story?"

He giggled, his sculpted face splitting into a lopsided grin. "Is it? Then why do you have one, Vinnie?"

She blinked and tried once more to convince him she didn't know what he was talking about. "But I don't. I swear on my day planner, I don't."

"Your unicorn—your-or unicooorn!" he sang in a maliciously gleeful imitation of Wayne Newton's "Danke Schoen." "Vinnie has a unicorn!"

Yep, that was Wayne Newton. Her biological father had loved him, and the few times she could remember spending with him, he always played his albums.

Still, Vinnie shrank from the man, up against a wall, a hard, fiery-hot wall, but he only leaned in closer until he was almost on top of her, his lithe movements uncannily like that of a big cat.

He draped himself over her lap, putting his lean body tightly against hers, and stared at her like something out of a deranged nightmare.

As she got a really close look at him—because let's face it, he was but an inch from her face—she couldn't get over how beautiful he was. From his clear skin, thick raven eyebrows, sharply angled cheeks and jaw, to his deep marble-like green eyes, his face was a literal masterpiece. Simply breathtaking.

And nuts. Literally the definition of nuts. From his crazy voices to his wild facial expressions—he was certifiable.

In that moment, while she cowered in fear, while whoever this was took her power, she hated herself. Hated her fears, hated her anxieties. Hated that she had no physical power to fight back with.

What else did Vinnie Morretti hate? She hated that she lacked the chutzpah to tell him to fuck right off. Just the way Nina would were she in Vinnie's predicament. If she was going to go out, was this the way she wanted to leave this Earth? Sniveling and whimpering?

The only thing she had was her smarts. Handing out her SAT scores wasn't likely to help with the kind of foe that could transport her to a place like this.

Speaking of a place like this—she, of course, knew where she was, and it was everything she'd expected and more.

Hot. Dry. Lots and lots of flames. It was hellish in Hell.

But as he gazed at her, his eyes glassy and wildly dilated, Vinnie decided it was better to keep whoever this was talking while she tried to figure out how to get away from him.

Summoning up some of the facts she'd tucked away about Hell, she inhaled deeply, looked him in the eye and asked with as much sincerity as possible, "Where are we?"

He giggled like a coquettish schoolgirl, complete with coy glance and fluttering eyelashes. "Heeeell," he answered on a long, dry exhale.

She sighed forlornly despite the fact that he was inches from her face and his body was pressed so closely to hers, she felt every ridge of his abs against her belly.

She made a mockery of rolling her eyes in exaggeration. "Well, I know that, silly. The flames climbing the walls were the first indication we weren't in Kansas anymore. And if that didn't do it for me, then the temperature in this room cinched the deal. What I meant was, what *level* of Hell?"

"How do you know about Hell, little lady?" he asked in a peculiar, yet spot-on imitation of John Wayne.

Straightening her spine, Vinnie tilted her head up and attempted to exude confidence. "I read about it, of course. I read a lot... Anyway, the seventh level. That's where the demons that were created by Satan, versus a human turned into demon, live. Am I right?"

He gave her an exaggerated bulge of his glassy green eyes. "Why, I do declare, Ouiser, we got us a smart girl here! I say, she's a very smart girl!"

It was then she realized the reason he mimicked voices from movies and music. By watching TV, he'd learned how to interact with people on the earthly plane. She'd read Jackie Chan had learned English that way.

She'd also read a lot about Satan's *creations* versus one-time humans who'd sold their souls for riches or whatever. Demons like this one were childlike, less cynical than a human turned demon who had been coerced into giving up his soul. They were definitely as frightening, but not nearly as bitter with regret.

Regardless, his choice of interaction certainly was odd, but if using that angle stalled him long enough to amuse him, maybe help would arrive in the meantime.

"That was Olympia Dukakis as Clairee from *Steel Magnolias*, right?"

He winked at her and leaned back just enough to allow another inch between them. "Darn tootin'."

"*Fargo!*" she shouted with a pleased grin. Being socially awkward had lent to plenty of free time to watch lots of movies and TV. When she didn't have her nose buried in a book, it and the rest of her face were in front of the television. Who knew rather than helping her win trivia games, it might help save her life.

He clapped his hands together in obvious joy as he rose to tower over her. "You're sooo good at this, but…"

Her eyebrow shot upward. "But?"

"E-noooough!" he screamed in her face with rage-filled eyes, gathering her up by the material of her shirt until her neck was forced to arch backward.

Vinnie swallowed hard—so hard it was audible. Sweat beaded on her upper lip and her brow, but she let herself go limp in his grip, let her legs melt until he was forced to hold her up.

"*Please let me go,*" she rasped, hating the utter terror in her voice, but her neck felt like it might snap and her head would explode if he didn't let her up.

"Yo, Adrian! I'm not lettin' you go until your boyfriend shows up. Hear me? I'm goin' fishin' and you're my bait. Got it?"

As he spoke the infamous Sylvester Stallone words, he jammed his face in hers—and that was when Vinnie realized nightmares really do come true.

His face morphed, an ability she knew existed, but had never personally witnessed and hoped never to witness again. His skin went deep red, pockmarked and dripping pus, his tongue slithered in and out of his mouth once more, only this time it was forked.

Vinnie fought with everything she had not to scream, not to let the welling rise of hysteria consume her. She forced her eyes to stay open, to stare him down while he dripped pus and drooled saliva.

"How do ya like me now, Vinnie?" he screeched down at her, making her teeth rattle.

Then without warning, he changed back and smiled beautifully again, seconds before he dropped her to the hot floor by spreading his fingers and simply letting go.

She clattered to the ground in a crumpled heap, which knocked the wind out of her, but he wasn't done —not by a long shot.

Scooping her up by the length of her long hair, he dragged her across the floor while she attempted to dig her heels into the ground.

"No more fun and games for you, Vinnie! The

party's over!" he yelled, moments before her threw her against the wall.

Okay, whether she had superhuman strength or not, that would have hurt. Her head slammed into the wall—which, for a wall of flames, was surprisingly hard. Her nose smashed up against it and her shoulder crumbled under the incredible force.

She rolled over with a groan of pure agony, clenching her eyes shut, fighting the pain, only to force them open when she heard the heavy thump of feet.

"You useless fucking shitstain!" a voice yelled—Nina's voice, to be precise. "I'm going to deflate those raisins of yours and feed them to my goddamn neighbor's dog if you lay one more finger on her! Hear me, Godfrey?"

Nina was on him in a blur of limbs and hair, driving a single finger up under his chin to balance him then lifting him high.

He looked down at the vampire, his legs dangling, his body visibly trembling. "Lemme go!" he cried in panic, kicking his sneakered feet. "You're killin' me, Smalls!"

"I'll kill you all right, you fucking jackoff!" Nina yelled up at him, flashing her fangs. "Who the fuck do you think you're messing with, asswipe? Just who the fuck do you think you are, snatching my friend from her goddamn kitchen like you have some rights or some shit?"

Godfrey's expression took on an agonized look. He tore at Nina's wrist with both hands, gazing down at her, his eyes filling with tears. "I need it. Pleeease, please, please, please, pleeeease. I need the unicorn! It's my ticket to ride, vampire!"

Oliver dropped out of nowhere—like, out of *nowhere*—right from the ceiling, crashing to the floor with Darnell right behind him.

Godfrey caught sight of Oliver and his sparkling horn, and his face instantly changed from agony to ecstasy. Vinnie was sure it was because it dawned on him that unicorns truly did exist.

Godfrey stopped struggling and yelled in excitement, "I knew it! I knew it! Give me my unicorn. Give me liberty or give me my unicorn!"

His twisted version of the Patrick Henry quote would have made her laugh if it weren't for the pain her shoulder was in.

Oliver scurried to his feet with Darnell right behind him.

"Vinnie!" Oliver called out, his voice ringing with panic as he knelt beside her and pulled her into his arms. He brushed the hair out of her face and looked down at her, his horn glowing, his eyes concerned. "Are you all right?"

She didn't think twice about what she did next. Under normal circumstances, she would have analyzed all outcomes with the thoroughness of an actuary.

But not today. Right now, right this second, she was just grateful to see a familiar face. So grateful.

Vinnie threw her good arm around Oliver's neck

and squeezed tight, clinging to him as he gathered her closer and pressed his lips to her forehead.

"I'm okay. Are *you* okay?" she whispered, her voice trembling.

"Is this…Hell?" Oliver asked in wonder, blinking his eyes.

"Y'all get up now," Darnell said, urging them to take his hands as he looked around. "C'mon. We gotta get you two outta here before anybody else shows up."

Nina dropped Godfrey to the floor and shoved him across the length of it with a hard kick before scooping him back up again and giving him a hard shake. She sneered at him, her eyes wild and on fire.

She had hold of him so tight, her fist shook. "Who knows about this, freak? How did you find out about him? Tell me, or I'll smear you from one end of Hell to the other!"

"I say, I say, that's for me to know and you to find out!" he jeered in Porky Pig's voice, followed by a giggle.

"Nina!" Darnell roared, putting a hand on her shoulder and squeezing. "Let him go. We hafta get outta here before somebody sees us. We don't have time to question him. Drop him and hurry yo'self up now!"

Just before she launched him across the room, Nina gave him one last warning with the point of her finger. "Look at her face, you weasel motherfucker! If I ever catch you anywhere near her or anyone I know, I'll kill you, Godfrey. You hear me, Cuckoo Puffs? I'll fucking kill you. Stay the fuck away, and tell all your little friends or whoever else knows about this to do the goddamn same!"

Vinnie's last glance of Godfrey was of him battered and bruised on the floor, his perfect eyes sad, his shoulders drooping and dejected, before Darnell took Nina's smaller hand in his big one and instructed Vinnie and Oliver to hold on to her hoodie.

And in the blink of an eye, they were back in her kitchen as though nothing had ever happened.

Except something had.

Something Vinnie knew would forever change her.

CHAPTER 16

"Vinnie, you okay?" Oliver asked as she sat in his backyard in a chair on the patio under the watchful eye of Darnell, the chilly wind blowing, the leaves dancing about.

She swiped her finger under her eyes and tugged her knit cap down over her ears. "I'm fine. I just needed a moment of quiet." She burrowed under the blanket Arch had brought her and looked up at the starless sky, appearing so close, she felt like she could touch it.

"It's late," Oliver reminded as he pulled up a chair across from her and held out his hand. When she took it willingly, Oliver began to rub some warmth into her fingers. "And cold."

She nodded and looked down at her lap with a shrug. "I like the cold. It helps me think."

"So what are you thinking about? Do you mind if I ask?"

Vinnie stared off into the distance, not really seeing

anything at all but Godfrey's face, and it wasn't the face you'd think would stay with her. "I know it's ludicrous, but that demon's face…Godfrey's face when we were leaving him there? It's haunting me."

"But the pus-dripping one you told us about isn't?"

"Okay, that was gag-worthy scary. Yes. But I mean the one just as we were zapped out of there. He looked lost, sad. I realize he probably wanted you because he wanted to use your horn as leverage to barter his way out of there, but if it was because he was trying to escape Hell, who could blame him?"

Godfrey's helplessness, the dejected slump of his shoulders, his green eyes so full of sorrow, was what was had driven her outside. The image refused to leave her brain.

"He's a bad demon, Vinnie. You heard what Darnell said, didn't you?"

She'd heard all about Godfrey and how bad he was. "I did, and I totally understand what he's capable of."

Oliver tilted her chin up. "So you feel sorry for him?"

"I guess I do. I mean, you did hear Darnell's story about how he was tricked into selling his soul all those years ago, right? Darnell did what he did for the financial health of his family, but he's not a bad demon. Don't we all, somewhere along the way, do things like that?"

Oliver clucked his tongue. "I can't say I remember the last time I sold my soul, Vinnie…"

She looked at him then, her voice determined when

she spoke. "You know what I mean, Oliver. We all do things for survival, and sometimes they're not so nice. Godfrey didn't have a choice about who he is. He was created for the express purpose of evil, but maybe he's evolved enough that he doesn't want the life—the only life he knows—that the devil forced on him."

Oliver visibly shuddered and nodded. "I do know what you mean, and I'm sorry you're so sad. I don't know that there's anything I can do, but I'm here if you think I can help."

"Forget it. I know I have to let that sleeping dog lie. So, let's talk about how *you're* feeling."

"Like everyone under the paranormal sun wants a piece of me and these people have lives they need to get back to. You do, too. They—you—can't stay here forever."

Vinnie gazed at him, her expression soft as she tilted her lips upward in a small smile. "I have every faith they're going to figure this out, Oliver. I know it doesn't feel like it, but people are working behind the scenes as we speak."

He lifted a hand and cupped her cheek, leaving her insides warm despite the cold. "But will they work fast enough, Vin? I don't ask that because I want them to get it together. I ask that because I'm terrified someone's going to get hurt when the next evil whatever comes for my horn and me. Namely, you."

"But I'm fine," she protested. "Really." Admittedly, a little banged up, but fine.

Oliver made a face. "Vinnie, he slammed you up against a wall. A wall of *flames*. I've never seen anything like that place and I never want to again. You have a bruise the size of Texas on your shoulder and one side of your face looks like you ran into a semi. What if the next time you're not bruised, but dead? I can't live with that. I won't."

Her hand instantly went to her face, which was indeed swollen and bruised from her run-in with the wall. "I can only tell you that I believe these women are going to figure it out before it comes to that. But there's no way they'd leave you now anyway. No way *I'd* leave you to your own devices. So if that's where you're going, forget it."

He dropped her hand and sat back in the lawn chair. Closing his eyes, he ran his hand through his hair with a grating sigh. "I don't know where I'm going. I only know people are crawling out of the woodwork to get to this horn, and I happen to be the unfortunate fool who owns it. For all the effort put into keeping it quiet, that mission failed. In the process, you've ended up hurt and who knows how many people know I exist. You heard what the ladies said, Vinnie. People are going to keep coming for me unless something's done. I don't have to worry about just one lunatic, I have to worry about all of them."

The dark night felt as though it were closing in on them, its midnight claws reaching out to grab at her until she squirmed in her chair. "If I ever discover who found out about you and told everyone else and started this whole mess, I'll kill them myself. But I'd sure like to know the snitch of origin."

"Still the million dollar question," Oliver responded, though his voice was filled with defeat. "But does it matter if we have an answer anymore? The question is still the same. Who's coming for me by way of you or one of the girls—or, God forbid, Carl—next? And would it be long before they discover where my family is? I gotta be honest, Vinnie. That terrifies me. How could I explain this horn to them, let alone the paranormal?"

Vinnie swallowed hard. She couldn't imagine having to explain to the people she loved a world they thought only existed in the movies.

"You're right. You're absolutely right. But if you'd like, when things calm down, I'd be happy to go with you to talk to your family. To ease them into this."

Oliver rubbed his forehead, but she saw the war he was waging about this displayed in his eyes.. "Thanks, Vinnie."

Vinnie eyeballed his horn, beautiful and glittery under the moonlight, still growing by the day. "Hey, how does the horn feel these days, anyway? Does it still hurt if you bump into it?"

Oliver grimaced, his chiseled face and deep dimples accentuated. "It's sensitive, for sure. I mean, I definitely know it's there, but other than that, it's just the weird thing on my head."

She grinned at him, tucking her scarf tighter around her neck. "You know, on the bright side, that horn would make a badass Halloween costume. You'd definitely win for most authentic costume."

He laughed good-naturedly. "You have a point. Hey, you know, I was wondering something else. It's been bugging me since this started, and it might sound silly, but I guess we're beyond that and well into the outlandish now."

She cocked her head and gave him a questioning look. "What's that?"

"Am I going to turn into a horse when this thing is done growing? Like, will I need to DIY a stable out back and fill it with some hay? Every unicorn I've ever seen isn't some random guy with a horn sticking out of his head. It's a horse with a rainbow-colored horn. Maybe I haven't finished shifting and that's what my end result is going to be?"

Vinnie snorted a laugh as a picture of Oliver as a horse with a sparkly horn, prancing around in his backyard, flashed in her mind's eye. "You know, I never thought of that, and I don't have an answer. And here we were wondering how you were going to live with this horn, but maybe you just answered your own question. I think you've found your new calling in life, Baldwin. You can do princess parties. Every princess needs a unicorn, right?"

"A unicorn definitely needs a princess. Will you be my princess?" he asked, giving her a lascivious wink.

Her cheeks flushed and her heart skipped a beat, but she somehow kept her cool. "Maybe. But I have conditions," she teased.

"Oh yeah. Like?"

"Like, only if I get a castle. It's off if there's no castle, buddy. Oh, and a turret. There must be a turret so I can survey my kingdom from on high. And a moat. Can you DIY me a moat?"

"I'd be happy to. I mean, there must be a How-To vid on YouTube for a moat, right? But one question."

"Shoot," she said, amused.

"As a unicorn, will I have opposable thumbs?"

That's when they both started to laugh. Laugh until Vinnie's stomach hurt and she had to bend over at the waist and gasp for breath.

"Hey, you two," Wanda called from the doorway, stepping out into the cold night. "What's so funny?"

They looked at each other and began to laugh all over again.

Wanda smiled, but her smile was brief as she came to stand near Vinnie's chair. "So, I have some news, guys," she said softly—hesitantly.

"About?" Oliver asked, sitting up straight.

"What to do next. We've heard from the council."

Every muscle in Vinnie's body stiffened to the point of painful. "And?" she asked before she held her breath.

"They want to see you, Oliver. Now, before you get upset, just listen. Greg and Keegan met with select members they'd trust with their lives and negotiated a deal that they'd meet with you just to set some sort of precedent. You know, like an edict sent out to everyone that you're not to be harmed in any way until they can figure out what to do with this power you've acquired.

So don't worry on that front. They'd never go back on their word with Greg and Keegan. Of that, you can be sure. And we'll go with you, of course. No one will hurt you with us there. I promise you."

Oliver blew out a breath. "And Alice?"

Vinnie warmed at his question. Even in a time of dire crisis, he didn't want her mother to get in trouble. He was such a good guy.

Wanda pulled her oatmeal-colored shawl tighter around her shoulders and reached out to squeeze his hand. "We didn't even breathe her name. I swear. We told them if they wanted to meet with us, we'd be happy to give them the details. But I want you to know, we had to do this, Oliver. We can't have these continual attacks on you. You, or even Vinnie, could end up dead at this rate. You have to be protected. The power that horn wields is enormous. Life-changing. So we talked long and hard about it, went through all the pros and cons, and made a decision. That's why Nina asked how you felt about finding help outside of OOPS, if we could find someone we trusted enough to handle it. I mean, we don't even know how word got out about you, let alone how to deal with this. It's all just too risky to leave to luck and the universe."

Oliver exhaled and gave her a small smile. "It's a relief, really, Wanda. I couldn't live with myself if one of you were hurt looking out for me. I'm fine with going to this council."

Wanda smiled at him with deep warmth in her eyes. "You're a lovely man, Oliver, and we've all grown so fond of you. I swear as I'm standing here, if it's the last thing we do, we won't let them run roughshod over you. But that horn of yours feels like it's growing by the hour. We have to do *something*. We'll make a deal to have you protected somehow and still have a life semi intact. I don't know what that means, or how that'll evolve, but we'll help all the way."

Vinnie gulped away her emotions. Man, this had been some journey, and now it sounded as though it might come to a decent enough end, and that warmed her heart. She was so glad she'd met these people. It had changed her life in more ways than one.

"I'll help, too, of course, Oliver. I might not have superpowers, but I know way more than anyone should about every faction of the paranormal."

Oliver grabbed her hand and squeezed it. "When does this meeting happen?"

Wanda winced, but then her earlier smile returned. "In two days. And we're all going with you. All of us. Greg and Keegan, and my husband Heath—" Wanda stopped speaking quite suddenly, her hand going to her belly.

And that was when Vinnie saw the puddle at her feet, glistening in the moonlight.

She hopped up and grabbed Wanda's hand. "Wanda! Are you all right?"

But Wanda bit her lip and winced, shaking her head.

Oliver rose, too, and gave Vinnie a questioning glance. "What's going on?"

Wanda patted both of them on the arm and turned, but she stopped for a moment to look over her shoulder and say quite calmly with a wink and a smile, "I think I'm in labor. Hallelujah!" Before she waddled off back into the house.

∽

"Shouldn't we be at a hospital for this?" Oliver whispered to Vinnie at the doorway to his bedroom. Though, he wasn't sure why he was whispering, because no one else was, that's for sure.

"Puuush, pushpushpushpush, Wanda!" Nina hollered as she and Marty held one of their friend's hands and Wanda's husband, Heath, held the other.

"Apparently, they were going to have a home birth anyway. That's what Nina told me," Vinnie whispered back. "She said Arch got his birthing doula certificate or something like that, just for this occasion. I guess he's not just an amazing cook. I heard Heath say he couldn't get in touch with the midwife, but what are you going to do? If a baby is ready, a baby's ready. There was no time to get her to the hospital. She went from zero to a hundred in like five seconds."

Arch pushed his way past them into Oliver's master bedroom, where Wanda lay on his bed, knees up and still looking as elegant as anyone can be when they're in agonizing pain.

But all that changed when a contraction hit her so

hard she yanked her hands from Heath and Nina and clenched the sheets with white-knuckled fists.

Arch propped himself on the edge of the bed next to Heath and wiped her brow with a cool cloth. "Miss Wanda, you must listen to me. With the next contraction, you must bear down. Do you understand me?"

"Yes!" she yelled up into his placid face, rearing upward, seething and red-faced. "I fucking understand, okay? What about plain English don't you think I understand?"

Both Vinnie and Oliver blanched. Wanda didn't swear. She didn't even get angry. Holy Toledo. Giving birth must really, really suck.

"Right on, Potty Mouth," Nina said on a laugh, patting her friend's hand. "Now I know you're in this shit to win it."

Wanda's eyes went wide and wild as she grabbed Nina by the front of her hoodie and hauled her close. "Shut the fuck up, Mistress of the Night, or I'm going to rip your lips off your body!"

Nina peeled Wanda's fingers from her hoodie and kissed her forehead, her tone appeasing. "I'm so fucking proud of you right now, and that's why I'm gonna let your preggers ass live."

"Here it comes," Wanda panted, sweat dripping off her forehead. *"Heeere—it—coomes!"* As she grunted and sat forward, Heath pushed his way in behind her and cradled her between his legs to brace her body.

"Push, honey!" he urged. "That's it! Push!"

Oliver grimaced, because Wanda looked like

someone was severing her limbs. He wasn't much for seeing someone in pain, but this cinched the deal. Also, he really liked Wanda. He'd hate to see anyone in this much pain, but especially not someone as nice her.

Looking over his shoulder and down the hall, he checked to see how Carl was faring. He held Heath and Wanda's other child, a toddler named Sam. Carl rocked him on a chair Darnell had brought with him so he could read.

Now, he read *Goodnight Moon* to little Sam, and he was slow and stilted, but so damn amazingly persistent in his effort to learn how to talk, Oliver's breath caught in his throat seeing them together.

Sam, according to Nina, was half zombie, but Oliver had to admit, he'd have never known. Heath had brought him along so he could meet his new brother or sister and they could bond, and he was the sweetest kid. Chubby, happy, and healthy.

Vinnie's animals had gathered on Darnell's lap next to Calamity, somehow sleeping through the ruckus in his bedroom, and Baloney slept contentedly in Carl's pocket.

This picture, the one he'd always had in his mind when it came to having a family, was exactly what he'd imagined.

Okay, maybe someone having a baby on his bed hadn't been part of that picture, and the players weren't paranormal at the time he'd dreamed them up, but he had no trouble at all adjusting his vision of what a family should be.

Now more than ever, he knew this was what he wanted, and he hoped to be able to find it—to fill his life with these kinds of people. People you could trust beyond keeping secrets and confidences.

He hoped to pursue this thing with Vinnie, too. His attraction to her grew with each passing day, and today, when that crazed demon had her in his clutches, he realized he had a real crush on her. A crush he wanted to pursue when this was all settled.

But first he had to get this thing with the council out of the way—he had to figure out how to live with this thing sticking out of his head without having to worry everyone and their werewolf was going to come gunning for him.

He also had to understand it. Oliver knew there would be choices he had to make, if what had happened with Arch's hand was any indication of what might *always* happen when he used his horn to help others. But he hoped to find someone to help him with that.

Someone a lot wiser than he'd ever be.

"I think the baby's coming!" Vinnie said, tugging on his arm in excitement.

He refocused his attention on Wanda once more to find Arch was now at the foot of the bed, the tuft of hair on his head falling forward, his glasses on, hands at the ready.

"Push, Miss Wanda! I can see the head. Push now!" he ordered in his cultured British voice.

Marty got in close to Arch and cheered her friend

on, too. "Push, honey! One more time! You're almost there!"

Nina placed her hand on Wanda's stomach as it rolled and moved with the movement of the baby. "C'mon, Wanda, gimme a niece or a nephew!"

With one last scream—a blood-curdling one, if Oliver was honest—Wanda pushed and, all of a sudden, there was a tiny dark head jutting from the end of the bed.

Wanda cried out as the baby entered the world...but there were no other cries as Marty grabbed a blanket and Arch placed the baby on it.

Vinnie let out a small gasp as total silence invaded the room, and then she grabbed his arm and squeezed.

He hadn't ever seen a live birth of anything, but wasn't the baby supposed to cry upon entry to the world?

And that was when all hell broke loose.

Wanda sat straight up, letting her legs flatten as she looked at the baby. "What's going on?" she squeaked, and Oliver saw the effort it took for her not to scream the question. Her eyes were wild, and in an instant, tears began to fall down her face.

Oliver's heart pounded in his chest as he looked to Vinnie.

Arch and Marty looked at each other for no more than a second, horror in their eyes, and then Oliver knew. He knew what that look meant.

Arch began CPR, pressing his mouth to the baby's, but the infant's skin remained blue and mottled.

"No," Vinnie whispered in horror from behind her hand. "Dear Goddess, no!"

Heath was up and off the bed in seconds, pushing Arch out of the way and reaching for the tiny baby. He instantly began CPR, but the baby clearly wasn't responding.

Wanda looked at everyone, their faces somber, Marty's wet with tears, Nina's stricken with pain, and she threw her legs over the side of the bed, pushing the sheets out of the way as she grabbed for the baby. And when she saw the infant, blue and lifeless, she wailed, hoarse and raw, "*No! No! No! Nooooo!*"

Nina went to grab her friend by her arms, to keep her from seeing any more, but Wanda shoved her away with such force, she fell to the floor. "Stay away from me, Nina! Let me have my baby!"

Falling to her knees, Wanda scooped the baby up and held it tight to her chest, rocking back and forth and begging anyone who would listen. "Please, please, please don't take my baby! I'm begging you," she sobbed as she bartered with the universe. "I'll do whatever you want, but don't take my baby!"

In that moment, in that raw, horrific, life-altering moment, Oliver couldn't bear her pain.

He felt it course through him, rocking him to his very core. His soul shuddered inside him, his legs trembled with a sting so deep, he almost couldn't stand.

He didn't know what compelled him to do what he did next. He only knew this woman—this woman and her friends—had stopped everything in their lives to make his livable, to help him cope. To help him when he was helpless.

And he would repay them in kind.

Pushing his way into the room, Oliver didn't ask permission. He didn't shy away from the mother and her newborn, and he didn't worry about what would happen to him when he did what he did.

He went on instinct and instinct alone when he grabbed for the baby, making everyone scream in protest.

Wanda was on her feet in a flash, her eyes hot with anguish and anger as she reached for him, her hands ready to claw his eyes out.

Heath—incensed, judging by the look of death in his eyes—tried to grab him as well, but in some perverse reversal of power, Oliver managed to evade his grasp.

He held tight to the baby, tearing the infant from his mother's arms and, grabbing its tiny fist, he pressed it against his horn.

The thunder that struck his body ripped through him, brought him to his knees and, while his compulsion was to move the baby away to end the agony, he refused it. He welcomed the pain searing his gut. He ignored the blaze in his chest, the fire in his belly, and the feeling his head would explode in a million pieces.

And that's when the baby cried.

Thank Christ, the baby cried.

And that's how Oliver knew everything would be all right, just before he collapsed to the floor.

CHAPTER 17

"Oliver...good Goddess, you're an amazing soul," Vinnie whispered as she lay beside the unconscious man who'd saved the life of a baby, not knowing the risk to his own. She pushed the hair from his face and smiled down at him. "Wanda and Heath have gone off to the hospital, but you did it, Oliver. You saved the baby. It's a girl, by the way. A beautiful, robust, hollering-like-a-banshee-on-her-way-out-the-door girl, with hair the color of chestnuts in fall. And that's all due to you."

He didn't answer her, of course. After he'd saved the baby, as yet to be named, he'd collapsed and seized until his body calmed. Nina assured her that he was just unconscious, but saving Wanda's baby had taken a toll on him, no doubt.

She'd also assured Vinnie that he couldn't do this forever. His body could only take so much before it could take no more.

And that left her heartsick.

Oliver had proven over and over he was the kind of man who'd give you the shirt off his back. But having this healing power, coupled with a soul as sweet as his, could only lead to disaster.

How did you make the choice to hear a story on the news about a child in agony, dying of cancer, and not want to do something, knowing you likely had the power to fix it? What if you came across a car accident and someone in the wreck was dead? How did you walk away?

She'd bet Oliver couldn't, but his body also couldn't withstand the kind of seizures he was having for very long before it just gave out on him.

"Hey, you two okay in here?" Nina asked, poking her head in the doorway with Marty right behind her, both pairs of eyes filled with worry.

Vinnie sat up and smiled wearily. "I'm okay. You're sure we don't need to take him to the hospital?"

"I'm sure," Nina said again. "He's gonna be weak AF when he wakes up, but I won't say I'm not damn glad he did what he did. He saved that baby's life. He'll never want for a single thing as long as I have shit-all to say about it. You understand that? Not a single thing."

"Same," Marty said, her eyes tired and still watery with tears. "I saw my whole life pass before my eyes while Heath was administering CPR. Thank the Gods for Oliver. Thank the Gods."

Vinnie's heart clenched in her chest so tight, she almost couldn't breathe. Yes, thank the Gods and

Goddesses and whoever was in charge of this thing called life.

"Are Wanda and the baby still okay?"

Both Nina and Marty nodded, their smiles relieved. "Yep. Mama and baby are fine. Safe at the hospital and in a doctor's care. I don't know if Heath's ever gonna recover, but fuck all, that was scary."

Vinnie nodded. It was right up there with her experience in Hell, and if she had the choice, she'd do that a hundred times over if it meant saving Wanda's baby. "How's Arch feeling?"

Marty put a hand on Nina's shoulder and sighed. "He's so upset. We tried to reassure him that he couldn't have prevented whatever it was that happened. He was fully prepared to be her birthing doula, and Wanda did want to have the baby at home. Who knew it would come so fast? I mean, one minute she's as pregnant as you can get and the next, the baby's flying out of her life a bullet. She wasn't due for at least another month—which is why we couldn't get in touch with the midwife, I guess. But he can't hear any of that right now. So he's in the kitchen making bread. Baking always soothes him."

Vinnie sighed, deciding once she felt better about leaving Oliver alone, she'd find a way to cheer Arch up. "Do the doctors even know what happened—why the baby stopped breathing? Was the cord wrapped around her neck?"

Marty shook her head, tucking her hair behind her ears. "Apparently, our little buddy is a medical mystery.

They're still running tests, but so far, no one has an answer."

Nina entered the room, giving her shoulder a nudge. "Listen, kiddo, you've been up for a thousand years. You look whacked. Try and get some sleep. He's probably gonna be out for a while."

Vinnie smiled up at Nina as she slipped off the bed. "I'll do that," she whispered as tears began to fall down her face.

"Aw, honey. What's wrong?" Marty crooned, rushing to her side and wrapping an arm around her shoulder.

But Vinnie shrugged and laugh-cried. "I don't know. It's silly to cry now. But I think it's just really hitting me. I mean, the stuff with the baby... I don't know how you guys keep it together the way you do."

Nina wrapped an arm around her neck and dropped a kiss on the top of her head. "It's all right, Almost-Goddess. You just need some sleep. You had a shit day, too."

A vision of Godfrey flashed in her mind, but she clenched her eyes tight and warded it off. "That was nothing compared to tonight."

"Hey," the vampire said, frowning down at her. "You're not afraid Godfrey will try and take you again, are you? Because he knows I'll fuck him up till the end of time if he does."

She threw her arms around Nina's neck and reached for Marty, too, clinging to them. Planting a kiss on Nina's soft cheek, she shook her head. "No. I'm just really fried, vampire. Thank you for today. Thank you for saving my life—*again*."

"It's just what we fucking do," Nina said, untangling herself from Vinnie with a thump to her back. "Now get some rest. You need to be sharp for fucking council."

Marty hugged her tight. "Sleep is the ticket for all tired princesses. Get some. You want me to stay with Oliver?"

There was no way she was leaving this man now. Not when she was so afraid he wouldn't wake up, despite what Nina said. She pointed to the large chair Oliver had in his room, complete with an attached ottoman. It was big, wide, and puffy, and it looked like a perfect place to snuggle up.

"No. I'll sleep on the chair or something. I'm short enough to fit. You guys go do whatever you have to do with the kids. I'm fine."

Marty tweaked her cheek and winked. "All ya gotta do is yell if you need us."

Nina grazed her cheek with her knuckles. "Don't let the bedbugs bite, kiddo."

As they left the room, their footsteps fading, Vinnie sat back down next to Oliver and closed her eyes, resting a trembling hand on his chest, careful to avoid his glowing horn. "Please be all right. That's all I want. I just want everyone to be safe—especially you."

With a sigh, she leaned back against the headboard and closed her grainy eyes.

When she woke again, it was pitch black and

someone had covered them. Somehow, she was lying on Oliver's broad chest, her nose buried in his sweater, his arm around her.

Her eyes popped open and she stiffened, horrified she'd been so forward. But Oliver wrapped his arm tighter around her.

"Would you mind staying?"

She settled back against him, not that it was a chore, mind you. "How did I get here?"

"You looked exhausted, and you were sleeping so soundly, but your neck was crooked. I didn't want you to get a crick in it, so I slid you down, and this is where we landed," he offered sleepily. "Too soon?"

"No," she whispered, so content. So safe. So warm. "How are you feeling? Are you okay?"

"Drugged," he muttered. "I feel like someone tranq'd me. I can hardly keep my eyes open."

"You spent a lot of energy saving Wanda's baby. I'm not surprised."

He stiffened at her words and tried to sit up. "The baby? Is it okay?"

She patted his chest and hushed him. "She's fine. Wanda's fine. It's a girl, and everything's okay. They're safely in the hospital, the baby's doing well. But that's all because of you. You did a wonderful thing, Oliver. It was amazing. *You* were amazing."

She would never forget that lifeless baby. She'd never forget how blue and stiff she'd been. She'd never forget how, the moment Oliver pressed her tiny fist to his horn, she instantly breathed, how she was immediately rosy-pink and healthy and screaming her tiny head off.

She'd never forget how the room erupted around them, or how Heath ran to grab the baby as Nina and Marty ran to catch Oliver. Tears had flown, great gulping sobs had ensued, a hum of pervasive joy spread throughout the room as they packed Wanda up to take her and the baby to the hospital.

All because of Oliver.

He expelled a deep breath at her explanation, his words hitching when he said, "Thank God."

Snuggling closer to him, she patted his cheek. "Sleep now, okay? Nina said you would be exhausted, but I promise everything's okay. Baloney's with Carl and everything's right as rain."

"Hey, Vinnie?" he murmured, giving her arm a squeeze as he tucked her closer still.

"Uh-huh," she replied, feeling drowsier by the second in this cocoon they'd created.

He rested his chin on top of her head and sighed deeply, the sound lingering in her ear. "We're almost at the end of this. You still up for a castle and some coffee?"

Her cheeks went hot, but she smiled to herself in the dark. "I've already looked up moats on YouTube, and as long as you have a crocodile, it's on like Donkey Kong."

"A crocodile? What does that have to do with building a moat?"

She tweaked his chest and giggled sleepily. "We

have to protect the castle somehow, don't we? That's what moats are for."

He chuckled, his words slow. "Note to self, look up where to purchase a crocodile in Buffalo."

She could no longer keep her eyes open, and as they slid closed, her heart happy, she whispered, "Night, Oliver."

"Night, Vinnie."

∽

The next time Vinnie woke, it was to a bump and a long groan. Her eyes were reluctant, but they opened—and when she saw what was in front of her, she bolted upright, her jaw unhinging.

"Well, shit. Look who's awake." A man stood at the end of the bed, wearing a ski mask, with Oliver slung over his shoulder like a sack of potatoes, his horn glowing pink and purple in the dark. "Welcome to the party, Nerd."

Vinnie squinted into the dark room. She knew that voice. Why did she know that voice?

Instantly, her mind raced. With the past few days rife with demons and vampires, she could only imagine which faction of the paranormal was next.

"Who are you? What are you doing in here?" she asked, her voice trembling as she began to slide off the bed.

"You make a sound and I'll shoot your fucking face off, and then that cute little rug rat out there, sleeping like a little angel? I'll kill it, too. So if you were going to call your friends to save you this time, you'd better hope they're quicker than my little friend here."

The man in the ski mask held up something shiny, and if her heart weren't already beating out of her chest, it would be now. He had a gun.

Vinnie's mouth went suddenly dry, her throat threatening to close as her hands grew clammy and her legs wobbled.

Still, she forced the words from her mouth. "What do you want?"

"What the fuck do you think I want, Nerd? Don't be a fucking idiot," he whispered roughly, flashing the gun again. "I want your sparkly motherfucking unicorn. I'd take the hot vampire, too. But I'm all outta garlic, and I bet she's a biter." And then he hissed a laugh at his own joke.

Nerd? How did he know who she was? Was this another random attack or something more calculated?

God, why was his voice so damn familiar? "Wait!" she whisper-yelled as he turned toward the French doors off the master bedroom, leading to Oliver's backyard. Hopping off the bed, she fought panic and tried to make her brain find a way to reason with him.

But her words just weren't working tonight. She was sluggish and slow, and as she reached out toward him, she tripped and fell, knocking over a small table with a potted plant. It crashed to the ground and smashed to smithereens.

But it sounded more like fireworks had gone off.

The house had been so quiet, but that was all it took to rile Frank and Mario, who began to yap.

The man in the ski mask tucked the gun in his waistband in a flash and reached down for her, his eyes glittering in the dark, angry and hot.

"You're such a fucking asshole, Vinnie. Still the same old clumsy, misfit dipshit you always were!" he spat, grabbing her by the arm and yanking her upward.

He dragged her to the edge of the patio, her bare feet scraping on the concrete, proving he was no slouch. He wasn't only carrying Oliver as though he weighed no more than a toddler, he dragged Vinnie, too, and she was no lightweight.

But Vinnie wasn't going out without a fight. Not this time. She went limp for a moment, letting him tug her dead weight as the dogs barked and Sam cried and she screamed, "Oliver! Oliver!" seconds before she launched herself at him, fingernails ready to rip his face off.

It might be all she had, but she was going to give it her all anyway.

Just as the lights in the kitchen went on, as she heard Nina scream out her name, Vinnie managed to rip the ski mask from the intruder's head—and it stunned her so badly, she lost her footing.

"*You?*" she sputtered in disbelief as she stumbled, still managing to somehow cling to his dark jacket.

"Yeah, *me*, bitch," he sneered, before he snapped his fingers and everything went blank.

CHAPTER 18

"Vinnie," Oliver whispered, pressing the flashlight app and holding up his phone. Though, he didn't really need to. His alicorn acted as a torch in the dark. "Wake up. You have to wake up. Do you hear me?"

She was slouched against his shoulder, her beautiful pale face bruised, her flame-red hair wild around her face. But she was out of it and he'd been trying unsuccessfully for what felt like forever to wake her.

He looked around at their surroundings, a corrugated steel shed of some kind with a couple of padlocks on the *inside* of the door, leaving him to wonder how someone had locked them in from the insid*e*, yet the perp was nowhere to be found.

Then he tried to remember what the hell happened and understand why he felt like he'd been drugged. One minute he was snuggled next to Vinnie in the warmth of his bedroom, and the next, he was being dumped on the hard floor with little to no memory of getting here.

Was it another demon? Maybe a werewolf this time?

He listened closely to hopefully determine where they were, but heard no sounds of traffic, water, nothing. Leaning forward, her wrapped an arm around Vinnie's shoulders and lay her limp body on his lap, then pulled his sweater off to give her something to cushion her head so he could get up and look around.

But there wasn't much to see. It was a box, probably eight by twenty in size.

As his horn glowed, and his eyes adjusted, Oliver paused as he felt the walls.

Wait. Maybe this wasn't a shed. Maybe it was a…a shipping container? Looking around again, that felt more accurate.

But what difference did it make what they were being held captive in?

They were being held captive.

His heart sped up despite how sluggish he felt. Had someone captured him, and now had plans to ship him off to some exotic place—like black market stuff?

The women and Vinnie had talked a lot about the kind of money his horn could bring to someone greedy enough. What if whoever did this planned to sell him? But to what end? Would they keep him in a cage and use him at will? And what did they plan to do to Vinnie?

Jesus Christ. He had to wake Vinnie. She needed to

be ready for whatever they were facing, but by hell, he wasn't going down without a damn fight.

Kneeling beside her, Oliver gave her a gentle nudge. "Vinnie! Vinnie, you have to wake up." He was reluctant to pat her face, it was so swollen, so instead, he pinched the flesh of her arm, instantly regretting it when she twisted away from him.

"Ow! What the heck?"

As her eyes opened and focused on him, he brushed her hair from her face. "I'm sorry. I didn't know how else to wake you, but you have to get up, Vinnie."

She groaned and fought to sit up, using his thigh as leverage. Upon looking around, she asked, "Where are we?"

"In a shipping container, I think. Do you know how the hell we got here?"

Vinnie blinked as though she was remembering something, and then she yelped, "Byron!"

"Who?" he asked, gripping her shoulders.

"Byron, Dorinda's son," she said again, as though she still couldn't believe it.

Oliver frowned. "The one who had fairies at his birthday party? That Byron?"

She bounced her head, her eyes hard chips of ice. "That's the one. Just as he was hauling you out of your bedroom, and I was clinging to him for all I was worth to try to stop him, I managed to get his ski mask off. I'm as surprised as anyone. Byron's not exactly Mr. Motivated or even terribly smart. He's just always gotten by on his parent's money. This makes no sense."

"Is this the same guy who was in the driveway with the Corvette and the blonde?"

"That's him," she spat.

Damn, damn, damn. "Aw, hell, Vinnie," he grated out.

She froze on the spot, her eyes wide. "What?"

Dread filled the pit of his stomach. For all the warnings, for all the care these women had taken in keeping him hidden, he was the one who'd fucked up all that effort.

"*He saw me.* He must have. He roared up beside Marty's car so quickly, he caught me off guard. I tried to duck, but I ended up whacking my horn and it damn well hurt. My head reared backward, but honestly, I thought he was too drunk to notice because he kept right on walking. But he must have seen me. I forgot all about that. Shit. Shit. Shit!"

Vinnie rasped a long sigh. "Still, I'm telling you, Oliver, he's the last person I would have suspected would kidnap you. He's always only done what he had to in order to skate by. He had his friends do his homework, when there was a test, there was always someone to copy from and his parents never took him to task. Even when he got caught. So, I don't know why he'd want you or your horn. He has plenty of money. Other than being an asshole all the time, I don't get his motive. Also, he has a gun. *A gun.*"

Oliver gulped. A gun. "Okay, let's not think about his motivation now. Let's think about how the hell we're going to get out of here. Do you have your phone? Mine's not getting a signal."

She nodded, pulling the phone from the back pocket of her jeans, but she didn't have any bars, either. "Damn!"

He squeezed her hand. "It's okay. Listen, save the battery and turn it off for now. I have mine. If we need yours for the flashlight, we'll turn it back on, but my horn seems to be doing the trick. Now, any idea how we got in here, and how we got locked in here with a padlock on the *inside* of the door?"

She made a face—an angry face. "Byron is capable of magic, Oliver. That's how he got us here in the first place. He snapped his fingers and wham! I don't know how strong his magic is. I don't know what he knows in terms of spells and such, but he's capable."

Shit. More magic. Exactly what he didn't want to hear. "Okay, next. Do you have anything on you to fight back with? Because I've got nothing but the clothes on my back. You said he had a gun, right?"

Damn, that scared the shit out of him. They might have immortality on their side, but that didn't mean they were infallible. They weren't like Nina, who could take a bullet.

Vinnie began to dig in the pockets of her jeans and came up with a safety pin. It was a big one, but it certainly wasn't going to do much damage against a gun. "This is it. But maybe we can stab him with it and catch him off guard?"

His mind raced, but there wasn't a whole lot to be

done with a safety pin. "Not a great plan, Vinnie. He has a *gun*..."

She rubbed her forehead and winced. Clearly her injuries were aching, judging by her pained expression. "Okay, you're right. He has a gun. Listen, he doesn't want me. I just happened to come along for the ride, right? Because I latched onto him and the transport spell took me with you both by proxy. He wants *you*, but he wouldn't hurt you because it could hurt the alicorn, and he can't take that chance."

"But he *would* hurt *you*, Vinnie. So whatever you're hatching in your head, no. End of."

"Way to DIY this, pal. Listen, I know exactly how to get to him. He's got a weak spot when it comes to his parents and their money. Nina stuck her finger in that wound when she met him, and if I rub salt in it just enough to distract him—"

"No, Vinnie!" Oliver growled, his stomach turning at the thought. "Do you hear me? No poking the bear. He's got a *gun*. I can't impress upon you enough, *he has a gun*. He also knows, in terms of magic or whatever he has, we're weaker. Maybe he'd just shoot me to disable me, but he'd kill you. *Kill you.*"

She gripped his hand, her fingers freezing cold. "You're right. But listen, I saw lights go on in the house when I yelled your name to try to wake you up. The dogs were barking their head's off. Let's just pray Nina can smell him and she'll find us. It's all we have."

The shipping container shifted then. Not enough to be terribly noticeable unless you were already on edge, but the air became thick and smelled like Sulphur.

And out of nowhere, Byron appeared, his hair slicked back, his eyes cunning, his clothes impeccable... a shiny gun in one hand and a flashlight in the other.

~

From the light of Oliver's horn, she could see Byron was pointing the gun at her head and smiling the smile she remembered so well. Even aged, it was still the same. Beautiful but sneaky. So sneaky.

"That won't happen. She's super fucking hot, but not so smart. She gave her hand away when she said she could smell my rotten soul. I'd forgotten vampires could track you by scent. It's been a loooong time since I hung out with one—especially one that looks like her. Jesus, she's hot...but she'll never track you by your scent, Nerd."

"So you masked our scents with a spell?" Vinnie asked, pushing her way up from the floor with Oliver's help. He tried to push her behind him to shield her, but even as she trembled, her rage grew and she rooted herself to the spot.

Byron shrugged his shoulders and grinned. "Yeah. But what would you know about that, Vinnie? You're a half-breed, aren't you? No magic spells to speak of. In fact, nothing of any consequence to speak of, not if you inherited your mother's abilities, anyway."

God, she was so tired of being labeled and called names for something she didn't even care about. She was tired of being the paranormal world's joke because her mother shoved them both down everyone's throats. She'd hidden away from these people for a very long time to avoid them and now, here she was, all up in the paranormal world's face.

But enough was enough.

Without warning, Vinnie lifted her chin, a rage from nowhere slithered up her spine, and she took a deep, long breath.

Before she exploded.

Which was a very un-Vinnie thing to do.

She lifted both her hands and flipped Byron the middle finger, her face hot with rage. For all the days he'd made fun of her because they were poor and she didn't have a father, for all the times he made her feel like a joke, she wanted to say the one thing she'd wanted to say since she'd met him in kindergarten.

"Fuck you, rich-boy elitist weasel! Fuck you and your fucking entitlement, you sorry-ass excuse for a man! Why are you doing this, Byron? Is it because your sissy ass wants a unicorn horn to call his very own? Don't you have enough toys to play with? Don't *Mommy and Daddy* buy you everything your little boy heart desires?"

To anyone else, it might not have appeared to ruffle his feathers much, but she knew Byron. She knew what he was like back on the playground when someone bested him. He was pretty good at hiding it, except for that tic in his jaw. It was small, and it didn't last long, but she'd gotten under his skin.

What she was going to do now that she'd managed to work her way under his skin was another story. There was no backup plan, but she knew one thing for sure—he wouldn't kill Oliver because he didn't know what it would do to the unicorn alicorn.

So this was her one chance to get him to come at her, and she was going to take it by humiliating him—even with Oliver gripping her shoulders from behind as a clear signal to stop poking the bear.

But Byron surprised her by leaning back against the door of the container, crossing his feet at the ankles. "Will it really matter what an elitist I am when I hack this motherfucker's horn off and sell it to the highest bidder, Vinnie? You stupid, stupid bitch. Always with the high and mighty. Did you think I'd forgotten what a bitch you were? Not a chance. I saw the way you and your hot friends looked at me at my mother's house like I was some pathetic sack of shit. Fuck you!"

But Vinnie shrugged out of Oliver's grip and raced right up to Byron, jamming her face in his, so close she could smell his breath.

"They wouldn't look at you that way if you *weren't* a pathetic sack of shit, would they, Rich Boy?" she screamed, her spit flying from her mouth, her head on the verge of exploding with her rage. "What are you going to do with an alicorn anyway, you useless gob of shit? You're just barely potty-trained."

He grinned down at her, salacious, wide. "I might be

a pathetic sack of shit, but somehow I still managed to get my hands on *him*, didn't I? And after others failed, too. I just had to bide my time and wait for the right opportunity. Everyone's talking about him in our circles—you know, the *pure paranormal* circles. But don't worry, Vinnie. I don't think I'll have to use my big brain to figure out what to do with an alicorn that has the kind of power his does."

Her eyes must have flown open, because he leered at her. "I know, I know. I'm a useless gob of shit, but not so useless I didn't sit up and take notice when your boy here was in my driveway. Not so useless that I didn't make contact with people who'd want a unicorn horn. Not so *useless* I wouldn't spy on you and your fucking hot friend. That Oliver can heal people just upped my asking price. Don't bother to deny it. Saw it with my own eyes tonight when he healed that half-breed kid. You think someone won't pay top dollar for your boy here?"

Vinnie gulped and licked her dry lips, but she refused to let him see how terrified she was. And she didn't know what it was—but something shifted in her.

She didn't know if it was because she'd had dirt kicked in her face one too many times by him, or maybe it was watching Nina deal with scum like this, but she cared about nothing other than calling him out for what he was. A lazy, entitled, weak little boy.

Her heart screeched in her chest. Her face hurt from the last encounter she'd had with a wall in Hell, but she reared up at him and screamed, "Fuck you, Mama's Boy!"

Byron's arm swerved then, and he positioned the gun directly in front of her face, right between her eyes, his lips a thin line. "Talk shit some more, why don't you, Nerd? See if that doesn't get you dead, *bitch*."

Oliver grabbed for her and shoved her behind him, his chest heaving. Yet, his words were surprisingly steady as a rock. "*Enough.* Leave her alone. Take me. Take me wherever you want to go, but leave her out of this. You don't have to kill her if you have me."

Byron rubbed his fingers together, making the padlocks snap open. "Like you have a fucking choice what I do to her? Shut the fuck up and move," he ordered sharply. "Or I swear to Christ, I'll blow her fucking Einstein head off. Hear me, Ollie the Unicorn?"

Using the gun, he motioned for them to get in front of him. "Push the door open and walk, motherfuckers. Time's up. Now walk!" he yelled.

Grabbing her hand, Oliver pushed the door open with a creak and they stepped out into what was most definitely a shipping yard. Row after row of shipping containers were stacked three of four high. But if he wasn't shipping Oliver off somewhere, where was he taking them?

It was cold and dark, and as they began to move, her legs stiff and sore, the rain started to pelt them. Icy droplets of cold, hard rain.

Oliver's horn shone brightly, the pink and purple sparkles ironically cheerful despite their predicament, lighting up the path to what she was sure was going to be their death. How else could this end?

"Walk faster! Walk or I start shooting, little bitches!" he hollered with glee. "I'll take out her legs first, Oliver. You wanna watch your bitch bleed out?"

Oliver pulled her to his side as Vinnie scanned her memory for some movie or a TV show she'd watched where a gun was being held at the hero's back, yet, somehow, he managed to escape. But she couldn't think for the throb of her face and the burning ache of her muscles.

What she *could* do?

Talk. She could talk. It didn't seem to make much of a difference, but maybe she'd get lucky and hit on something, anything that would help.

"Where are you taking us, Byron?" she yelled as they ate up more and more of the gravel-filled pathways of the shipping yard, taking them to who knew where.

"Shut up, Brainiac. Shut up, or I'm going to take your fucking red head right off while your boyfriend watches."

She didn't even know where they were. She didn't know Buffalo had a shipping yard. Did Buffalo have a shipping yard? Did it make a damn bit of difference if it did?

And then she saw it, up ahead—a car with its headlights on. She prayed it was someone who'd come to help, but she feared the reality was, it was whoever Byron had found to buy Oliver and his alicorn.

And that was when she made a decision. Her mother had dragged Oliver into her crazy matchmaking game, and she was going to get them out. Oliver wouldn't like it, but it would give him the chance he needed to escape, because there was no other way out.

As they walked, she tried to keep her focus enough that when she saw the next big rock, she'd trip and fall, and while Byron was busy screaming about how he was going to kill her, Oliver could make a break for it. But she'd have to do it before they got any closer to that damn car.

Her lips were almost frozen together, but somehow she made them move. She turned around and started walking backward, slapping a smile on her face even though it hurt.

"Hey, Byron! Do you remember that time on the playground when Christopher Hennicutt fell off the monkey bars and broke his arm? I was just thinking about that the other day when I was at my job. You know, the one where you earn money all by yourself? Jesus, his arm was all bent up and crooked. Remember?" She turned back around and skipped as well as she could along the path, the car's headlights getting brighter by the second.

"Shut up!" he howled into the whistling wind.

"Vinnie," Oliver hissed. "*Stop.*"

And right there, in all its glory, her opportunity arose in the way of a pothole just up ahead. She calculated approximately where she'd have to walk to hit it just right, and then she turned back around and called out to him, "Do you remember what you said when you saw him? You said—"

She hit the pothole like a ton of bricks, and as a by the by, it was a helluva lot deeper than she'd first thought, so when she went down, her ankle twisted so sharply, it was probably better off she was going to end up dead.

Because in the infamous words of her most favorite vampire, that shit was gonna hurt.

As she crashed into the pothole, she screamed out, "Run, Oliver, run!"

And that was when the first shot was fired.

~

Oliver's eyes flew to where Vinnie fell, his heart crashing so hard in his chest he thought it would explode.

Byron aimed the gun at her, but the headlights of the car must have impaired his vision, or he was a really shitty shot, because he fired the gun and the bullet pinged one of the shipping crates with a sharp report.

That was the moment Oliver took his opportunity —the only one he'd probably have. As Byron ran toward Vinnie, gun pointed at her while she lie helpless on the ground, her ankle twisted behind her, Oliver ran.

He didn't stop and think about Byron and the gun.

He didn't stop and think about who was in the car up ahead. He didn't stop and think, period.

He simply refused to allow the woman he'd come to care for, the woman he loved talking to late into the night about, of all things, shiplap, the woman he'd held in his arms while she'd slept, to die.

Not today, Satan. *Not. Today.*

Oliver roared a howl so loud, so guttural, he almost couldn't believe it came from his mouth. Head down against the battering rain, legs pumping, he charged Byron like a bull in a china shop.

"I'll kill you, you sonofabitch!" he screamed into the wind seconds before he rammed into Byron's lithe, athletic body, driving his horn right into his midsection.

His body strained, his head pounded, his muscles flexed, and his chest threatened to implode when he made contact.

Byron's gun went flying, clattering off to the side of the gravel pathway as Oliver knocked him over with the force of his rage, stabbing him hard in the gut with his horn.

Oliver steamrolled him, using every ounce of strength he had—and that was when the strangest thing of all the things that had happened since this all began, happened.

His alicorn burned, so hot, so fierce, he was sure it would fry his brain and sizzle the very skin from his forehead. He heard Bryon scream in agony, writhing against him as he collapsed forward with a grunt and an "oompf!"

And then Byron exploded—exploded into a million particles of pink and purple, scattering everywhere, flying up into the air as though he were embers of a burning flame, shooting sparks, lighting up the sky.

Along with Byron, Oliver's alicorn exploded, too.

He felt it release from his head with a force so strong, it knocked him to his back, where he stared up at the starless sky with a quarter moon winking down at him as purple and pink glitter mingled with the ret rain, showered down on them.

God, all that wet glitter was going to be a nightmare to get out of their clothes.

"Oliver!" he heard Vinnie cry out hoarsely. "Oliver, oh my God! Are you okay? Answer me, damn you! Answer me!"

He forced his elbows under him and pushed himself all the way up to a sitting position, only to find Vinnie crawling to get to him, her ankle precariously twisted, her body battered.

"Stay there, Vinnie. Don't move or you'll hurt yourself even worse," he yelled back to her, rising to his feet, slipping in the mud and soaking wet.

But that was exactly the moment they heard the roar of the engine of the car up ahead.

In that second, just when he thought they were home free, Oliver saw the terror in Vinnie's eyes as she sat helpless to do much but try to crawl out of harm's way, and it shredded him, nearly ripped him apart.

Until he saw Byron's gun in the headlights of the car, still growing ever closer. It was off to the side in the gravel. Oliver dove for it, hitting the gravel with a crunch and scraping his cheek, latching onto the pistol's handle he rolled to his feet.

He held it up to the tune of Vinnie screaming, "Oooliver!"

He'd never used a gun before. He had no damn idea what he was doing, but he fired off a shot that nearly stopped his heart, aiming it at the driver of the car, whom he couldn't see, but prayed he'd hit anyway.

A flash of a shadow flew out in front of the car, a blur of colors and very little sound, but it screeched to a halt—and then the vehicle flew high in the air, arcing over them to crash land on top of a stack of shipping containers.

And then someone yelled, "Fuuck! I'm never gonna get this shit outta my hair, Sparkle tits! And put that GD shit down before you hurt yourself!"

Nina. It was Nina, stomping toward him with Marty and Darnell hot on her heels. She stopped in front of him, her raven hair plastered to her skull with wet glitter, and held out her lean hand.

"Give that to me, John Fucking Wayne. Jesus Christ and a bottle of Dos Equis, you're gonna get yourself fucking killed."

He sighed in relief, the biggest relief he'd ever felt in his entire life, as he threw an arm around her neck and squeezed her tight before letting go. "You came."

She batted him away, as always, uncomfortable with

any form of gratitude. "Of course I came, dipshit. Darnell tracked your phone. How much patience do you think I have to listen to Chatty Cathy talk about her elementary school days? Jesus, what kind of stall tactic was that, Almost-Goddess?" Nina asked as she turned around to look down at Vinnie, but she was smiling.

Vinnie choked out a cry as Oliver knelt to scoop her up. "You are one helluva sidekick, Princess Vinnie. What the hell were you thinking, talking all that smack, but worse, tripping on purpose like that?"

As he lifted her soaking-wet body, cradling her next to him, she moaned, but her sense of humor was still intact. "I was thinking if you died, I'd never have a moat, and we had a deal, Glitter Shitter. I'd be your princess if you'd build me a castle with a moat."

But he couldn't laugh. Instead, he gathered her as close as he could without hurting her and hugged her to him as the rain spat at them, cold and wet.

"You could have been killed, pulling that stunt, Vinnie. Jesus Christ, I saw my life flash before my damn eyes when he aimed that gun at you."

But she simply shrugged and wrapped her arms around his neck. "Well, that was the point. A distraction. I did mention that back in the shipping container. And all for what? Your alicorn is gone, Oliver. It exploded. All this glitter falling on us must be the fallout from your alicorn."

Oliver blinked. He'd forgotten the sensation of it leaving his forehead. "Gone? Really?"

"Yep. When you hit Byron, he exploded in a million colors, and so did your alicorn."

A moment of grief shot through him for the alicorn that had become so much a part of him these last several days, but it passed as quickly as it came, because along with its leaving, the heavy weight of who to heal was now gone, too. If he didn't have a horn, he couldn't heal anything.

That was a relief so intense, it shook him to his core.

"Sure is gone, Oliver. Shoulda seen it from where we were sittin'," Darnell said on a chuckle as he came up behind them and clapped Oliver on the back. "Lit up the damn night like the Fourth o' July with all that glitter, brother. You're a beast, man. A total beast."

"Okay, ladies and gentlemen," Marty said, clapping her hands, leaving drops of glitter-rain flying in the air. "I'm thrilled to itsy-bitsy bits everyone is okay. But the party's over. Darnell? You get these two back home, and Nina and I will do cleanup."

Oliver smiled at Marty and chuckled. "I'm not even gonna ask what that entails, but I'm guessing it has something to do with the guy in the car."

"Two guys in the car, to be fucking exact, and it's best you don't, Sparkle Tits," Nina said with her infamous cackle, pushing her sodden hair from her face.

"You can't call me that anymore, vampire. You're going to have to come up with something more original now," he teased.

Nina reached up and tweaked his cheek. "Fuck you

and your original. You'll always be Sparkle Tits to me. Now get the fuck out of here and go make googley eyes at each other while you see about that ankle or I'm gonna beat your ass for shitting all this glitter on me." She held up a strand of her soaking wet hair, covered in shiny glitter.

Mouthing a thank you to the women, Oliver clung to Vinnie as he turned to follow Darnell. The wind blew and the rain picked up, but he didn't care. Vinnie was alive. That was all he needed.

As Darnell popped open Marty's SUV doors, Vinnie tugged on his soaking-wet sweater. "Hey, what did Nina mean when she called me Chatty Cathy? How did she know what I yammering on about with Byron?"

Oliver grinned down at her. "My phone. I turned the sound down and dialed her number while you were screaming at Byron about what a mama's boy he is…er, *was*."

"Ooooh, crafty unicorn is crafty. Well played, buddy. See? I *was* distracting him. Now, let's forget about Byron and talk about that moat. Just because you're not a unicorn anymore doesn't mean that you can get out of—"

Oliver planted a kiss on her soft lips, one that deepened the longer it went on, and when she sighed, when she melted against him, he knew this journey, this crazy, wild, sparkly journey, was meant to lead to this.

To Vinnie.

EPILOGUE

One not-such-a-glitter-shitter-anymore guy who'd inherited some Godlike powers; an almost-Goddess who's the shit with a paint brush with no powers to speak of but a mighty-mighty brain; a vampire with a fresh mouth and an attitude; a mother for the second time of a half-werewolf, half-vampire baby girl; a fashionista bleached-blonde werewolf who loves makeup and jewelry; a teddy bear demon who happened to really like DIY as much as his new friends; a gentle, slightly green zombie; a spiffy manservant who had given up being a doula for good; three spouses of the aforementioned; a poodle named Muffin, a talking cat named Calamity, a dog named Mario and yet another named Frank, a cat named Brenda and a chipmunk named Baloney, all gathered almost a year later at a moving-in-together party/surprise reveal...

. . .

"He did not either," Marty said on a chuckle, bouncing Wanda's beautiful dark-haired, blue-eyed baby on her skinny-jean-clad hip. She shook her signature bangle bracelets, making the baby grab at them with her chubby fists.

Nina smiled at the baby and cooed as she dropped kisses on her. "Tell Auntie Marty, Sparkle Tits did too. Uncle Darnell and Daddy and all the guys helped. Ask him."

"He did, Marty, and it's magnificent, if I do say so myself. The craftsmanship of it all is simply stunning," Wanda, looking as slim and fit as anyone ever had in a pencil skirt, low heels and a lavender silk shirt, assured Marty as she cuddled a sleeping Sam to her chest. "They're just putting the finishing touches on now. He wanted to have it ready for move-in day for Vinnie."

"I can't believe he did that," Marty murmured with a smile. "He's such a great guy."

Vinnie stuck her head into the circle the women made and asked with a smile, "Who did what?"

"Mind your funky business, lady," Nina chided, flicking her fingers in Vinnie's face.

Vinnie frowned at the vampire and made a face. "My *what* business? Who are you?"

Nina tweaked her cheek and grinned like a cat that ate a mouse. "You heard me. I don't swear in front of the kids. I said, mind your *funky* business. Now mind it and don't make me break my rule."

Vinnie tucked Baloney into her sweater pocket and tried to see out the back windows to Oliver's...er, *their* backyard by standing on tiptoe, but he and Darnell, Carl, Greg, Keegan, and Heath had covered them with brown paper to keep her from seeing whatever he was doing.

Alice, who sat with little Charlie in her lap while Hollis played on her iPad and Calamity snuggled next to her, stood guard to keep Vinnie from peeking out.

"Aw, c'mon, meaniebutt," Vinnie whined. "Lemme see. They've been out there for two days doing whatever they're doing. I've been on an Oliver's-house ban for what feels like forever."

"Yeah," Nina agreed. "And Sparkle Tits said it was a surprise. So let it be a surprise, nosy."

"Miss Vinnie, you will leave this kitchen now, or I shall boil you in oil!" Arch teased from the stove where he, as always, prepared a feast fit for kings to celebrate Vinnie's big move.

With her free arm, Marty grabbed one of the last boxes Carl brought in from the moving van, and Vinnie followed her to Oliver's den, the last room left to unpack to officially make this *Vinnie* and Oliver's house.

They'd been dating for almost a year now, and every second of it had been amazing. She was never happier than when she was with Oliver, Baloney and her pets.

They'd decided to take it slow and really get to

know one another instead of rushing into anything—to truly learn about each other without any false pretenses. Oliver admitted he was guilty of doing exactly what Denise had done, trying to turn his ex-fiancée into something she simply wasn't, and he didn't want to make the same mistake twice.

Denise hadn't wanted the lifestyle he'd wanted, and he hadn't wanted hers. This time around, he promised to genuinely listen to Vinnie and what she wanted, instead of only *hearing* what he wanted to hear, and Vinnie promised to speak up without fear of rejection or retribution if she didn't want the same thing, instead of keeping her emotions hidden while she buried her nose in a book.

But it turned out she did want the same things Oliver wanted, and most everything she wanted, he wanted, too. Except for more throw pillows. He'd firmly stated he didn't want more of those. But she'd won that playful argument.

And they'd been making it work for almost exactly a year today, which is why they'd decided a couple of months ago to move in together and see how they fit as a couple sharing the same space. She'd put her house up for sale, and with some luck and a great realtor Heath knew, she'd sold it for quite a hefty profit.

During that year, they'd even gone to couple's counseling so Vinnie could learn to deal more effectively with her social anxiety and OCD, and Oliver could learn to be an effective partner to her.

Alice had gone with Vinnie, too, and they were making real strides in their relationship. Vinnie, after her long talk with Marty that night, a night that now seemed so long ago, finally understood what it was her mother had been trying to do all along.

And Alice finally understood that what *she* thought was good for Vinnie, wasn't so good at all, even if her heart was always in the right place.

And somehow, the twain had begun to meet.

They often had lunch after a session or went shopping, and nothing pleased her more than the time she and Alice spent together and with Oliver, who, her mother gloatingly reminded her, had been her pick for Vinnie all along.

Vinnie'd met Oliver's parents and his sisters on a trip to Colorado, where they'd skied and drank tons of hot cocoa, and she'd liked them as much as they'd liked her. They still didn't know about Oliver's ordeal, but he promised when the time and place were right, he'd explain…and maybe even show them what he could do now since that night in the shipyard.

It wouldn't be easy, but Vinnie promised to help him when he was ready.

"So, while we have a moment alone, I don't want to pry, and you can tell me to bug off, but everything's good with you two, you know… I mean, you'd have come to me if you needed to talk about anything personal, right? You can talk to any one of us. I hope you know that," Marty encouraged.

Ah. She meant sex and Vinnie's virginity. The big elephant in the room.

Oliver had respected that aspect of her life like no one before him. She'd confessed the humiliating secret of her almost first time to him, and how it had shamed her enough not to want to try again. Coupled with her social anxieties and her fears, the actual thought had become almost bigger than her.

But with patience and understanding on Oliver's part, and some awkward moments when she'd halted things due to her anxiety, even though it left poor Oliver wanting more, they'd worked it out by talking to each other. And when the actual time arrived, it had been filled with love and tenderness, and those emotions only grew with each intimate moment they shared. And they'd shared plenty since—plenty that she often smiled about secretly to herself at the most inopportune times.

"I do know I can come to you. But everything on that front is really great. *Really great.*"

She squeezed Vinnie's arm and smiled warmly. "Oh, and hey," Marty said with a nudge and a wink. "I see your biggest fan talked you into hanging your stuff up?" She pointed to the wall above Oliver's desk, where Brenda the cat sat in her favorite spot, right in the middle of everything.

Oliver had indeed talked her into hanging her paintings in his den, a space he'd deemed the place he liked to spend the most time, cuddling and watching

TV with her. So why wouldn't he surround himself with pictures painted by his favorite girl in the world?

There was an entire wall above his desk devoted to Vinnie's art. All of Oliver's favorites, in fact. She'd had them framed and gave them to Oliver for his birthday, and every time she came over to binge watch one show or another with him, her heart swooned at the idea he'd hung them.

Vinnie smiled, secretly pleased. "Oh, by the way, I have a little bit of news on the painting front."

Marty grinned as she set the box down and handed the baby off to Vinnie so she could begin to unpack. "Do tell."

Vinnie pressed her cheek to the baby's and inhaled, loving the scent of her rosy skin. "I submitted some of my work to a couple of comic book publishers—small places, mind you. I didn't go all Marvel/DC or anything."

Marty rolled her eyes and giggled. "Whatever that means. If it's not foundation and lip gloss, I don't understand. But keep talkin'. I like what I'm hearing, kiddo."

"Anyway, I heard back this week, and a place in Texas is interested in my art. The money's not huge, but they loved my work."

"Shut the front door!" Nina yelped from behind her, giving her shoulder a nudge with the flat of her palm. "Way to rock a dream, kid."

"Oh, Vinnie, I'm so proud of you," Wanda said with a warm smile. She took hold of the baby's fist, kissing it, and said, "And so is little Olivia, aren't you? Tell Auntie Vinnie how proud you are!"

Olivia giggled and nestled her soft head into Vinnie's neck. In honor of what Oliver had done to save this precious life Vinnie and Oliver had grown to love, Wanda and Heath had decided there was no other name for their little girl than a take on Oliver's.

When they'd had Olivia christened, they'd of course invited Vinnie and Oliver and, at the big party afterward, where they met almost everyone the women of OOPS had helped over the years, Wanda and Heath announced the baby's name. And for the first time since she'd met him, Oliver choked up.

As everyone had toasted his heroic act, he'd fought to stand up straight, but Vinnie knew how much he loved little Olivia, and having her named after him brought him great pride.

They'd grown close to all the women, their spouses, Carl, Darnell, and Arch. They Skyped often, texted, shopped, talked, played board games and cards, and had meals together at least once a month.

Her world had become so much bigger than she ever imagined it could be—filled with people who knew what it was to be labeled misfits and spit in the face of that label by living their best lives in spite of the purist haters.

Vinnie had learned from them, she'd grown because of them, and there would never be a time she wouldn't be grateful they'd come into her life. They'd brought her Oliver, the greatest gift anyone could have ever given her.

Marty grabbed her around her shoulders and gave her a warm hug. "I'm so pleased for you, Vinnie! What an amazing thing to happen. To see all of your beautiful paintings shared with the world. Speaking of, there's something Keegan and I want to talk to you about. We're thinking of starting a line of cosmetics geared toward superheroes. Or superhero-ish. You know, they're all the rage these days, and of course, we'll need an artist for packaging. It's a bit of a ways off, but if you think you might be interested, we'll talk prelims and such over dinner one night next week at the house?"

Vinnie grinned. Honestly, how had she gotten so lucky? "Are you kidding? Of course I'm interested."

Marty squeezed her, dropping a kiss on her cheek. "It's a date then," she said before she went off to unpack some more.

Then Wanda eyed her with a critical glance. "Any more noise from that hag Dorinda about killing her son?"

Vinnie shook her head. After some digging, Wanda had found Byron owed a pretty hefty debt to some ogre loan shark, which was why he'd kidnapped Oliver in the first place—in the hopes of trading his debt for Oliver's powers.

That ogre and his henchman were the unfortunate souls who'd landed on top of the shipping crates when

Nina launched their car across the night sky like she was lobbing a tennis ball.

Both were in council custody, still terrified Nina would hunt them down. Neither Oliver nor Vinnie had asked Nina and Marty what they'd done to them, because they'd both had a taste of Nina angry, and that was plenty, thank you very much.

But Vinnie and Oliver had their final meeting with the council only last week. They hadn't told the others, simply because the council had assured them Dorinda's complaint that Oliver and Vinnie had murdered her son was rendered invalid due to irrefutable evidence.

Apparently, the shipping yard had a CCTV, and what Byron had done was all on video. There really wasn't much to talk about, according to the elders of the council.

Well, except Oliver's new powers.

In the explosion, he'd lost his alicorn, but when he'd crashed into Byron, he'd somehow absorbed his magic, leaving him with some pretty neat tricks he'd found he could perform quite by accident. It had also most likely left him as immortal as Vinnie.

He'd had a great time popping in and out of her house with the snap of his fingers, and why drive to Manhattan to spend the weekend when they could skip rush hour and just appear in Times Square, bags in hand?

So instead of worrying her friends—because they were a lot like mother hens when it came to her safety and well-being—Vinnie just shook her head.

"Nope. All's well that ends well. Except for Oliver and his penchant for zapping us places. He's like a kid in a candy store with that power. He said all he has to do is think of a place and boom, he's there—which worries me. Because he's going to end up on the track of the Indy 500 or the Audubon…or worse? The Dalai Lama's lap."

Nina cackled a loud laugh. "That's almost cooler than being able to fly."

Then Vinnie broached the subject she most wanted to avoid. Ezekiel. "What about our favorite viper in a middle-schooler's clothing, Ezekiel? Hear anything about his sentencing?"

They'd finally gotten some answers from Ezekiel about how he'd found out about Oliver. Apparently, he often took pleasure in taunting people like Mikey, people who hunted for all manner of myths with the kind of passion Mikey had.

It was a game for Ezekiel to follow them around and frighten them then wipe their memories. He'd simply happened upon Mikey the night they'd been at Byron's—sheer dumb luck was what he'd called it.

But the council had called it something else entirely. They'd called it prison worthy and then locked him in a cell while they debated his sentence.

Nina popped her lips. "Yep. That dink's gonna be locked up for a long time, kiddo. A coupla lifetimes long. So nothing to worry about, okay?"

"What about Godfrey?" To this day, his face still haunted Vinnie from time to time.

Yes, she knew he was created for the purpose of evil and he'd certainly made good use of his purpose with her, but…a small part of her still felt sad.

"You mean how did he find out about Oliver's existence?" Nina asked, cocking her head. "Your buddy Byron wasn't exactly discreet about fucking asking around about my favorite Glitter Shitter. Word gets around in our world. You know that, Vin."

Vinnie nodded. "Have you seen Godfrey since that all went down?"

Nina grazed her cheek with her knuckles. "You want to know if he's okay, huh?"

She gave her a sheepish look. "I do."

"You're a good fucking kid, Vin. Yeah. He's okay. Darnell's been sort of mentoring him and he's making real progress, I hear. There's not much that can be done about where he comes from, but he can definitely change what the fuck he does with his powers."

Vinnie smiled because clearly Nina saw what she'd seen in Godfrey or she'd have left him to rot in Hell. "You're a good fucking vampire, Nina. Thanks."

Carl stuck his head inside the den and waved his hand, making her forget all about Ezekiel. He'd been duct-tape free for a month, and it looked like his record was holding steady.

"Come…o—ou—t…side. Now, please," he said with his lopsided grin.

Vinnie reached for his hand and gently squeezed it before she handed him Olivia. "Carl, how are you? Did I thank you for being such an amazing help today? I never could have gotten this done without you." She dropped a kiss on his cheek before they headed to the backyard.

"Hold up there, Almost-Goddess. I gotta cover your eyes. Sparkle Tits said so."

"Cover my eyes? Geez, what are they *doing* out there?"

Nina placed her cool, pale hands over Vinnie's eyes, walked her toward the door off the kitchen and led her to her favorite place of all—Oliver's arms.

The cool, crisp air of fall, their favorite season, greeted her nose. She smelled the scent of mesquite wood in the fire pit they'd built together with a six-pack of beer, a pizza, and a YouTube video. And the delicious smell of Arch's homemade lasagna and garlic bread drifted from the open window in the kitchen.

Oliver brushed a warm kiss over her lips, making her heart skip a beat. "Honey?"

"Uh-huh?"

"I made a promise to you almost exactly a year ago today. Do you remember what that promise was?"

"That I could bring my throw pillows. No, wait. That was only last week. That we could repaint the guest bath because that horrible moss green has got to go?"

Oliver chuckled, the rumble of it landing in her ear as she pressed her cheek to his broad chest. "Well, there was that, but no. Do you remember how we talked about unicorns and princesses?"

"Did you get me a crocodile, Oliver Baldwin?

Listen, I love animals, but I don't know if I have enough Steve Irwin in me to handle a croc."

Everyone began to laugh, a sound she welcomed with open arms.

"It's not a crocodile. Remember I promised if you'd be the princess to my unicorn, I'd build you a castle and a moat?"

Vinnie frowned and latched onto the material of his Bills sweatshirt. "I do remember that. But it was made under duress, so the fact that I have no castle with a turret and a moat to date is not a problem. A garden will be just fine."

He leaned down and pressed his lips to her ear, making her shiver. "Open your eyes, honey."

Vinnie forced her eyes open to find all the people she'd fallen so deeply in love with smiling at her as they yelled, "Surprise!"

Her eyes welled with tears as she focused on her surprise.

"Nooo. You really did it? You did this for *me*?"

Oliver chuckled and pulled her closer. "You refused to take the den as a place to paint, because you didn't want to usurp me out of my man-space, as you called it. And you wouldn't choose one of the guestrooms because you want to fill them with friends and babies—which is why we decided to move in here, instead of your place, because it's bigger. But I wanted you to have a place you could call your own, honey. A place where you can organize everything the way you like it, because I know organization is important to you. It's a place where you can paint those incredible works of art for your new publisher or just paint to paint. But it's all yours."

She put her hand to her mouth to keep from ugly-crying.

There before her, in all its purple-and-pink-shingled glory, arched stained-glass windows, and not one but *two* turrets, was a castle with a unicorn carved from wood above the door, and a tiny flag flying on a pole at the top of the turret that read, Castle Vincenza Raphaela Morretti.

Someone had planted pink and white mums in planters to set on the tiny front porch, and there was even a wishing well right next to it with a cotton candy machine in the center, spinning the sugary delight in purple and pink.

But that wasn't all. The wishing well had a fairy and carousel wind chime hanging from the roof, the tinkling chimes dancing in the light breeze of late afternoon.

And almost the entire way around the perimeter, there was a moat. A moat with pink and green lily pads and a blowup crocodile.

It stood proudly under the buttery autumn sun, glistening and perfect.

It was the most perfect thing *ever*.

She couldn't hold back anymore, tears flowed down her cheeks in salty drops as she threw her arms around Oliver's neck, burying her face in his collar. "I...I don't know what to say. It's the most amazing thing I've ever seen! This is why you kept me away for the last week? I was starting to think you were having second thoughts about shacking up."

He squeezed her tight, wrapping her legs around his waist. "I'd never do that, but I had to have someone come in and install the heating unit. I'm pretty good, but I'm not *that* good."

"It has heat?" she squeaked, making Baloney poke her head out of her sweater.

"Uh-huh. And air. It's kind of like my version of a she-shed. Or as we've all been calling it, a Vinnie-shed. So you'll always have something that's all yours with no interference from a big oaf like me."

She dropped kisses all over his face, bracketing his jaw with her hands. "I love it, Oliver. I love it, and I love you. No one has ever done anything like this for me. Not ever. It's beautiful. You're all so amazing. All of you, thank you!"

He leaned back in their embrace and smiled his gorgeous smile. "I love you, Vinnie. I always want you to have fairies and dancing carousel horses. *Always.*"

"And I always want you to be my unicorn. *Always.*"

As everyone gathered around them, as gold and rust leaves fell from the trees, as the fire in the pit they'd built burned and glowed, as Frank, Mario and Muffin chased each other in the backyard, as Arch called them to say it was time for family dinner, Vinnie wiped her tears and let Oliver carry her inside.

To their home.

To their future.

To their always.

The End

I hope you'll come back next year and join me for another adventure with the women of OOPS. I don't know what it'll be about yet, but you can bet it'll be filled with laughter, too much cussing, and most of all, eternal, ride-or-die friendship. *Always.*

PREVIEW ANOTHER BOOK BY DAKOTA CASSIDY

Chapter 1

"So, Sister Trixie Lavender, how do we feel about this space? Open concept, with plenty of sprawling views of the crumbling sidewalk from the leaky picture window and easily room for eight tat chairs.

"Also, one half bathroom for customers, one full for us—which means we'd have to share, but there are worse things. A bedroom right up those sketchy stairs with a small loft, which BTW, I'm calling as mine now. I like to be up high for the best possible views when I survey our pending tattoo empire. A tiny kitchenette, but no big deal. I don't cook anyway, and *you* sure don't, if that horse pucky you called oatmeal is any indication of your culinary skills. Lots of peeling paint and crappy plumbing. All for the low-low price of...er, what was that price again, Fergus McDuff?"

Short and chubby, a balding Fergus McDuff, the landlord of the current dive I was assessing as a candidate for our tattoo parlor, cringed and visibly shuddered beneath his limp blue suit.

Maybe because Coop had him up against a wall, holding him by the front of his shirt in white-knuckled fists as she waited for him to rethink the price he'd quoted us the moment he realized we were women.

Which was not only an outrageous amount of money for this dank, pile-of-rubble hole in the wall, but not at all the amount quoted to us over the phone. It also looked nothing like the picture from his Facebook page. I know that shouldn't surprise me. He'd probably used some Snapchat filter to brighten it up. But here we were.

A bead of perspiration popped out just above Fergus's thin upper lip.

Coop's dusky auburn hair curtained his face, but his stance remained firm. "Like I said, lady, it's three grand a month—"

Cutting his words off, Coop tightened her grip with a grunt and hauled Fergus higher. His pleading gray eyes darted from her to me and back again in unadulterated fear, but to his credit, he tried really hard not to show it.

Coop licked her lips, a low hum of a growl coming from her throat, her gaze intently focused on poor Fergus. "Can I kill him, Sister Trixie Lavender? Please, please, pleeease?"

"*Coop*," I warned. She knew better than to ask such a question. "She's just joking, Fergus. Promise."

"But I'm not. Though, I promise I'll clean up afterward. It'll be like it never happened—"

"Two thousand!" Fergus shouted quite jarringly, as though the effort to push the words out pained him. "Wait, wait, wait! I meant to say two thousand a month with *all* utilities!"

That's my demon. Overbearing and intimidating as the day is long. Still, I frowned at her, pulling my knit cap down over my ears. While this behavior worked in our favor, it was still unacceptable.

We'd had a run-in with the law a few months ago back in Ebenezer Falls, Washington, where we'd first tried to set up a tattoo shop. Coop's edgy streak had almost landed her with a murder charge.

Since then (and before we landed in Eb Falls, by the by), we'd been traveling through the Pacific Northwest, making ends meet by selling my portrait sketches to people along the way, waiting until Coop's instincts choose the right place for us to call home.

Cobbler Cove struck just the right chord with her. And that's how we ended up here, with her breathing fire down Fergus McDuff's throat.

Coop, who'd caught on to my displeasure, smirked her beautiful smirk and set Fergus down with a gentle drop, brushing his trembling shoulder with a careful hand to smooth his wrinkled suit.

"That's nice. You're being nice, Fergus McDuff. I like you. Do you like me?"

"Coop?" I called from the other end of the room, going over some rough measurements for a countertop in my mind. "Playtime's over, young lady. Let Mr. McDuff be, please."

She rolled her bright green eyes at me in petulance and wiped her hands down her burgundy leather pants, disappointment written all over her face that there'd be no killing today.

Coop huffed. "Fine."

I looked at her with my stern ex-nun's expression as a clear reminder to remember her manners. "Coop…"

She pouted before holding out her hand to Fergus, even though he outwardly cringed at the gesture. "It was nice to meet you, Fergus McDuff. I hope I'll see you again sometime soon," she said almost coquettishly, mostly following the guidelines I'd set forth for polite conversation with new acquaintances.

Fergus brushed her hand away, fear still on his face, and that was when I knew it was time for me to step in.

"You do realize she's just joking—about killing you and all, don't you? I would never let her do that," I joked, hoping he'd come along for the ride.

But he only nodded as Coop picked up his tie clip and handed it to him in a gesture of apology.

I smiled at her and nodded my head in approval, dropping my hands into the pockets of my puffy vest. "Okay, Fergus. Sold. Two grand a month and utilities it is. A year lease, right? Have a contract handy?"

Fergus nodded and scurried toward the front of the store to get his briefcase. It was then Coop leaned toward me and sniffed the air, her delicate nostrils flaring.

"This place smells right, Trixie Lavender. Yes, it does. Also, I like the name Peach Street. That sounds like a nice place to live."

I looked into her beautiful eyes—eyes so green and perfectly almond-shaped they made other women sick with jealousy—and smiled, feeling a sense of relief. "Ya think? You've got a good vibe about it then? Like the one you had in Ebenezer Falls before the bottom fell out?"

And you were accused of murder and our store was left in shambles?

I bit the inside of my cheek to keep from bringing up our last escapade in a suburb of Seattle, with an ex-witch turned medium named Stevie Cartwright and her dead spy turned ghost cohort, Winterbottom. It was still too fresh.

Coop rolled her tongue along the inside of her cheek and scanned the dark, mostly barren space with critical eyes. Any mention of Eb Falls, and Coop grew instantly sullen. "I miss Stevie Cartwright. She said she'd be my friend. Always-always."

My face softened into a smile. I missed Stevie and her ghost compatriot, too. Even though I couldn't actually hear Winterbottom—or Win, as she'd called him—Coop could, and from what she'd relayed to me, he sounded delightfully British and madly in love with Stevie.

Certainly an unrequited love, due to their circumstances—him being all the way up there on what they called Plane Limbo (where souls wait to decide if they wish to cross over)—and Stevie here on Earth, but they fit one another like gloves.

Stevie had been one of the best things to ever happen to me; Coop, too. She'd helped us in more ways than just solving a murder and keeping Coop from going to jail. She'd helped heal our hearts. She'd shown us what it meant to be part of a community. She'd helped us learn to trust not just our instincts, but to let the right people into our lives and openly enjoy their presence.

"Trixie? Do you think Stevie meant we'd always be friends?"

I winked at Coop. "She meant what she said, for sure. She always means what she says. If she said she'll always be your friend, you can count on it. And I miss Stevie, too, Coop. Bet she comes to visit us soon."

Coop almost smirked, which was her version of a smile—something we worked on every day. Facial expressions and body language humans most commonly use.

"Will she eat spaghetti with us?" she asked, referring to the last meal we'd shared with Stevie, when she'd invited her friends over and made us a part of not just her community, but her family.

"I bet she'll eat whatever we make. So anyway... We were talking the vibe here? It feels good to you?"

"Yep. I can tattoo here."

"Gosh, I hope so. We need to plant some roots, Coop. We need to begin again Finnegan."

We needed to find a sense of purpose after Washington, and this felt right. This suburb of Portland called the Cobbler Cove District felt right.

Tucking her waist-length hair behind her ear, Coop nodded her agreement with a vague pop of her lips, the wheels in her mind so obviously turning. "So we can grow and be a part of the community. So we can blend."

"Yes, blending is important. Now, about threatening Fergus…"

Her eyes narrowed on Fergus, who'd taken a phone call and busily paced the length of the front of the store. "He was lying, Trixie Lavender. Three grand wasn't what he said on the phone at all. No, it was not. I know what I heard. You said it's bad to lie. I was only following the rules, just like you told me I should if I wanted to stay here with you and other humans."

Bobbing my head to agree, I pinched her lean cheek with affection and smiled. "That's exactly what I said, Coop. *Exactly*. Good on you for finally listening to me after our millionth conversation about manners."

"Do I win a prize?"

I frowned as I leaned against the peeling yellow wall. I never knew where Coop was going in her head sometimes. She took many encounters, words, people, whatever, at face value. Almost the way a small child would—except this sometime-child had an incredible figure and a savage lust for blood if not carefully monitored.

"A prize, Coop?" I asked curiously, tucking my hands in the pockets of my jeans. "Explain your thinking, please."

She gazed at me in all seriousness as she quite visibly concentrated on her words. I watched her sweet, uncluttered mind put her thoughts together.

"Yep. A prize. I saw it the other day on a sign at the grocery store. The millionth shopper wins free groceries for a year. Do I get something for free after our millionth conversation?"

Laughter bubbled from my throat. Coop didn't just bring me endlessly sticky situations, she brought me endless laughter and, yes, even endless joy. She's simple, and I don't mean she's unintelligent.

I mean, sometimes she's so black and white, I find it hard to explain to her the many levels and nuances of appropriate reactions or emotions for any given situation, and that can tax me on occasion. But she's mine, and she'd saved my life, and I wasn't ever going to forget that.

And I do mean *ever*.

She'd tell you I'd saved *hers*, but that's just her innocent take on a situation that had been almost impossible until she'd shown up with her trusty sword.

I gazed up at the water-stained ceiling and thought about how to explain the complexities of mankind. I decided simple was best.

"Trixie? Do I get a prize?" she inquired again, her tone more insistent this time.

"No free groceries. Just my love and eternal gratitude that you restrained yourself and didn't kill Fergus. He's not a bad man, Coop. And when I say *bad,* I mean the kind of bad who kicks puppies and pulls the wings off moths for sport. He's just trying to make his way in the world and get ahead. Just like everybody else. It might not be nice, but you can't kill him over it. Them's the rules, Demon."

"But he wasn't being fair, Sister Trixie Lavender."

"Remember what we discussed about my name?"

Now she frowned, the lines in her perfectly shaped forehead deepening. "Yes. I forgot—again. You're not a nun anymore and it isn't necessary to call you by your last name. You're just plain Trixie."

Plain Trixie was an understatement. Compared to Coop, Angelina Jolie was plain. My mousy, stick-straight reddish brown (all right, mostly brown) hair and plump thighs were no match for the sleek Coopster. But you couldn't be jealous of her for long because she had no idea how stunning she was, and that was because she didn't care.

"Right. I'm just Trixie. Just like Fergus isn't Fergus McDuff. He's just plain old Fergus, if he allows you to call him by his first name, or Mr. McDuff if he prefers the more formal way to address someone. And I'm not a nun anymore. That's also absolutely right."

My heart shivered with a pang of sadness at that,

but I'm finally able to say that out loud now and actually feel comfortable doing so.

I wasn't a nun anymore, and I'm truly, deeply at peace with the notion. My faith had become a bone of contention for me long before I'd exited the convent, so it was probably better I'd ended up being kicked out on my ear any ol' way.

In fact, I often wonder if it hadn't *always* been a bone of contention for the entire fifteen years I'd lived there. I'd always questioned some of the rules.

I'd never wanted to enter the convent to begin with—my parents put me there when they could no longer handle my teenage substance abuse. They'd left me in the capable, nurturing hands of my mother's dear friend, Sister Alice Catherine.

But after I'd kicked my drug habit, and decided to take my vows in gratitude for all the nuns of Saint Aloysius By The Sea had done for me, I came to love the thick stone walls, the soft hum and tinkle of wind chimes, and the structure of timely prayer.

They'd saved me from my addiction. In their esteemed honor, I wanted to save people, too. What better way to do so than becoming a nun in dedicated service to the man upstairs?

Though, I can promise you, I didn't want to leave the convent the way I did. A graceful exit would have been my preferred avenue of departure.

Instead, I left by way of possession. Yes. I said *possession*. An ugly, fiery, gaping-black-mouthed, demonic possession. I know that's a lot of adjectives, but it best describes what wormed its way inside me on that awful, horrible night.

"Are you sad now, Trixie? Did I make you sad because you aren't a nun anymore?" Coop asked, very clearly worried she'd displeased me—which did happen from time to time.

For instance, when she threatened to kill anyone who even looked cross-eyed at me—sometimes if they just breathed the wrong way.

I had to remind myself often, it was out of the goodness of her heart she'd nearly severed a careless driver's head when he'd encroached on our pedestrian right of way (the pedestrian always has the right of way in Portland, in case you were wondering). Or lopped off a man's fingers with a nearby butter knife for grazing my backside by accident while we were in a questionable bar.

Still, even while Coop's emotions ruled her actions without any tempered, well-thought-out responses, she was a sparkling diamond in the rough, a veritable sponge, waiting to soak up all available knowledge.

I tugged at a lock of her silky hair, shaking off the memory of that night. "How can I be sad if I have you, Coop DeVille?"

She grimaced—my feisty, compulsive, loveable demon grimaced—which is her second version of a smile (again, she's still practicing smiling. There's not much to smile about in Hell, I suppose) and patted my cheek—just like I'd taught her. "Good."

"So, do you think you're up to the task of some remodeling? This place is kind of a mess."

Actually, it was a disaster. Everything was crumbling. From the bathroom that looked as though it hadn't been cleaned since the last century, to the peeling walls and yellowed linoleum with holes all throughout the store.

Her expression went thoughtful as she cracked her knuckles. "That means painting and using a hammer, right?"

I brushed my hands together and adjusted my scarf. "Yep. That's what that means, Coop."

"Then no. I don't want to do that."

I barked a laugh, scaring Fergus, who was busily rifling through his briefcase, looking for the contract I'm now positive changes with the applicant's gender.

"Tough petunias. We're in this together, Demon-San. That means the good, the bad, and the renovation of this place. If you want to start tattooing again, we can't have customers subjected to this chaos, can we? Who'd feel comfortable getting a tattoo in a mess like this?"

I pointed to the pile of old pizza boxes and crushed beer cans in the corner where I hoped we'd be able to build a cashier's counter.

Coop's sigh was loud enough to ensure I'd hear it as she let her shoulders slump. "You're right, Sis...um, *Trixie*. We have to have a sterile environment to make tattoos. The Oregon laws say so. I read them, you know. On the laptop. I read them *all*."

As I said, Coop's a veritable sponge, which almost makes up for her lack of emotional control.

Almost.

I patted her shoulder as it poked out of her off-the-shoulder T-shirt, the shoulder with a tattoo of an angel in all its magnificently winged glory. A tattoo she'd drawn and inked herself while deep in the bowels of Hell.

"I'm proud of you. I'm going to need all the help I can get so we can get our license to open ASAP. We need to start making some money, Coop. We don't have much left of the money Sister Mary Ignatius gave us, and we definitely can't live on our charm alone."

"So I've been useful?"

"You're more than useful, Coop. You're my right-hand man. Er, woman."

She grinned, and it was when she grinned like this, when her gorgeously crafted face lit up, I grew more certain she understood how dear a friend she was to me. "Good."

"Okay, so let's go sign our lives away—"

"No!" she whisper-yelled, gripping my wrist with the strength of ten men, her face twisted in fear. "Don't do that, Trixie Lavender! You know what happens when you do that. Nothing is as it seems when you do that!"

I forced myself not to wince when I pried her fingers from my wrist. Sometimes, Coop didn't know her own demonic strength. "Easy, Coop. I need my skin," I teased.

In an instant, she dropped her hands to her sides and shoved them into the pockets of her pants, her expression contrite. "My apologies. But you know I have triggers. That's what you called them, right? When I get upset and anxious, that's a trigger. Signing your life away is one of them. We have to be careful with our words. You said so yourself."

She was right. I'd poorly worded my intent, forgetting her fears about the devil and Hell's shoddy bargains for your soul.

As the rain pounded the roof, I measured my words and tried to make light of the situation. "It's just a saying we use here, Coop. It means we're giving everything we have to Fergus McDuff on a wing and a prayer at this point. But it doesn't mean I'm giving up my soul to the devil. I promise. My soul's staying put."

At least I thought it was. I could be wrong after my showdown with an evil spirit, but it felt like it was still there. I still had empathy for others. I still knew right from wrong—even if all those morals went directly out the window when the evil spirit took over.

Coop inhaled and exhaled before she squared her perfectly proportioned shoulders. "Okay. Then let's go," she paused, frowning, "sign our lives away to Fergus McDuff." Then she smirked, clearly meaning she understood what I'd said.

Our path to Fergus slowed when Coop paused and put a hand on my arm, setting me behind her. There was a commotion of some kind occurring just outside our door on the sidewalk, between Fergus and another man.

A dark-haired man with olive skin stretched tightly over his jaw and sleeve tattoos on both arms yelled down at Fergus, who, after Coop, had probably had enough of being under fire for today. But holy crow, this guy was angry.

He waved those muscular arms—attached to lean hands with long fingers—around in the air as the rain pelted his sleek head. His T-shirt stretched over his muscles as he gestured over his shoulder, and his voice, even muffled, boomed along our tiny street.

I couldn't make out what they were saying, but it didn't look like a very friendly exchange—not judging by the man's face, which, when it wasn't screwed up in anger, was quite handsome.

Yet, Fergus, clearly at his breaking point after his encounter with Coop, reared up in the gentleman's face and yelled right back. But then a taller, leaner, sandy-haired man approached and put a hand on the handsome man's shoulder, encouraging him to turn around.

That gave Fergus the opportunity to push his way past the big man and grab the handle of our door, stepping back inside the store with a bluster of huffs and grunts.

Coop sniffed the air. She can sometimes smell things the rest of us can't. It's hard to explain, but as an example, she smelled that our friend Stevie isn't entirely human. She's a witch. Or she was. Now, since her accident, she only has some residual powers left.

But Coop had smelled her paranormal nature somehow—which, by definition, is crazy incredible and something I can't dwell on for long, for fear I'll get lost in the madness that demons and Hell and witches and other assorted ghouls are quite real.

"The man outside is not paranormal. He's just normal, as is the other man, and Fergus, too. If you were wondering."

I popped my lips in Coop's direction. "Good to know. I mean, what if he was some crazy hybrid of a vampire who can run around in daylight? Then what? We'd have to keep our veins covered or he might suck us dry."

Coop gave me her most serious expression and sucked in her cheeks. "I already told you, you don't ever have to worry anyone will hurt you. I'll kill them and then they'll be dead."

Ba-dump-bump.

"And I told *you*, no killing." Then I giggled and wrapped an arm around her shoulder, steering her past the debris on the floor and toward a grumpy Fergus, feeling better than I had in weeks. We had a purpose. We had a mission. Above all, we had hope.

We were going to open Inkerbelle's Tattoos and Piercings. I'd pierce and design tattoos, and Coop would handle the rest. We'd hopefully hire a staff of more artists as gifted as Coop. If the universe saw fit, that is.

And then maybe we'd finally have a place to call home. Where I could nest, and Coop could ink to her heart's desire in her tireless effort to protect every single future client from demonic harm with her special brand of magic ink.

During her life under Satan's rule, Coop had tattooed all new entries into Hell. She'd been so good at it, the devil left her in charge of every incoming sinner. But it was a job she'd despised, and she eventually escaped the night she'd saved me.

Lastly, I'd also try to come to terms with my new status in this world—my new freedom to openly share my views on how to get through this life with a solid code of ethics. Oh, and by the way, it has more to do with being the best person you can, rather than putting the fear of scripture quotes and fire and brimstone into non-believers.

I don't care if you believe. I know that sounds crazy coming from an ex-nun once deeply immersed in a convent and yards and yards of scripture. But I don't. You don't have to believe in an unseen entity if you so choose.

But I do care deeply about the world as a whole, and showing, not telling people you can live your life richly, fully, without ever stepping inside the hallowed halls of a church if you decide that's what works for you.

I want anyone who'll listen to know you can indeed have a life worth living—even as a low-level demon escaped from Hell and an ex-communicated nun who suffers from what Coop and I jokingly call demoniphrenia.

Also known as, the occasional possession of an ex-nun cursed by a random evil spirit.

And I was determined to prove that—not only to myself, but to this spirit who had me in its greasy black clutches.

NOTE FROM DAKOTA

I do hope you enjoyed this book, I'd so appreciate it if you'd help others enjoy it too.

Recommend it. Please help other readers find this book by recommending it.

Review it. Please tell other readers why you liked this book by reviewing it at online retailers or your blog. Reader reviews help my books continue to be valued by distributors/resellers. I adore each and every reader who takes the time to write one!

If you love the book or leave a review, please email **dakota@dakotacassidy.com** so I can thank you with a personal email. Your support means more than you'll ever know! Thank you!

ABOUT THE AUTHOR

Dakota Cassidy is a USA Today bestselling author with over fifty books. She writes laugh-out-loud cozy mysteries, romantic comedy, grab-some-ice erotic romance, hot and sexy alpha males, paranormal shifters, contemporary kick-ass women, and more.

Dakota was invited by Bravo TV to be the Bravoholic for a week, wherein she snarked the hell out of all the Bravo shows. She received a starred review from Publishers Weekly for Talk Dirty to Me, won a Romantic Times Reviewers' Choice Award for Kiss and Hell, along with many review site recommended reads and reviewer top pick awards.

Dakota lives in the gorgeous state of Oregon with her real-life hero and her dogs, and she loves hearing from readers!

OTHER BOOKS BY DAKOTA CASSIDY

Visit Dakota's website at http://www.dakotacassidy.com for more information.

A Lemon Layne Mystery, a Contemporary Cozy Mystery Series
1. Prawn of the Dead
2. Play That Funky Music White Koi

Witchless In Seattle Mysteries, a Paranormal Cozy Mystery series
1. Witch Slapped
2. Quit Your Witchin'
3. Dewitched
4. The Old Witcheroo
5. How the Witch Stole Christmas
6. Ain't Love a Witch
7. Good Witch Hunting
8. Witch Way Did He Go?

9. Witches Get Stitches

***Nun of Your Business Mysteries*, a Paranormal Cozy Mystery series**

1. Then There Were Nun
2. Hit and Nun
3. House of the Rising Nun
4. The Smoking Nun

***Wolf Mates*, a Paranormal Romantic Comedy series**

1. An American Werewolf In Hoboken
2. What's New, Pussycat?
3. Gotta Have Faith
4. Moves Like Jagger
5. Bad Case of Loving You

***A Paris, Texas Romance*, a Paranormal Romantic Comedy series**

1. Witched At Birth
2. What Not to Were
3. Witch Is the New Black
4. White Witchmas

Non-Series

Whose Bride Is She Anyway?
Polanski Brothers: Home of Eternal Rest
Sexy Lips 66

***Accidentally Paranormal*, a Paranormal Romantic Comedy series**

Interview With an Accidental—a free introductory guide to the girls of the Accidentals!

1. The Accidental Werewolf
2. Accidentally Dead

3. The Accidental Human
4. Accidentally Demonic
5. Accidentally Catty
6. Accidentally Dead, Again
7. The Accidental Genie
8. The Accidental Werewolf 2: Something About Harry
9. The Accidental Dragon
10. Accidentally Aphrodite
11. Accidentally Ever After
12. Bearly Accidental
13. How Nina Got Her Fang Back
14. The Accidental Familiar
15. Then Came Wanda
16. The Accidental Mermaid
17. Marty's Horrible, Terrible Very Bad Day
18. The Accidental Unicorn

The Hell, a Paranormal Romantic Comedy series

1. Kiss and Hell
2. My Way to Hell

The Plum Orchard, a Contemporary Romantic Comedy series

1. Talk This Way
2. Talk Dirty to Me
3. Something to Talk About
4. Talking After Midnight

The Ex-Trophy Wives, a Contemporary Romantic Comedy series

1. You Dropped a Blonde On Me

2. Burning Down the Spouse

3. Waltz This Way

***Fangs of Anarchy*, a *Paranormal Urban Fantasy* series**

1. Forbidden Alpha

2. Outlaw Alpha

Made in the USA
Coppell, TX
29 September 2020